I0679459

FINALLY HOME IN DESTINY

The Destiny Series Book 6

EMMA EASTER

Finally Home in Destiny
by Emma Easter

Paperback Edition

CKN Christian Publishing
An Imprint of Wolfpack Publishing

6032 Wheat Penny Avenue
Las Vegas, NV 89122

Paperback ISBN: 978-1-64734-711-6
Ebook ISBN: 978-1-64734-710-9

FINALLY HOME IN DESTINY

ONE

Lily hurried up the stairs in the House of Refuge carrying her duffle bag. At the top of the stairs, she greeted a group of women who were leaning on the railing chatting and two other acquaintances who passed by her. She hastened down the long hallway, annoyed that it felt longer than usual to reach Rachel and Keith's apartment. At last, she stood in front of their door and knocked.

"Open the door, guys," she whispered as she tapped her foot impatiently. Her heart was drumming with excitement and anxiety. Soon, by God's grace, she would be reunited with her sister, Stella. Hopefully, after that, she would be able to find a clue that would lead her to their parents.

The door opened, and Lily immediately flew into Rachel's arms. She hugged her sister-in-law tightly and walked into the living room. Keith was sitting on the sofa with Emily on his lap. She smiled at him as he stood up with Emily and came to hug her.

She pulled away slightly, kissed Emily's chubby cheeks, and smiled at Rachel.

"So where is Daniel?" She looked around the small living room as though he were hiding and at any minute would pop out from behind the sofa. "I need to go see my sister immediately."

Rachel smiled at her. "Lily, you have just arrived and you are already set to go. At least sit and rest for a while. Besides, look at the time. It's late. You cannot possibly go to Tucson right now."

Lily glanced at the ornate gold clock on the wall. It was almost nine p.m. She sighed. "Okay! Fine. I'll wait until tomorrow to leave for Tucson. But where is Daniel? I need to ask him how exactly Stella was doing when he saw her and let him know we will have to leave as early as possible tomorrow."

Rachel chuckled. "You do know that Daniel doesn't live here, don't you?"

Keith gave Emily to Rachel, dug his hand into his pocket, and took out his phone. "Let me call him and tell him to come over."

After Keith had called Daniel and asked him to come to the apartment, Lily took a deep breath and tried to release the adrenaline rushing through her veins. She sat down on the couch and exhaled again. She had left California for Arizona the minute Daniel had informed her he'd seen Stella. Her plan had been to go to Tucson with Daniel as soon as she arrived so she could see her sister, who she'd not seen for over two years. Unfortunately, she'd arrived later than she'd thought she would, though she should have known that would be the case. She pressed her lips together. If only she could see Stella today... But Rachel was right. It was late. Tomorrow, she and Daniel would leave for Tucson first thing in the morning.

"So, how is my dear brother?" Rachel asked as she sat beside Lily. She ran her fingers through Emily's hair and kissed the toddler's forehead.

Lily smiled widely. "He's great. I wish he were here. Unfortunately, he could not come because he had to go to Florida for a business meeting. But he said he will try to come once the meeting is over."

"What about the kids?"

"I left them with their nanny, Irene. They have gotten so attached to her over the months she's been working with us, and she's great. Taylor and I trust her with them." Lily reached out and caressed Emily's cheek. "Though I already miss them. I don't think Taylor will need to come here. I can't stay away from the kids for long. I'll probably head back to California to be with them and Taylor the day after tomorrow." She sighed as she remembered she also wanted to use whatever clues she got about their parents' location from Stella to search for them. "I guess that depends on what I find out about my parents from Stella."

Rachel opened her mouth, clearly to say something, but turned as the front door opened.

Daniel walked in, and Lily grinned. "You are finally here." She stood up as he walked toward her.

"I am." He smiled and gave her a brief hug.

She sat again. "So, since it's already late, we cannot go to Tucson today. We will have to leave first thing in the morning.

Lily looked up at him as he sat on the sofa facing her. He shook his head. "I don't know if that will be possible, Lily. Vina and I just got married, and I don't want to leave her so early in the morning. And I doubt she would like that either." He smiled.

"Even though we are still in Fallow Creek, we are on our honeymoon now, you know."

Lily blinked in surprise. "Did you just say you got married to Vina, Daniel?"

Daniel grinned. "Yes."

"When did this happen?"

Keith and Rachel laughed. "They got married yesterday," Keith said. "Crazy, I know."

Lily studied Daniel's face, confused. "But I spoke to you just a few days ago and you told me Vina was in Los Angeles and engaged to someone else. Are we talking about Davina Brooks, or some other Vina that I don't know?"

Rachel chuckled. "No, we are talking about the Vina you know."

Lily turned away from Rachel and faced Daniel again. "Tell me how that happened."

Daniel laughed. "It's a really long story, Lily. Right now, I want to go back to my wife, but I will tell you all about it on our way to Tucson."

Lily smiled. "So, you agree that we can leave early tomorrow?"

Daniel sighed. "How early are we talking about?"

"As early as possible. How about around seven o'clock?"

"Umm, no, Lily Hunter!"

Lily raised her eyebrows. "Dalton."

"Sorry... Dalton." Daniel smiled. "You got married less than two years ago, so you know how it is. I just got married, and I would like to stay in with my wife until at least nine o'clock." He looked at Rachel and grinned. "My boss as well as Vina's gave us a few days off after we got married so we could spend some alone time together. Vina will not be pleased if I leave her alone, especially so early in the morning, and then stay out all day. How about I come out here around ten o'clock and we can go then?"

Lily chuckled and smiled. "I understand, Daniel. I'm sorry for insisting that we leave so early. It's just because I have been so eager to see my sister after being separated from her for years. But you need to spend as much time as you can with Vina. We can head out at noon if you like."

"No, ten o'clock is okay."

"I'm so happy for you, Daniel. I think you and Vina make a lovely couple." Lily beamed at him. "Where is Vina now?"

A bright smile appeared on his face. "At our house."

Lily nodded. "Okay, then, it's settled." She smiled at Emily, who was still sitting on her mother's lap and playing with her necklace. Emily reminded her of Bree. Her little stepdaughter had grown very attached to her, which was not surprising seeing as she was the only mother Bree knew. And she really saw Bree as her daughter now. She couldn't wait to see her again and kiss her soft cheeks. She ran her fingers through her niece's silky soft hair and looked at Daniel. "We leave by ten o'clock tomorrow."

Daniel nodded and stood up. "I have to go now." He left before Lily could say anything more.

Lily turned to Rachel and chuckled. "I remember how that was — just getting married and awash with the glow of a newlywed."

"Well, you're still somewhat of a newlywed," Rachel said. "And you definitely still have that glow."

Lily smiled. "In a way, I still feel like Taylor and I just got married. Every day when I wake up beside him, I ask myself how I got so lucky. I still get giddy whenever he comes home from work."

"I know how that feels," Rachel said, looking over at Keith, who was scanning a Home Repairs magazine.

Clearly sensing his wife's eyes were on him, Keith raised his head and gave Rachel a heart-melting smile before going back to his reading.

"And how are you getting on with Taylor's kids, Lily?" Rachel asked her. "You told me the other day that you and Bree have a close bond. But I know you are just starting to get along well with Josh."

Lily grinned. "Josh and I are getting closer every day, and I am so glad he doesn't feel like I came to replace his mother anymore. I love those kids so much, and I already miss them. I'll have to call them before they go to bed to know they are okay."

Rachel rubbed Emily's back as they began to talk about children — how difficult they could get sometimes but how easily they stole one's heart. Lily hoped to have another child with Taylor one day, but for now, she was totally satisfied with the ones they had.

Soon, the conversation moved to Stella, and Rachel said, "I can't imagine how eager you are to see your sister again."

"I can't wait. I'm really eager to finally see her after such a long time. I know Daniel said Stella doesn't know where our parents are, but I am holding out hope that she has some information that might help us find them."

They continued talking about Stella and Lily's parents until Rachel got up and told Lily she was going to serve dinner. "I didn't even ask if you were hungry, Lily. I should have served dinner an hour ago," she said. "I just got carried away with our conversation."

Lily smiled and got up. "Let me help you."

"No, sit. I'm not cooking anything. I am just serving the leftover fried rice from yesterday." Rachel began to hand Emily to Keith, but Lily insisted on taking her. When Rachel left, Lily got into a conversation with Keith about how different living in California was from Arizona, while Emily sat on her lap playing with her doll. Minutes later, she and Keith got up to set the table and Rachel set the food on the dining table.

Emily sat in her highchair and tossed around her food, while Lily sat talking with Rachel and Keith while they dined on the rich and flavorful rice. After they finished eating and cleared the dishes, they sat in the living room and continued reminiscing about Lily's and Rachel's childhoods in Fallow Creek compared to Keith's in Destiny.

Half an hour later, when their conversation died down, Rachel looked at Emily, who was now asleep in her arms, and smiled. She looked at Keith, who was also yawning, and then turned to Lily. "It's time to put this little one to bed. It's long past her bedtime."

Lily stretched and stood up. "And it's time for me to go to bed as well. I've got an early day tomorrow." Once more, she kissed the top of Emily's hair and then hugged Rachel and Keith. She headed straight to the small guest room where she'd stayed the last time she was here, got her pajamas out of her duffel bag, hastily brushed her teeth, and then fell into bed.

TWO

When she woke up the next morning, Lily frowned. Her dreams had been filled with heated conversations with her parents. She glanced at the clock on her bedside table and saw it was only six o'clock. Brushing aside her troubling dreams, she quieted her heart enough to pray and study her Bible, and then she went to take a shower. She finished preparing to leave for Tucson by eight o'clock and then heard a scraping sound coming from the kitchen.

She headed to the kitchen and found Rachel standing with Keith, preparing breakfast. She smiled as she watched them hold hands and grin at each other as they worked. They were clearly enjoying their time alone and she didn't want to intrude. She turned around and began to walk away, then stopped when Rachel called her name.

She walked back to the kitchen and greeted Rachel and Keith. "I didn't want to disturb you guys," she said.

Keith smiled. "That's okay. I have to go visit some

people now anyway. Let me leave you girls to talk."

He began to walk away, but Rachel called to him. "Do those people include Dennis Hamilton?"

"Yes, why?" he asked.

Rachel sighed. "Nothing. You know what I feel about you visiting that man."

"I know. But like I told you, he's harmless now. I have to share God's word with whomever I feel called to share it."

"I know," Rachel said. She opened her mouth, clearly to protest, and then shrugged. "Hurry back, Keith."

He walked back to Rachel, planted a kiss on her cheek, and left.

"So Keith visits Dennis Hamilton regularly?" Lily said. "I am not surprised, since Keith has a pastor's heart, but it's the same Dennis that tried to kill both of you. How is he able to do that?"

Rachel sighed heavily. "I have asked him about that a few times, but he always says the same thing he said now." She thinned her lips and waved her hand. "I don't feel like talking about Dennis Hamilton right now. Let's talk about something else." She asked Lily if she'd made any friends in California, and Lily began to tell her about some of the women in her new church she was friendly with. After that, they talked about the new staff Rachel had had to hire to help her run the House of Refuge and Fallow Creek as a whole. Most were people from outside the town, but a few were residents of the House of Refuge.

Some minutes later, Rachel leaned against the cabinet, covered her mouth, and yawned loudly.

"You're tired," Lily said. "You didn't sleep well

last night?"

"I did," Rachel answered. "I just get really tired these days, especially in the morning. I always think I sleep well, but maybe I don't. I guess I have so many responsibilities in Fallow Creek that even when I am asleep, my mind is fully active."

"Maybe try going to bed earlier so you can get in more hours of sleep… and then you will wake up refreshed."

"Maybe." Rachel smiled and began to stir the grits cooking on the burner.

They continued to talk while Rachel cooked. Some minutes later, she added cooked shrimp, sausage, and spices into the pan of boiling grits.

Keith came back just as Lily was setting the table. He went to give Emily a quick bath while Lily dished out the food with Rachel. Keith came out with Emily a few minutes later, and they sat at the table and ate quickly, as they all had a full day ahead of them. This time, Rachel fed Emily and got most of the food into her mouth.

After breakfast, Lily sat on the couch and glanced at her wristwatch. It was almost half-past nine. She sighed and willed the time to go faster.

When it was five minutes to ten, she stood up and announced that it was time for her to leave. Keith and Rachel wished her Godspeed, and she left the House of Refuge and stood at the gate waiting impatiently for Daniel.

Daniel sauntered up to her at five minutes past ten, and she shook her head. "You are late, Daniel Bacon."

He chuckled. "I'm not late. It's only," he glanced at his wristwatch, "four minutes past ten."

"My watch says six minutes past ten now," Lily told him.

He grinned. "Well, are we going to leave now or stand here talking about my being three minutes late?"

"Five minutes late," Lily teased him.

He shook his head and sighed. "Fine. Five minutes." He pointed at her rental, the white Range Rover parked in front of the House of Refuge. "I stayed up really late yesterday, and I didn't sleep as long as I wanted." He smiled. "I'm going to make up for it while you drive."

"No, you are going to drive us, Daniel," Lily said, chuckling. "I had to drive from Prospect to Fallow Creek. I don't feel like driving now."

Daniel groaned as she tossed him the car key and stepped past him. He got into the driver's seat while she got into the passenger's.

She closed the door and smiled at the look on his face. "Cheer up, Daniel. You will be back in Fallow Creek before you know it, and back with your bride." She turned to him as he started the car and they began to pull away from the House of Refuge. "Talking about your bride, you told me yesterday that you would tell me how you and Davina got married so quickly when she was engaged to someone else the last time I heard."

As he sped toward the town border, he began to tell her everything, from Vina's decision to hold off on getting married to his going to L.A to win her back, and then to the utter joy he'd felt when she'd returned to Fallow Creek. "I knew I had to marry her immediately so she could not slip through my hands again. I asked her if she would marry me that same day, and as outrageous as my request was, she happily agreed. I just wish I had taken control of my anger issues and jealousy sooner. We would not have suffered most of the heartache we did."

"I think as long as you are still working on your anger issues and not letting it control you anymore, you are on the right path. I am happy you have the girl of your dreams now."

"I do. I feel so incredibly blessed to have Vina."

Lily smiled. "I understand. I feel the exact same way about my husband."

They continued to talk as they got to Prospect, and then stopped to top up the tank at a gas station. After that, Lily called Taylor and told him they had left for Tucson. When he told her he missed her and couldn't wait to see her, she beamed. "I miss you too," she said. "I will call to let you know how it all went after I see my sister."

As Daniel continued to drive, Lily asked him about his time as the assistant leader of the security squad, and he asked her about life in the House of Refuge before Rachel took over. She wasn't surprised when he told her how regimented their lives had been. Her everyday life at the House of Refuge had been just as regimented.

Lily said, "I think that was one of the ways Dennis Hamilton used to keep everyone in line in Fallow Creek. No matter what your job or position was, you had to follow strict rules and regulations."

They finally drove into Tucson, and Lily's heart began to gallop. Excitement ran through her as she thought about seeing Stella again.

Daniel turned onto a long, narrow street with different kinds of houses lining each side. He parked in front of a small, grey bungalow and got out of the car.

Lily got out as well and took a deep breath before following Daniel to the front of the house. When Daniel rang the doorbell, she started praying silently that Stella would be here. Even though Daniel had seen her here only days ago, there was still a small chance that she'd moved away with her husband, John, considering how disgustingly sneaky and unpredictable John was. It would be awful if that were the case, especially if Daniel's brother didn't know or was told by Stella's husband not to tell where they'd gone.

The door opened, and a bearded man she recognized as Steven Bacon, Daniel's older brother peered at them. His mouth turned up, and he stared at Daniel with a mixture of amusement and scorn. And then he reached out and pulled his brother into a hug.

"So, you finally came to your senses, little brother," Steven said. "I am glad you've finally left that town."

Daniel pushed away and shook his head. "No. Actually, I still live in Fallow Creek." He tilted his head toward his brother. "Are you going to invite us in, Steven?"

"You still live in Fallow Creek!" Steven stared at him for a few seconds and then sighed loudly. He turned to look at Lily, and his eyes widened in clear surprise. "Lily Hunter! Wow! Stella will be so happy to see you. All she's done for weeks is talk about you and your parents." He smiled and stepped back from the door. "Come in."

Lily thanked him and walked into the house

with Daniel. She looked around the small living room for just a second and then said to Steven, "Where is she? Where is my sister?"

"Wait here. Let me go get her for you," Steven said, and left the living room.

Lily turned to tell Daniel how thrilled she was to be able to finally see her sister again and then gasped as a loud scream startled her. She stood up as Stella flew into the living room toward her. Opening her arms wide, she folded Stella into a hug and sighed with joy and relief. She hugged her sister tightly with tears in her eyes, and for a long moment, they both stood holding on to each other, Stella clearly not wanting to let go just as she didn't. At last, she pulled away so she could inspect Stella closely.

Stella looked Lily over and smiled. "You look so different, Lily. You are absolutely beautiful. More beautiful than I have ever seen you." Her smile widened. "And very radiant."

Lily laughed. "Very radiant?"

Stella shrugged, still smiling. "That's the only word I can think to describe how you look." She laughed. "You're glowing." She put her hand on Lily's arm, leaned in, and whispered in Lily's ear, "I know you married Taylor Dalton last year, the most desirable man in Fallow Creek."

Lily grinned.

Daniel shook his head and chuckled. "I heard that, Stella. I am the most desirable man in Fallow Creek, not Taylor Dalton."

Lily and Stella laughed out loud, and Daniel joined in.

Steven walked into the living room again. "Why

are you three laughing so hard?" he asked, looking at them suspiciously but with a smile on his face.

"It's our secret," Daniel said.

Stella put her arms around Lily and beamed at her. And then the smile suddenly melted off her face as footsteps sounded behind them. She stepped slightly away from Lily and bit her lip.

Lily turned around and rolled her eyes. John, Stella's always-scowling husband, had walked into the living room. She turned to look at Stella again and frowned. Her sister looked frightened. What had John done to her to make her so scared simply because he'd walked into the room? The Stella she'd known growing up was exuberant and playful. This Stella was timid and withdrawn and seemed wary even before John had come in here.

Stella began to move toward her husband, but Lily took hold of her hand and held her back. "Stay here beside me, Stella. We still have a lot to talk about." She glared at John. There was no way she could leave her sister with a man that made her so scared. After this visit, she would try to talk Stella into going away with her. But the problem was that Stella might not agree to do that.

Stella sat beside her on the couch, while Daniel and Steven sat at the dining table, not far away from the living room, talking. John sat on the sofa near the door, clearly to listen in on their conversation. With the men here, especially John, Lily could not ask her sister exactly what she wanted to. For a long time, they shared stories about their childhood, how strict their parents had seemed when they were growing up, and then about Lily's marriage to Taylor and her relationship with his children.

Stella smiled and whispered again, "I cannot get over how great you look, Lily. Are you sure you're not pregnant? I know you're glowing because you are deeply in love with your husband, but it could also be because you are pregnant."

Lily laughed. "No, I'm pretty sure I'm not pregnant, Stella."

"Well then, I guess you look radiant simply because you are happy and in love."

Lily nodded and looked into her sister's eyes. Once again, a thread of worry ran through her at the apprehension in Stella's expression. She glanced at John, who was seemingly reading a book but was clearly just pretending to do so while he listened to their conversation. She frowned in annoyance and said to Stella, "What about you? Are you happy in your marriage?"

Stella blinked and shifted slightly away from Lily. "What do you mean?" she asked. Her eyes flickered to her husband.

Lily looked at John as he stood up and came to stand at the window behind Stella. He opened the curtains and looked out, but Lily could see he was looking at Stella from the corner of his eye.

Anger simmered in her heart. With John standing behind Stella, almost hovering over her, it was unlikely that Stella would tell her anything about her marriage. Her anger began to boil over, but she pushed it away and focused on Stella again. There was no point trying to push Stella to tell her about her marriage right now. It would only make Stella upset and probably get her in trouble with John. And she was bound to be if she said anything that John did not like. Which really worried Lily.

Without a doubt, from the look on his face and Stella's, John would give Stella some kind of grief once Lily left. What that grief would be, she didn't know.

Once again, she fumed, and then she sighed and pressed down her anger. She turned the conversation back to their parents and the fact that they still didn't know where they were. Once more, the constant worrying that had become a part of her after she'd found out her parents had disappeared without a trace began to press in on her. She knew Stella didn't know where their parents were either, but she didn't know why Stella had been in Fallow Creek when everyone started leaving the town. "You have not told me why Mom and Dad left Fallow creek without you knowing, Stella. What really happened?"

Again, Stella looked a little scared, and she glanced briefly at John before looking at Lily again. She pressed her lips together and looked down at the tiled floor.

Lily turned and scowled at John. Without a doubt, the man had something to do with why Stella didn't know where their parents were. Once again, her stomach burned with anger, and this time she didn't try to push it away or hide it. She spat out, "John, I haven't seen my sister in a very long time. I would like to have a private conversation with her. Do you think that would be possible?"

John glowered at her without saying anything.

Lily narrowed her eyes. "Can you please excuse us?"

John shook his head. "No, I can't. Stella's my wife. I think anything you want to say to her is also for my ears."

"Not true," Lily said. "I have a right to have a private conversation with my sister without you breathing down her neck."

John did not move an inch.

Lily bit her lip and tried to hold her anger in check. She took a deep breath and said to John as evenly as she could, "We want to talk about women stuff."

He raised his brows and stared at her with a curious look. "Women's stuff?"

"You know, things like our..."

John lifted his hand and shook his head. "Don't say it." He glared at her and then looked at Daniel and Steven, who were still sitting and chatting at the dining table. "What about them? Why are they allowed to still be here?"

Daniel and Steven looked over at them. Daniel stood and said to Steven, "Let's go outside and talk. We still have a lot to talk about, like the fact that I got married to Vina two days ago."

Steven's mouth dropped open as he stared at Daniel, and then he said, "Wait, did I just hear you say you got married to Vina two days ago?"

Daniel grinned. "Yes."

"What? And you are just telling me now. Why?"

Daniel took his brother by the shoulder. "Come on. Let's go outside." They walked past Lily and Stella and went out of the house.

John glowered at Lily once more and then walked out of the living room.

Lily sighed with relief after he left. "Now tell me everything that happened Stella. When exactly was the last time you saw Mom and Dad, and why don't you and your husband know where our parents are?"

Stella pressed her lips together, and for a long moment, she said nothing. Just before Lily could ask her about their parents again, Stella sighed heavily. She began to tell Lily everything: how their parents had come to their house and John had promised them that they would all leave Fallow Creek together; how she'd discovered that he'd lied to her parents and never intended for them to leave together; and how he had made her pack up and leave town, making sure their parents didn't know where they were moving.

"I tried to reason with him, but he didn't listen. He didn't want Mom and Dad knowing where we were moving, or us knowing where they were going. It broke my heart."

Lily could not contain her anger after Stella finished speaking. She stood up and paced the living room, fuming. That evil John. She looked over at her sister. Stella was staring at the space in front of her, but Lily could see shame and hurt in her eyes. She sighed. John had turned her sister into someone who could not speak up for herself... But wasn't that what most of the men in Fallow Creek did to their wives? She sighed again and went and sat down beside Stella once more.

Stella put her hand on Lily's shoulder. "Are you angry with me, Lily?"

"Of course not!" Lily turned to face her. "It's that husband of yours that I am angry with. Because of him, we don't know where Mom and Dad are and might never know. When you got married in Fallow Creek, I knew he wasn't a good guy. In fact,

I sensed there was something wrong with him. But I didn't know how bad he was. Yes, most of the men in Fallow Creek don't treat their wives well at all, but John is cruel, Stella. What kind of husband willfully separates his wife from her parents?"

Stella seemed to bristle, and Lily sighed. "I wish I could take you away from here," she said, and took her sister's hand. "Away from that man you call a husband."

Stella shook her head. "I can't leave him, Lily. No matter what he has done, he is still my husband, and my place is by his side."

Lily placed her hand on her forehead, feeling weary and helpless. She wanted to tell Stella that her place was anywhere she felt safe and happy, and that clearly wasn't with John, but she stopped herself from speaking. There was no use. Her words would accomplish nothing. Knowing what she knew about the women of Fallow Creek, especially those who'd left with their men, there was no way Stella would ever consider leaving John. Not unless Lily physically carried her out of this house. And she would have tried if she didn't know that John and Steven would not let her and that Stella would resent her for it.

"Lily, are you sure you are not angry with me?"

"No," Lily said again. "I am not angry with you, Stella."

"Are we ever going to find Mom and Dad?" Stella asked.

Fear gripped Lily at the thought that they might not, and then she forced a smile. "We will, Stella. I promise that I will do everything in my power to find them."

"But you told me that you have been looking for them for a long time and you still haven't found them."

"I know, but I will keep looking. They are somewhere. They cannot have disappeared into thin air. I am pretty sure that someone from Fallow Creek knows where they are. I just have to find that person."

Lily spoke confidently to Stella, but deep in her heart, she felt anything but. Taylor had asked everyone from Fallow Creek who he was still in contact with if they knew where their parents were, but none of them did. Just like Stella said, she and Taylor had been looking for a long time and still hadn't found them. But she would not give up.

She reached out, pulled Stella into a hug, and silently asked the Lord to help her find their parents quickly, just as he had helped her find Stella. She also asked that she would one day, soon, be able to get her sister out of her awful marriage.

THREE

Hours after Lily came to see her sister with Daniel, she finally got up to leave. She hugged Stella tightly and then stepped back to look into Stella's eyes. There were tears there, and Lily felt tears fill her own eyes and stream down her cheeks. She bit her lip and asked, "Are you sure you won't come with me, Stella?"

She glanced at John, who was standing just outside the door, looking eager for her and Daniel to leave.

Stella shook her head. "I'm sure, Lily. I can't leave John."

Lily tried once more to convince Stella to come with her. "But what about Mom and Dad?"

"What about them?"

"It would make more sense for us to look for them together. Don't you want that?"

"I do... but like I told you before, my place is beside my husband. I can't leave unless he gives me permission to do so."

Lily's temper rose. "What husband are you

talking about, Stella? The one that caused all this? The one whose fault it is that we don't know where our parents are? How can you stay with such a cruel, selfish man?"

Stella looked away as tears flowed down her cheeks.

Lily felt remorseful for the way she'd spoken, though she did not regret the words she'd said about John. She sighed and wiped her sister's tears away with her thumb. She started to open her mouth to try to convince Stella one more time to go with her to Fallow Creek, then shut it again when the men opened the front door and walked into the living room.

Stella stepped back from Lily, a guilty look on her face. She went over to John, and he put his hands on her shoulders and gave Lily a look that clearly said he wanted her to know Stella belonged to him and there was nothing Lily could do about it.

Lily stared at him in anger and quickly wiped the tears from her eyes when Daniel approached her. She took a deep breath and forced herself to smile.

"Are you ready to go, Lily?" Daniel asked, smiling back.

"I guess so," she said. She looked at Stella again and said, "I'll come back soon. I promise." She smiled genuinely at her. "I'm really glad I found you after such a long time."

Stella beamed. She walked over to Lily, hugged her again, and then went to stand beside John.

Lily heaved a weary sigh and followed Daniel out of the house.

Outside, Lily bit her lip and swallowed the sob

that rose up in her throat. When Daniel asked if she was okay, she nodded. "I'm fine." And then she shook her head. "I am not really fine. After hearing that John's deception is the reason why we don't know where our parents are, and seeing in a small way how he treats my sister, I don't understand why Stella would stay with him. I wish I could convince her to leave that awful man and come with me to Fallow Creek."

"I felt the same way when I came here to find Steven," Daniel said. "Did I tell you she wanted to follow me to Fallow Creek and would have if her husband hadn't returned unexpectedly and stopped her?"

Lily blinked in surprise. "You didn't. I can't believe it. She nearly left with you? Then why didn't she agree to leave with me?"

"She wanted to go with me because I told her you come to Fallow Creek regularly and she was eager to see you. She did say that as soon as she did, she would have to return to her husband."

"I'm going to come back here to get her one way or another," Lily said.

"How are you going to get her? You cannot force her to go with you if she doesn't want to."

Lily shrugged. "I don't know how I am going to get her to come with me yet, but I'll find a way." Her heart ached as she thought of Stella suffering in silence with John. That there was emotional abuse involved in their marriage, she was sure, but she also had a heartbreaking suspicion that there was physical abuse as well, though she could not prove it. Hopefully, John would not pull the same stunt he had with their parents and move Stella out of the house to some unknown destination before she could find a way to get her sister away from him.

Lily ran her fingers through her hair in frustration. "I just hope Stella stays safe. For now, I have to focus on finding our parents, though I don't know what else to do."

Daniel looked up at the sky and then faced Lily again. "Well, it will soon start getting dark. I think it's a good idea for us to head back to Fallow Creek before it does."

Lily smiled at him. "We still have a few hours before it gets dark, Daniel. It's not driving in the dark you are worried about, is it? You just want to get back to your new bride."

Daniel arched his brows, and Lily chuckled. "I understand. You should definitely start back now."

Daniel stared at her. "Aren't you coming?"

"No, there is a friend in Tucson I need to see before I head back to Fallow Creek."

"Are you sure you won't go back with me?" Daniel asked. "You told me you don't want to drive."

"I don't really want to, but I need to see this friend of mine."

"Okay." Daniel bade her farewell and walked away.

For a short moment, she watched Daniel walk away, heading in the direction of the bus station, and then she got into the Range Rover and drove off.

***

Sofia rolled her eyes as she listened to the man sitting in front of her go on and on about his last relationship without letting her get a word in. She finally tuned him out and, as usual, her mind went to Jude and the day he'd left her. The day they were supposed to get married but hadn't because he'd basically left her at the altar... or at the courthouse to be specific. Overwhelming sadness settled over her like a dark cloud, as it usually did whenever she thought about Jude and the marriage that had never happened.

Where was he now? She shuddered as she thought about the fact that he might have been deported back to his war-torn country. She preferred to think that he had developed cold feet and left her for some reason best known to him than that he had been deported back to Bakali. With the last news she had heard about that country and how dangerous the place had become, Jude would be in serious danger or worse if he'd been sent back there. She shut her eyes, unwilling to follow that line of thought any longer.

He had left her on their wedding day, she was sure. As painful as the idea was, it was definitely better than thinking he was dead.

Once again, a cloud of depression began to smother her. *Lord, please help me,* she silently prayed. She briefly shut her eyes and took deep breaths to try to shake the depression and anxiety pressing in on her, and then she opened her eyes again. She stared at her date and hid a groan. He was still talking about his ex and hadn't even noticed that she'd stopped listening to him. Why, oh why, had she accepted Edith's offer to set her up with this guy, and why did she agree to go on a date with him?

After more than a year of pining for Jude and grieving over their broken engagement, her friend, Edith had decided it was time she moved on, and she had reluctantly agreed. She could not remain miserable forever, longing for a guy who was clearly not coming back to her. She had to find a way to continue without Jude. And so, she had agreed for Edith to manage her love life and find a suitable guy for her as she had no strength to do it for herself. So far, she had gone on four dates, all set up by Edith, and all had gone badly. This fifth one was definitely going to be added to the list of disastrous dates.

The waiter brought their food and set it on the table. Her stomach cramped as she looked at her chicken salad. She wasn't hungry, and the thought of eating left her slightly queasy. She looked at Brandon, her date. He was already tucking into his steak and grilled potatoes. She watched him as he cut into the sizeable slab of meat and put it in his mouth while still talking. Pursing her lips, she looked away. Today was the one-year anniversary of her almost-marriage to Jude, and she'd agreed to go out on this date specifically to escape the misery that had begun to swallow her up. But maybe she should have stayed at home.

Brandon looked up at her as he put another large piece of meat into his mouth. He frowned as he looked at her plate. "Aren't you going to eat your food?"

She looked down at her chicken salad. "I am not really hungry."

His eyes lit up. "Can I have it then?"

Before she could answer, he reached out, took her plate, and transferred all the food onto his. He cut into the chicken with his knife and put a large forkful into his mouth. Looking up at her again, he nodded and grinned. "It's really good." With surprising speed, he finished the chicken, and then went back to eating his steak again. "So, Sofia, tell me all about yourself," he said.

She raised her eyebrows, surprised he had asked. She had decided he wasn't capable of listening to anything other than his own voice. But she did not want to talk about herself, and certainly not with him. She wanted the date to end. Still, in order to be polite, she said, "There isn't much to talk about. As I told you, I am an artist. A starving artist."

He laughed and then blinked as he looked at her. "You are serious?"

"Yes."

"You don't look anything like a starving artist. In fact, you look like a spoilt heiress or something."

She arched her brows and chuckled. "I don't know if I should be offended or flattered."

"Oh... definitely flattered." He grinned. "My cousin is an artist." He began to tell her about his cousin and how his paintings never sold, and then he talked about something else, which was mostly about himself.

Sofia groaned and soon stopped listening to him.

The date thankfully ended half an hour later, and before Sofia hurried out of the restaurant, Brandon asked if he could see her again. She politely told him she wouldn't go on a second date with him and quickly strode out of the place. She got into her waiting taxi and sighed in relief, glad to see the end of the date. Maybe she wasn't giving any of these guys a fair chance, and she knew she should instead of holding on to the memory of her relationship with Jude. But she could not help comparing them all to him.

You cannot go on like this, Sofia. The earlier you move on and find someone else, the quicker you'll stop feeling constantly miserable.

She got to her apartment building, paid the cab driver, and walked into the building. She rode the elevator to the penthouse suite that Lily and Taylor graciously allowed her to stay in and plopped down on the plush sofa. Since she'd moved in last year, Lily had not visited, but they exchanged phone calls and text messages regularly. She missed Lily. Since she'd stopped working at her former job, her circle of friends had gradually decreased. When Jude had left her on their wedding day, she'd stopped communicating with the rest of her friends. Now, she had only Edith and Lily. They were the two friends that never stopped calling and didn't give up on her. And Lily always had words of encouragement for her that made her feel much better whenever they talked.

I wish Lily were here now.

She began to reach into her purse to get her phone so she could call Lily and blinked when it began to ring. She dug her fingers into her purse, brought out her phone, and smiled widely. *Talk about the saint!*

"Hey, Lily! I was just thinking about you. In fact, I was just about to call you."

"Well, then I'm glad I called," Lily said. "Are you home now?"

"Home now? Yes. Why?"

"How would you like to come with me to Fallow

Creek?"

Sofia leaned back on the couch. "I don't know, Lily. Right now I am..." She jerked her head as a loud knock sounded at the door. Rising from the sofa, she headed toward the door with her phone. "Hold on, Lily. Someone is at the door. Let me see who it is." She opened the peephole and her mouth dropped open. Quickly, she threw the door wide open and shouted. "Lily!" She drew her friend into a tight hug and then pulled back again. Laughing, she looked Lily over. "What in the world are you doing here?" She shook her head and laughed again. "You are such a silly girl. And you called me, pretending to be in California."

Lily laughed. "Hey, I wasn't pretending." She reached out and hugged Sofia again and then stepped into the house. "The thing is, I came here about half an hour ago and found you were not home. I decided to get some dinner at that Italian restaurant down the road since I was hungry."

They plopped down on the sofa, and Sofia giggled. "You don't know how happy I am to see you," she said. "I've missed you so much, Lily. I know we speak on the phone regularly, but it's not the same as having my best friend here in person."

Lily nodded. "I know."

"So, how have you been?"

"I have been good," Lily said. She looked Sofia over. "You always look good, Sofia, but today you look amazing." Lily smiled. "Where did you go? On a date?"

Sofia grinned. "Yes. I went out on a date."

Lily leaned forward and smiled, looking really excited. "And how was it? Tell me everything."

"Disastrous, just like the others have been. Why can't I find a decent guy?"

Lily gave her a tender smile. "You mean a guy like Jude, don't you? You shouldn't be comparing all these guys to Jude, Sofia. Just give them a chance. You will never find someone new if you don't. And I really want you to."

"Is it so bad to want to find someone like Jude, or even like Taylor?"

Lily touched Sofia's arm and smiled sympathetically. Taking Sofia's hand, she said, "You will soon find someone great who will truly love you. I promise."

Sofia sighed wearily. "I miss Jude so much, Lily. Not a day goes by without me thinking about what life would be like if he was still here. If we had gotten married. And I cannot stop worrying about him. You know how I told you I prefer to believe that he left me on our wedding day rather than that he was deported back to his country?"

"Yes." Lily nodded.

"The thought that something bad may have happened to him is unbearable." She shut her eyes and pictured Jude's face, how happy he'd looked the day before they were supposed to get married. She sighed sadly.

Lily squeezed her hand. "You cannot go on like this, Sofia. I think you need a real break from your life here and from constantly worrying. Why don't you come with me to Fallow Creek?" A huge smile appeared on her face. "I have great news. I found my sister, Stella. She lives right here in Tucson."

Sofia gasped and then beamed at Lily. "You did?" She pulled Lily into a tight hug. "I am so happy for you. Wow! You have been searching for your sister for so long." She drew back and looked into Lily's eyes. "What about your parents? Have you found them too?"

"Unfortunately, I still haven't found them, and Stella doesn't know where they are either. But I will keep looking for them. At least I have found my sister."

"You have. God is so good." She put her sadness aside and focused completely on her friend. "So, what about Taylor? Did he come with you to Fallow Creek? And the kids? How are they doing?"

"No, Taylor didn't come with me. He was in Florida on a business trip when I got the news about my sister. The kids are with their nanny. It's why I have to go back soon. They love her, but I can't be away from them for more than a few days. Before I go, I'm going to try to see if I can find any clues in Fallow Creek — clues that could lead me to where my parents are. If you come with me to Fallow Creek, you could see where I grew up and the town that I have told you so much about. And then we can leave for California together and you can stay with us for a while. We can even travel out of the country together. Remember how you used to like to travel? It will be good for you."

Sofia sighed and searched Lily's eyes. "How long are we talking about?"

"For as long as it takes you to get back to a good place mentally and emotionally."

Sofia shook her head. "Are you sure I won't be extra baggage?" She smiled.

Lily laughed. "Of course not. Please, Sofia. I want you to come with me. It will be fun. You'll see."

"Okay, then," Sofia said. "As long as Taylor will be fine with it."

"He will be. He likes you, too. You know that."

Sofia smiled as her excitement rose. Lily was right. She needed to get away from all this sadness, especially at this one-year anniversary. "I'll go with you. You are right. I do need a break."

Lily shrieked and hugged her again. "We'll have so much fun, Sofia."

Sofia grinned. "When are we leaving on our fun vacation?"

"First thing tomorrow," Lily answered.

FOUR

The next morning, Sofia got into the passenger's seat of Lily's rental car. As Lily drove to Fallow Creek, she took a deep breath, glad she'd agreed to go on this trip with her friend. She enjoyed sitting beside Lily, chatting and laughing as the wind blew in her hair while they raced to Lily's hometown. She could not wait to explore the town Lily had told her so much about.

Lily laughed as Sofia filled her in on the details of her date the evening before. "He talked constantly about himself and didn't allow me to get a word in," she said. "The guy I went on a date with before that had nothing to talk about."

"Who knows, Sofia, you might meet someone new in Fallow Creek. Someone who you will connect with and who will be different from these guys you've been going on dates with. When that happens, don't forget to thank me."

Sofia laughed. "Lily, I doubt I'll meet anyone in your hometown. Weren't you the one who told me that Fallow Creek is now empty except for the women at the House of Refuge and a few families who came back not long ago? Most of the young, single men are gone, aren't they?"

Lily nodded. "That's true. I don't know what I was thinking."

"Besides, even if the single men are still there, they will not be the kind of guys I want to date." She grinned. "I am certainly not cut out to be a sister wife."

Lily chuckled. "You are right. I certainly don't want you to end up with a guy who will later acquire more wives like he was acquiring property." She glanced briefly at Sofia and faced the road again. "Anyway, it will be just us girls, and we'll have a great time. Maybe when you come with me to California, I will introduce you to one of Taylor's friends. There are two of them I have in mind right now who are single. They are great guys."

Sofia sighed. As much as she knew in her head that she needed to move on, she didn't want to. She didn't reject all the guys Edith had set her up with just because she didn't like them; she rejected them because they were not Jude. And none of the men Lily was going to introduce her to were him either. She bit her lip. *Oh, Jude, where are you?*

They continued chatting until Sofia looked up in surprise at a sign on the road that said, WELCOME TO FALLOW CREEK. She'd been so engrossed in her conversations with Lily that she'd not even noticed how the time had flown by.

Lily gazed at the sign and smiled widely. "We are here," she said. "This signpost wasn't here the last time I came. Rachel arranged for it to be put up about a month ago." She slowed down as they approached a two-story Spanish-style house, and Lily pointed. "That is, or used to be, Dennis Hamilton's house, but he doesn't live there anymore. His wives and children still stay there, though."

"Where does he live now?"

"A building on the other side of town that Taylor gave him. He lives there, or more accurately hides out there, with some of the ex-members of the security squad."

They drove past similar-looking single-story houses on both sides of the road.

As they continued on, Sofia noticed that apart from a few buildings, most of the homes looked the same. Apart from the fact that the town looked almost deserted, there wasn't much else that was peculiar about it. That surprised her. She didn't know why she'd expected the town to look different than it did. Maybe it was because Lily had spoken so much of how strange Fallow Creek was. Because of that, she had laughingly expected to see somewhat of a fantastical place. Or at the least, an exotic place.

They soon approached a massive white building, and Lily said, "That's theHouse." Sofia looked out the window and stared at the house. It was way bigger than she had imagined. But then, considering how many women lived in the house according to Lily, it was to be expected.

They finally stopped in front of the gates of theHouse of Refuge and got out of the car. There were a few women strolling around the grounds of the House, and Sofia followed Lily through the gates and up to the front of the building. Lily greeted some of the women and opened the large wooden door.

When they walked into the House, Sofia looked around her. They were standing in a large empty space, and in front of them was a long flight of stairs with polished wooden balustrades. Women walked up and down the stairs, and more were walking along the hallway at the top of the stairs.

Lily pointed to her right and said, "That is the common room. Do you want to see it?"

"Yes, please," Sofia said. Lily had also told her a lot about the common room, the room that had been empty before Rachel furnished it and made it a true common room for the women. Again, she was surprised at how big the room was, but even more surprised at how many women were seated on the many couches and sofas arranged around the room. Most of the women were chatting or just lounging and reading books and magazines. All of them were dressed in floor-length gowns that Sofia would never be caught dead in. She turned to Lily and giggled. "Now I understand where you got your peculiar fashion sense from. Of course, I should have known."

Lily smacked her arm playfully. "You cannot say I have not improved on my dress sense since I married Taylor."

Sofia chuckled. "And you have me to thank for that." She laughed when Lily rolled her eyes, and then pretended to inspect Lily's simple but beautiful knee-length navy blue dress. "Well, this is slightly better than what you used to wear, but…" She laughed again when Lily shook her head. "You know you look beautiful as always, Lily."

"Do you want to go upstairs to see Rachel and

Keith with me, Sofia, or are you planning to set up a fashion show here?"

"Hmm, setting up a fashion show isn't such a bad idea…"

Lily laughed. "Come along, Sofia!" She grabbed Sofia's hand and pulled her toward the stairs.

More women greeted Lily as they climbed the stairs. They walked down a long, carpeted hallway, and Lily again stopped from time to time to greet an acquaintance or friend of hers. Sofia peeked into some of the rooms with their doors open. From the little she could see where she stood, they were all elegantly furnished and bigger than she had imagined. Still, she somehow felt as though she had been here before because of how much Lily had told her about the place.

"This place is really nice, Lily," she said, after Lily waved to a woman who passed by them. "It's beautiful, in fact. From all that you've said, I imagined somewhere slightly… dreary."

Lily grinned. "It *was* dreary. You should have seen it when a constantly angry woman named Margaret was still in charge. It was more like a prison house than anything else. Rachel changed it all when she took over."

Sofia nodded. That made sense.

They finally reached the end of the hallway and stood in front of a door. Lily knocked on it and waited. Almost immediately, it opened, and a good-looking man stared at her. A huge smile broke out on his face as he looked at Lily. He reached out and hugged her and then opened the door wider to let them in.

"Keith, this is my very good friend, Sofia," Lily

said. "Sofia, this is Rachel's husband, Keith."

Keith greeted Sofia pleasantly and asked them to sit. "Let me go get Rachel," he said, and left the living room.

Sofia sat on the couch near the door and glanced at her surroundings. The living room was beautifully furnished in cream and white. Lily's sister-in-law definitely had good taste. But that wasn't surprising, as her brother Taylor also did. He had fully furnished the apartment in Tucson that he and Lily allowed her to live in, and she still marveled at how elegant every item of furniture was. She turned to Lily and smiled. Before she could say anything, a pretty young woman about her and Lily's age walked into the living room holding a staggering toddler.

Lily immediately stood up. "Rachel!" They hugged, and then she pulled back and grinned down at the toddler. "Emily, how are you today?"

The little girl looked up at Lily and gave her a heartwarming smile. "Good!" she said in a high-pitched voice.

Lily laughed and turned to Sofia. She said, "Rachel, this is my friend, Sofia. Sofia, this is my sister-in-law, Rachel."

Sofia immediately saw the resemblance between Rachel and Taylor. She smiled, pleasantly surprised when Rachel gathered her into a tight hug.

Rachel pulled back and said, "Lily has told me so much about you."

Sofia smiled. "And she talks about you all the time, Rachel. I feel as though I have known you for a while."

"I feel the same way, Sofia," Rachel said. "Lily

never stops talking about you."

Sofia beamed. "You look a lot like your brother. You're really pretty."

"Look who's talking," Rachel said, smiling. "Lily told me you were beautiful, but she didn't tell me just how beautiful you were." She looked Sofia over. "I love your dress."

Sofia looked down at her pink-and-white summer dress. "Thank you," she said.

Lily rolled her eyes. "Get ready to compliment this one every single day. She is always turned out as though she were going for a beauty pageant."

Sofia shook her head and laughed. "Lily! Thank you for making me look like a vain girl who cares only about her appearance in front of your sister-in-law."

"There is nothing wrong with caring about your appearance." Rachel smiled.

Lily grinned. "No, Rachel already knows that is far from who you are. I tell her all the time how sweet and generous you are. You just happen to also have great fashion sense."

"Well, thank you, Lily," Sofia said, shaking her head at Lily again. She sat down on the couch, and Rachel sat beside her. Lily sat on the other side of her and lifted Emily onto her lap.

"So, Daniel told me what happened when you went to his brother's house," Rachel said to Lily. "I'm really happy you've found Stella at last. I hope you can find your parents soon as well."

"I wish I could get Stella out of that house." Lily narrowed her eyes. "Away from that tyrant, John. Unfortunately, Stella refused to leave."

Rachel nodded. "Daniel told me."

Lily sighed loudly. "For now, I'll have to concentrate on finding our parents." She began to tell Rachel and Sofia everything that Stella had told her concerning their parents, how John had told them they would leave together only to order Stella to pack up their things and leave Fallow Creek without their parents' knowledge.

When she finished speaking, Rachel frowned. "I cannot believe your sister's husband would do such a thing, but then again, I know many men who lived in this town who would have done the same thing John did."

"And I thought my ex, George, was a singularly selfish person," Sofia said.

"We have many of those here in Fallow Creek," Rachel told her. "Or at least we used to. Most of them moved away when I took over."

Sofia nodded. "So I heard."

Soon, the conversation shifted to life in the House of Refuge, and Sofia listened with fascination as Rachel talked about running the House and the responsibility that came with being the leader of the town and in charge of all the women here.

As though to buttress her point, from time to time a woman came to the apartment to ask Rachel for something or deliver a message. Sofia noted how patient and thoughtful she was as she answered every question and concern, and how much of a responsibility she had. This was why Lily spoke about her sister-in-law with such admiration.

Ten minutes later, a guy called Daniel came into the house with his wife, a beauty named Davina. They sat on the couch facing Sofia, Lily, and Rachel. Sofia blinked and stared at Davina for a long moment. She looked really familiar. Sofia was sure she knew the woman, especially because the name Davina was also attached to this face in her mind. She just couldn't remember how she knew Daniel's wife.

And then it dawned on her, and she gasped. She clearly remembered where she'd seen Davina. But there was still a thread of doubt in her because why would Davina Brooks be here in this small town, married to this Daniel? She'd read in some celebrity magazine that the actress was getting married to a popular director. It suddenly seemed far-fetched that it would be Davina Brooks, but she decided to ask anyway. "I'm sorry," she said looking intently at Davina. "Were you in that movie, *The King's Treasure?* You look like the actress who played the supporting role."

Vina gave her a smile, but she looked a little embarrassed. "Yes, I was." She glanced at her husband and then looked at Sofia again.

"Wow!" Sofia smiled widely. She could not believe the actress was sitting right here in this living room in front of her. The magazine article had also said the movie was slated to be nominated for an Oscar for best picture and the leads for best actor and actress. She agreed as she'd enjoyed the movie. "You were amazing in that movie," she said. She wanted to ask how come Davina was here, especially since the film had been released not too long ago, but she changed her mind. Even though it was the strangest thing that Davina Brooks was living in this tiny town, married to a handsome but clearly regular guy, instead of in Hollywood or somewhere glamorous, it wasn't really her business.

Besides, Davina looked happy and content.

Rachel and Lily laughed. "You should see the look on your face, Sofia," Lily said.

Daniel chuckled and put his arm around his wife. "I am married to a movie star," he said, proudly. Vina grinned, and he kissed her cheek.

Emily was still sitting on Lily's lap and twisting her aunt's hair around her tiny fingers. Lily looked down at her and smiled before facing Daniel. "So, you asked your brother if he knew anything about where my parents were. What did he say?"

"He said he didn't know where they were," Daniel said. "Talking about your parents, Lily, I think I have an idea of someone who might know where they are."

Lily raised her eyebrows. "You do? Who?"

"I think Dennis Hamilton might know something about where your parents went. I am not totally sure, but you know how things were when Dennis Hamilton was still in charge of Fallow Creek. He seemed to know everything that happened in town. He knew who came and who went, and no one left the town without getting permission from him."

Lily shook her head slowly. "But most people believed he had left town a long time before the mass exodus started. I doubt my parents saw him before they left."

Daniel shrugged. "But there's no harm in asking."

Sofia frowned and whispered to Lily. "Dennis Hamilton. Isn't he the dictator who ran Fallow Creek like it was his personal property before your sister-in-law took over?"

"Yes," Lily answered.

"How come he is still here? I thought he had to

leave in order for Rachel and her husband to take over the town."

"It's actually a long story involving my husband, but I'll tell you about it later on." She looked at Daniel again. "If you think Dennis might know something, then we will go and see him tomorrow."

Daniel sighed loudly. "I am really not looking forward to seeing that man again. I have not seen him face to face since Rachel and Keith took over." He frowned. "I still wonder why you let him remain in Fallow Creek, Rachel."

Rachel shrugged.

"You don't have to go with me, Daniel," Lily said. "I will go and see Dennis with my friend, Sofia."

"No, Lily! There's no way I'm going to let you and your friend see Dennis Hamilton by yourselves. That man is dangerous."

"How dangerous can he be, Daniel?" Lily said. "Didn't Mike Cadwell seize all his weapons from him and his men last year before the police came and confiscated it all?"

"So? Just because he doesn't have weapons doesn't make the man any less dangerous." Daniel shook his head. "I'll go with you."

Someone knocked on the front door and then opened it. A young freckled-faced woman came in and whispered something in Rachel's ear.

Rachel stood up. "The cook has finished preparing our meal. I told her to prepare something extra special today so we could have a party — just something informal. We will eat in the general dining hall today with the other women and then show Sofia around the house." She smiled at Sofia. "I am sure you'd like to see how we live."

"Yes," Sofia said.

"So, everyone, to the dining hall for our little party. I'm sure everyone is hungry."

Lily stood, lifting Emily with her. "I am famished, and a party would be great." She grinned. "In honor of Sofia. I told you that you would have fun here, didn't I?"

Sofia nodded. "That you did."

"I know it's not what you are used to," Lily said, "but we do know how to make our guests feel welcome in our small town."

Sofia stood and laughed. "This coming from a California girl who lives in a mansion."

They all laughed while Lily shook her head.

They left the apartment together, and Sofia could not help smiling. For the first time in a long while, she felt as free as a bird. Linking her arm with Lily's, she silently whispered a prayer of gratitude to God. She was glad she'd agreed to come here with Lily. This was so much better than being at home, thinking about Jude and wallowing in self-pity. She let go of every residual sadness she'd carried here and happily walked down the stairs, determined to enjoy this tiny town she'd heard so much about. Hopefully, she would also carry this carefree joy with her when it was time to go back to her life in Tucson.

FIVE

As Lily wanted to show Sofia the whole town, they walked to Dennis Hamilton's house rather than take the rental car. Sofia walked on Lily's right while Daniel walked on her left. She half-listened as Lily and Daniel talked about how much Daniel loathed their former leader, but her attention was mostly focused on the town, the empty houses, the deserted streets. Once in a while, a woman from the House of Refuge passed by them, throwing a quick greeting their way, but most of the women who lived in the House of Refuge were still there for the small party Rachel had thrown. Lily had insisted they leave the house in the middle of the party because it was getting late and she wanted to see Dennis Hamilton as soon as possible to ask him about her parents.

They passed a house where a man and three women stood talking while more than a dozen children ran around the front of the house, and for a brief moment, Sofia stood and gaped at them.

"Sofia, what are you doing?" Lily put her hand on

Sofia's shoulder.

Sofia turned to her. "Are they one family?" she asked Lily.

"Yes, they are one family," Daniel answered. "That is James Bartlet, his wives, and their children."

Lily laughed. "Why do you look so surprised, Sofia? You knew this was a polygamous town."

"Seeing it with my own eyes is different," she said, frowning. She began to walk again, embarrassed that she'd stopped to gape at the family. She faced Lily as they walked. "I thought all the polygamists left when Rachel took over. How come these ones are here?"

"I don't know," Lily said. "Maybe they came back recently."

"They did." Daniel looked at Sofia. "A few families have come back, but mostly men with just one wife since they know about Rachel's stance on polygamy. But James Bartlet came back a few days ago." Daniel frowned. "Come to think of it, I know three other men with multiple wives who came back five days ago as well. I don't know why they decided to come back now, but I hope the men won't cause Rachel and Keith any problems."

"I thought all those men with many wives swore never to come back to this town because a woman was in charge," Lily said with disgust written on her face. "Why have they started to move back?"

"Maybe they realized that Fallow Creek is still their home no matter who is in charge here," Sofia said.

"Or maybe it is some sort of defiant gesture," Daniel said, scowling. "Maybe they want to cause trouble."

"Daniel, let's think positively." Lily chuckled. "You know how infectious Rachel and Keith's messages of God's unconditional love is. They probably heard about it and how Rachel and Keith have turned this town around with God's love. I think they just want to be a part of it all."

"I doubt it," Daniel said. "But we will agree to disagree, Lily. And yes, I have been touched by Rachel and Keith's messages, and I believe in showing love just like they do. It's just that I don't understand why Keith goes to visit Dennis Hamilton regularly, as though he doesn't know what type of man he is."

"Keith says he's a changed man," Lily said.

"I believe God can change anyone, but I don't know if Dennis is truly changed."

"You said you haven't seen him since the mass exodus?" Lily asked.

"Yes."

"Well, you will see him today and know if he has really changed. But I think if Keith says Dennis Hamilton has changed, then he truly has."

Daniel shrugged and said nothing else about it.

Lily and Daniel soon began to talk about Lily's life in California and how different it was from how her life had been when she'd lived in Fallow Creek. Since Lily had already told Sofia in detail about her life in Northern California, her mind soon strayed. She sighed softly as George's face flashed through her mind. She had not thought about him in such a long time. Maybe she did now because of all the talk about men with multiple wives. George didn't have multiple wives, but she had been his mistress for years even after his wife had found out about them.

Sofia shuddered as she remembered how stubborn and uncaring she had been at that time, how she had flaunted her sin. Where would she be now if the Lord hadn't had mercy on her and delivered her from that sordid relationship?

She sighed sadly as Jude's face settled in her mind. If only they were still together. If only things hadn't turned out the way they had.

Sofia, please forget about him, she silently scolded herself. She'd come to Fallow Creek with Lily to escape her misery and to try to forget about Jude. She could not let herself be sucked into a black hole of depression when she had finally decided to move on after such a long time of wishing and praying every day that he would return to her.

"Sofia!"

She blinked and turned to Lily. "Yes? Did you say something?"

"I said we are almost at Dennis's," Lily said, pointing at a building a short distance away that looked more like a warehouse than a home.

Sofia stared at the building. "So this is the place you told me Taylor gave your ex-leader to stay in after that flood?"

"Yes," Lily said.

Sofia nodded. Lily had told her about the supernatural events that led to her sister-in-law taking over the town, including the flood that had swept away the ex-leader and his men. She would not have believed the story if not for the fact that she'd just given her heart to the Lord then and knew God could do the impossible. He'd miraculously kept her from killing herself. Also, she knew Lily would not lie to her.

"It's huge," Sofia said. She gave Lily a teasing smile as they got to the gate of the building. "Taylor is addicted to giving out his property."

Lily chuckled. "Taylor is addicted to giving everything. But that's okay. That is one of the reasons why I love him so much."

The smile on Lily's face as she talked about her beloved husband pierced Sofia's heart. She'd had this once — a guy who she knew would give his life for her. She'd been lying to herself for too long in order not to fall apart. But she had to tell herself the truth. There was no way Jude could have left her at the courthouse on their wedding day simply because he'd developed cold feet. He had probably been arrested and deported back to Bakali, and since his country was in disarray now and his father had been seen as an enemy of the opposition, he was probably either rotting away in captivity... or dead.

She couldn't breathe as waves of sorrow washed over her. *Lord, please. It can't be.*

But she knew there was no other plausible explanation for why he had suddenly disappeared on their wedding day.

Daniel knocked on the gate, and they opened almost immediately. A young man, who looked about nineteen, stared at Daniel with his mouth open.

"Nate, are you going to let us in or just stand there gaping at me?" Daniel asked, glaring him.

"Yes... sir... umm... I didn't know you were going to come here today."

"I am not the only one here as you can see,"

Daniel said, exasperatedly.

The boy opened the gate wide and stepped back so they could walk onto the large grounds.

There were a few young men inside the compound. They all stopped what they were doing and gawked at Daniel. He stared back at them.

Sofia shifted closer to Lily and whispered in her ear, "Why are they all looking at Daniel as if he were a ghost?"

"They are all members of the security squad I told you about," Lily whispered back. "Daniel was their leader, and I think he refused to go with Dennis when Dennis planned that attack on Rachel and Keith. I don't think they knew that he knows they are all hiding out here with Dennis Hamilton. And I am sure they are wondering why on earth he is here."

Daniel finally turned away from the other young men and faced the one he'd called Nate. "Is Dennis home?"

"Umm… no… sir. He isn't." Nate glanced at the other men and then faced Daniel again. He said nervously, "He went to Prospect…" He looked down at his feet. "No… he went out, but he will be back tomorrow."

Daniel narrowed his eyes and stared at Nate with a suspicious look on his face. "When exactly will he be back tomorrow so we know when to come back here?"

Once more, Nate looked at his comrades and then said, "I am not sure when, sir."

Daniel sighed loudly, and Lily stepped closer to Nate. "It would be really helpful if you could simply tell us if he'll be back in the morning, afternoon, or evening. Just telling us he'll be back tomorrow doesn't help at all."

Nate's expression changed as he faced Lily. His brows knit and he gave her a disdainful look. "I can tell you now that Dennis Hamilton will not want to see you or speak with you." He turned to stare at Sofia with a condescending expression on his face and then looked at Lily again. "In case you have forgotten, our leader doesn't waste his time with women." A sneer appeared on his face as he looked Lily and Sofia over. "Unless he wants to take one of them as his wife."

Sofia's mouth fell open at the callous words and she gasped in shock when Daniel punched Nate.

"Daniel!" Lily glared at him.

Nate fell to the ground, holding his stomach and writhing in pain.

Fear gripped Sofia as the other men walked toward them, their gazes fixed on Daniel. Some of them balled their fists. All of them looked like they wanted to attack Daniel but were scared to.

Lily screamed Daniel's name again, but he ignored her. He glared angrily at the men as they approached, his own fists balled. "If you all want to fight me, come on then! But remember who I am."

They stopped in their tracks and looked at each other. None of them moved forward.

Lily grabbed Daniel by the arm while Sofia began backing away. "Come on, Daniel, let's go!" Lily yelled, and tried to pull him toward the gate. He stood his ground, refusing to move for a few seconds, and then he finally turned around and followed her.

Sofia was already at the gate when Lily and

Daniel reached her. She walked out the gate with them and held her breath until they were some distance away from Dennis Hamilton's abode. She sighed with relief as she turned and saw no one had followed them.

Lily also turned around and then stopped. She called out to Daniel, who was still marching on in anger, uncaring whether they were attacked or not. Daniel stopped, and Lily walked up to him. "What was that, Daniel? Why did you punch that guy?"

"He deserved it," he said, and then his angry expression fell away, replaced by guilt. "I am sorry. I know I shouldn't have. But when he insulted both of you, I didn't know what came over me." He sighed. "I just couldn't stand there while he said all those stupid things to you, Lily."

"I understand," Lily said, sighing. "But you may have ruined my chance to find out if Dennis Hamilton knows where my parents are. He will hear about what happened and refuse to even see me."

"I will apologize to him when we go tomorrow, Lily. Again, I am sorry."

"No, you won't!" Lily said. "You are not going with us tomorrow."

"It's not safe for you to…"

"It's safer than going with you," Lily said. "Just yesterday, you were telling us you had better control of your anger issues. What happened?"

"I do," he said, "but I am human." He shook his head. "Vina will kill me when she hears this."

Lily gave him a small smile. "She won't." He smiled at her, but she shook her head. "You have to do better, Daniel."

"I will."

Lily shook her head and took Sofia's hand. "We will head toward my house. You can go, Daniel."

Daniel sighed. "I still think it's not a good idea for you to go to Dennis's by yourselves tomorrow."

"We can take care of ourselves, can't we, Sofia?"

Sofia wasn't sure about that, but she nodded anyway.

"Okay, then," Daniel said.

They turned in the other direction.

"What about the car, Lily?" Sofia asked as they walked on, their arms linked.

"It will be safe in front of the House of Refuge. I will get it tomorrow."

"Well… that was a close call, wasn't it?" Sofia said to Lily.

Lily nodded. She looked distracted, and Sofia guessed she was thinking about her parents.

They got to a large three-story Victorian, and Sofia smiled as she admired the house. "Your home is beautiful, Lily," she said as they walked up the porch together.

"Thank you. Taylor built it years ago to look like a coliseum, and even though he loves our house in California, he talks about this one all the time."

They entered the house, and Sofia wasn't surprised at how lavishly but tastefully it was furnished, with expensive marble tiles, columns, and a breathtaking spiral staircase that went on and on.

They sat on the couch together, and Lily began to tell her how Taylor had insisted on replacing the furniture to suit her tastes more. Faye, Taylor's late wife, had been a minimalist and had furnished the house that way. But when they were watching a TV show one day and Lily had told him she liked the décor in a particular home in the show, he had taken note, as he usually did, and surprised her with a trip to an upscale furniture store in California where he'd told her to pick whatever furniture she wanted.

"At first, I didn't have the heart to change anything here, but Taylor said Faye wouldn't mind and he wanted me to be happy. So, I finally gave in and shopped to my heart's content." She beamed.

Lily kept gushing about Taylor, and Sofia didn't mind even though she felt a tinge of envy. Just because she wasn't with the man she loved anymore didn't mean she couldn't be happy for her best friend who was still head-over-heels in love with her husband.

Soon, the conversation changed and they chatted about mundane stuff. Sofia put away her sadness as she tucked her feet under her and listened with a smile as Lily told her about her stepchildren's funny antics. She couldn't wait to go and see the children with Lily when they left Fallow Creek. For now, she would enjoy being here and completely immerse herself in this getaway with Lily.

After a while, Lily stood and smiled at her. "Would you like to watch a movie? A chick flick, maybe?"

Sofia smiled. "Definitely. What movie do you have in mind?"

"I brought some classic movies from California," Lily answered. "Let me go and get them. You can put the TV on. I'll be back."

She left the living room and Sofia turned the

television on, eager to relax and watch a movie with Lily. And then she gasped and stepped back from the TV set. She stared at the images flashing on the television. Bakali burning. People dying. She shut her eyes as pain tore through her. *Oh, Jude!* Was he still alive and would she ever be happy again?

She turned the TV off and curled into a ball on the sofa, weeping softly.

SIX

Jude's eyes flew open and his heart thudded as a loud explosion reverberated through the air. He jumped up from the cold hard floor where he had been sleeping and hurried to look out the small window of the cell he shared with his father. He grabbed the iron window bars and peered through them. He could see smoke billowing in the sky some distance away from the cell, and he looked around the grassy land surrounding the prison block. As usual, there was no one anywhere around.

He shook the bars with anger and frustration, and smothered an urge to scream. He had done enough screaming the first few weeks he'd been here. Now, he knew it was useless and strength-consuming to keep doing it. He looked back at his father, who was still asleep on the floor, and sighed. He wasn't surprised his father had not been awakened by the sound of that explosion. He'd gotten used to it, as he had told Jude many times when they heard explosions or gunshots. Jude had not been able to get used to the troubling sounds of war. He sighed again and looked out the window. Another loud explosion sounded, followed by gunshots, and he jumped back. He heard his father stir behind him but did not turn around.

"Jude, come away from the window!" his father said in his usual hoarse voice. "A stray bullet might hit you."

Jude's heart raced as another series of gunfire pierced the air, but he did not step away from the window. Every day he felt as though being in this cell was driving him farther and farther away from sanity. The only solace he found was being in the company of his father and being able to look out of this window to see that there was still a world out there, even if he wasn't participating in it and hardly ever saw anyone outside.

But did he really want to participate in the world outside? The world had gone mad. Although he craved his freedom, the chance of him and his father ever regaining it was slim.

His mouth fell open as another loud explosion lit up the sky and shook the ground of their cell. Fire and smoke rose into the clouds from the distance, and then the fire seemed to creep closer and closer to the prison block. For a long moment, Jude stood transfixed in the same position he'd been minutes ago, his heart filled with dread. The fire was burning closer. Would it consume their cell? Would his dad and all the political prisoners locked in the prison be burned to death?

He shuddered as he watched the fire, and then, gradually, it began to wane until there was only billowing smoke. Gunshots rang through the air again, and the sound grew louder and louder, which meant the gunshots were being fired close by.

For a brief moment, he allowed himself to believe that perhaps someone, or a group of people, had been sent to free him and his father from this dreadful place and that they were engaged in a gun battle with the guards posted at the periphery of the prison block a mile away. And then the gunshots stopped, and he sighed in disappointment. No one was coming to rescue them or even see them, except for a guard or two. He hardly saw the guards, except twice a day when one came to bring him and his father food. He knew, however, that there were quite a number of them surrounding the prison block.

Jude crinkled his nose as the stench of urine and excreta wafted into his nostrils. There was no escaping the constant smell. For the first month or two after he and his dad were locked up in this place, it was one of the things he thought would eventually drive him insane. Now, he had gotten used to it, except for once in a while when the smell became almost unbearable. But there was no way to escape it, so he had learned to live with it.

Another round of gunshots.

"Jude!" his father called out harshly. "Can you please come away from that window?"

Jude backed away and went to sit beside his father. "How much longer do you think this war will go on?" he asked.

"I have no idea," his father said, and waved his hand. The man did not seem to care about the question.

He studied his dad. He looked older than his fifty-three years, but that wasn't surprising. He had been in captivity for much longer than Jude had. Jude had been in this cell for about a year, but his dad had been in captivity long before he'd found out his father was still alive. That was years spent locked up.

A flood of anguish had risen up from the pit of Jude's stomach as he thought about his father being in confinement for years. The fact that he did not know when this evil war would end or if they would ever get out of here made him feel even worse. For all he knew, they might die in captivity. One thing he knew was that starvation would not be the reason for their deaths. Felix had made sure that they got fed twice a day and that their meals were sizable. Clearly, he still held out hope that Jude would join him in his evil campaign to change the country by eliminating all those he thought where holding it back. It was why Jude and his dad had been locked here. Because he had refused to join the opposition or support them in any way. As far as they were concerned, anyone who refused to join or support them was an enemy and had to be eliminated. Felix had probably kept him and his father alive because they were once friends. But from their tense conversation the last time Felix was here, his patience was running thin.

Another loud explosion sounded outside, and Jude stood up and went to the window.

"Jude, I don't know why you keep going to look out the window whenever there is an explosion or gunshot. You should be used to them by now. It has been the same since we were brought here."

Jude didn't answer. Just because his father had gotten used to it all didn't mean he could. There was death behind the explosions and the gunshots. Soon, it would be their deaths.

Jude leaned his back against the filthy wall of the cell when the gunshots stopped. He was about to close his eyes when his father began to pray. Jude frowned as anger filled his heart. His father prayed continuously, and every single time he prayed, Jude got angrier and angrier. His dad's prayers had never helped them in any way. And it certainly hadn't helped his father at all.

He wasn't surprised that God refused to help him out, but his father had been a loyal Christian for years and a faithful pastor. And yet, here he was in captivity with the threat of death hanging over his head. Rage rose up in Jude and he felt like screaming at his father and telling him to stop praying. Instead, he went to the window and looked out again. Outside had grown deathly quiet once more, but he knew the explosions and gunshots would start all over again soon. He shut his eyes and took a deep breath. He was tired of constantly being afraid for his life and for his father's.

Maybe I should just give in and join Felix and Keziah's stupid party and their war.

But he knew he could never do so. He would not be part of the killing going on in the name of bringing balance to the country. Felix and Keziah, and all those who were part of this mess, were insane for believing in such a thing. He would never be a part of them, and his father definitely wouldn't, which meant they would not be released from this cell. They would rot away in this prison.

He thought about all the atrocities that had taken place during this war and a sob rose up his throat into his mouth. How could he ever have been associated with people like Keziah and Felix, who were two of the leaders of the opposition? The last time he'd seen them was when they'd come here about two months ago to try to convince him once more to join them. Even though it was hard for Jude to say no to him and his dad being released from this cell if he agreed to join the opposition, he had refused. He didn't know if or when they would come here again, but he was not looking forward to seeing them at all.

He started to walk back to where his father was sitting and then turned as someone banged on the heavy metal door of their cell. The handle twisted and the door opened. Two guards walked in, stern expressions on their faces, their guns held at their sides.

Jude frowned as he looked at the guards. This was strange. There were just standing near the door. Usually, only one armed guard came to bring food for him and his father. His heart sank. This probably meant that Felix and Keziah had come to pay him a visit and to lecture him on his need to join them. He groaned and turned his back to the door.

"Jude!"

Great! He groaned again. *Keziah.* He sighed loudly and turned around.

Keziah stood before him, the guard behind her looking intently at him, daring him with his eyes to come any closer to her so he could lash out. But Jude was not interested in coming any closer. He stepped back slightly, and she sighed.

"You look awful, Jude," she said, and stepped

closer to him. She crinkled her nose and made a face. "And you smell even worse." She looked him over with pity in her eyes.

He scowled at her. Looking past her, he stared at the door. Any moment now, Felix would walk into the cell and begin his patronizing lecture. But at this time, he preferred to have Felix here lecturing him rather than Keziah standing here and gazing at him with a mixture of sympathy and a look that he recognized from when they were together but did not welcome or want to acknowledge. She opened her mouth to speak, and he knew exactly what she was going to say from the way she was looking at him.

"Jude, please, I beg you. Please reconsider. I hate seeing you wasting away in this cell like this."

"How many times can I tell you that I am not interested in joining you in this disgusting war you people started?"

"Jude, it's not a disgusting war. The war is needful to bring change to our country. And we are winning. Soon, we will completely take over the country." Her sympathetic look turned to worry, and she placed her hand on his shoulder. "Please Jude, come and join us. I know that Felix and the other men in our party won't change their plans when we take over. Everyone who isn't for us when that time comes will be eliminated. I cannot bear to see you come to harm in any way."

Jude gritted his teeth so as not to show the fear running through his veins. So that was Felix's plan. They were going to kill everyone who was not for them. That included him and his dad. He looked back at his father, who was still sitting on the ground staring up at him and Keziah, and then he turned back to her. Her eyes were fixed on him, and she didn't seem to notice his father. "So, that means my father and I are going to perish in this cell?"

She shook her head. "Not if you join us." Her hands slipped off his shoulders to grip his fingers. "Jude, we need you. I need you."

"No, you don't! You just want to gather as many people as possible in order to validate this war of yours, but nothing you do will make it right. Nothing justifies killing so many people. I'm never going to join you." He turned away from her again.

She turned him around to face her and said, "What will it take to convince you to join us?"

"Nothing!"

"But you don't understand, Jude. If you don't join us now, you will die here with your father. Is that what you want?"

His chest squeezed with fear, and he pressed his lips together. No, that was not what he wanted. And yet he had no choice but to refuse her request. There was no way he would do what they wanted him to. If that meant he and his father would die here, then so be it.

He felt weak with fear, especially for his dad. He had suffered so much. Jude's heart raced with dread, but he took a deep breath and pressed down the fear. Squaring his shoulders, he looked her in the eye. "Listen, Keziah, you're wasting your time. I'm never going to join you. Please stop asking me to, and don't come back here again."

"Jude...!"

"Please go," he said to her. She began to plead with him again, but he shook his head. "Please go."

She stood her ground and then reached out and took his hands again.

He blinked and looked at their joined hands. He didn't know why she still had feelings for him after he'd told her more than a few times that he wasn't interested. If there had been any shred of feeling left for her because of their past relationship, it had all died — not just when he met Sofia, but after all this with the war and finding out how brutal she was.

She looked into his eyes and said softly, "You know I still love you. I still want you."

He shook his head. "I don't feel the same way, Keziah. I'm sorry. I cannot give you what you want. Please don't tell me you love me again." He stepped back. "I want you to go now, and don't come back again."

She shut her eyes and groaned. "Am I so undesirable that you don't ever want to see me again?"

"You know it's not because of that." He sighed. She was still as stunning as the first time he'd seen her, but he had no interest in her anymore. He loathed all she now stood for.

Her brows furrowed. "It's because of that American you were engaged to, isn't it?"

Jude shut his eyes as pain tore through him. *Sofia.* Every single day, her face stayed in his mind. Every night he dreamed about her. With every fiber of his being, he missed her and longed to see her. His heart ached not just because of how much he missed her, but also because of what he knew she would think about him. He'd suddenly disappeared without a word on their wedding day. She would probably think that he had developed cold feet and abandoned her at the courthouse. Or worse, she would think he was dead.

The thought had worried him constantly since he'd left the United States more than a year ago. She had tried to kill herself for less reason than this. When her ex had broken up with her, she had swallowed a couple of pills but luckily was found by a friend. He felt literally sick thinking of what she might have done to herself when she'd found out he was gone. Hopefully, she was okay, and hopefully, she had moved on and was happy. Even though thinking about her with someone else was intensely painful, he loved her enough to want her to have whatever would make her happy. Finding someone else who she could love would help her forget about him. He sighed sadly.

Keziah snapped her fingers and gazed curiously at him. "You're thinking about her now, aren't you?"

He said in a haunted voice, "I think about her every day."

For a long moment, Keziah stared at him without speaking. Finally, she heaved a loud sigh. "Please consider what I said, Jude."

"And please remember what I said," he told her. "I am never going to reconsider, and I don't want you to come back here ever again."

Pain flashed in her eyes and then it was gone as quickly as it appeared. Once again, she stared at him with a sympathetic look on her face. "Remember that you're not the only one involved in this." For the first time since she'd come into the cell, she looked at his dad, who was sitting on the floor behind him. "Remember your father as well."

Jude turned to look at his father and then looked at her again. She was right. Even though he didn't want to die, he was willing to accept whatever Felix and his group did to him rather than join in their immoral war. But if he could save his father's life, then maybe he should try to do so. He could save his dad's life by simply joining Felix's party and pledging his alliance to it. And yet, he could not bring himself to do it.

"My son will not join you in the civil war," his father said from behind him.

Jude turned and gave his father a sad smile and then turned and faced Keziah once again.

She gave him a curt nod and then turned around and walked out of the cell with the guards.

The metal door banged shut, and Jude groaned and went to sit beside his father.

"You did the right thing, Jude," his father said, placing his hand on Jude's arm.

Jude felt weak and leaned against his dad. He felt like weeping. He had sealed their fate. They were both going to die. "I'm sorry, Dad."

His father put his arms around Jude. "It's okay, Jude. God is still with us. I've been praying, and I trust that God will bring us out of here in due time."

Jude moved away from his father and stared at him in anger. "How can you say that? He has not delivered us since we came here. God hates us! Why would you still pray and trust Him?" He shut his eyes and let out his breath slowly. "Maybe there is no God."

"Don't say that," his father said. "You know there is, and He loves us. I know this is awful," his father's eyes traveled around their small cell, "but we need to have faith. I am going to hold on to my faith and believe that God will get us out of here soon. I want you to do the same."

Jude laughed harshly. God is not going to get us out of here! In fact, I think it's time to stop believing there is a God. Unless a miracle happens this week and somehow we are set free from this prison and I can go back to America to find Sofia, I will never believe in God again."

His father studied his face and nodded. "Maybe God will do that for us, and then you will know that He truly cares for us."

"Dad, I was joking. You know all that is not going to happen. If God was going to deliver us from this wretched prison, he would have done so a long time ago."

His father began to speak, but Jude held up his hands. "I have heard it all before, Dad. Please, don't say any more about it. I'm tired." He stood up and went to the window to look out again. All he saw, as usual, was the empty space before him. But he knew it was only a matter of time before Felix sent guards to kill him and his father. He wasn't sure which would come first, though — him going insane or being killed. Neither option was palatable.

He looked at his father again. As usual, he was praying. Jude groaned and looked away. No amount of prayer was going to save them from their fate. All they could do was hope for a non-violent end. He knew when that time came, he would hold tightly to Sofia's face in his heart and believe that one day, somehow, she would find out the truth about him.

SEVEN

Lily walked into Sofia's room to inform her she was leaving for Dennis Hamilton's and smiled when she saw Sofia was still asleep. She turned around and walked out of the room again. She didn't want to wake her friend up. Yesterday, just before they'd started watching the movies she'd brought from California, Sofia had looked excited and happy, which had made Lily happy. But by the time she'd changed and come back to the living room to put the movie on, Sofia's mood had changed. When Lily asked what was wrong, she said nothing was wrong. But Lily knew exactly why her friend was sad. Hopefully, she would be able to cheer her up during this time in Fallow Creek and then in California. Cheering Sofia up definitely didn't include taking her along to see Dennis Hamilton and putting her in any kind of danger.

As she walked to the front door, Lily thought about Taylor. She took her phone out of her purse and dialed his number. Her mood immediately lifted when she heard Taylor's voice on the other end of the line.

"How are you, baby?" Lily smiled and lowered herself on the sofa. She knew she had to leave to see Dennis Hamilton, but she couldn't help the relaxed feeling that came over her just hearing her husband's voice. Taylor always made her day better.

He answered, "I'm great now that I hear your voice."

She laughed. "I miss you so much, Taylor," she said.

"I miss you, too. I wish I was there with you, but I know you're having fun with Sofia."

Lily felt worried again. "I am, but I don't really know how to make Sofia feel better. She looked really happy when we got to Fallow Creek yesterday, but she seems to be feeling down again.

"I think she will feel increasingly better the more time she spends with you on your getaway. Anyone, no matter what's going on with them, will feel better just being with you."

Lily chuckled and then sobered again. "I hope Sofia can find someone else soon. I'm sure that would help her to get out of this cycle of depression. She told me she had been doing much better but that she'd started feeling down two days ago. Exactly a year after her ex-fiancé suddenly left her on their wedding day. She was deeply in love with him, but I think she can fall in love again. I'm thinking about introducing her to one of your single friends when we get to California. Do you have anyone in mind that you think Sofia would get along with?"

"Lily! Being the matchmaker as usual?"

"As usual? When have I acted as a matchmaker?" She smiled, remembering exactly when. Taylor hadn't let her hear the last of it since she'd set up a good friend of his with another friend of hers. The relationship had been short-lived and hadn't ended well. After that, he had made her promise not to act as a matchmaker again, but how could she stand by and see her friend so sad? She knew she could help Sofia feel better if she found someone new for her.

"Lily!" Taylor called out her name again. "I know what you're thinking. Remember you promised to stay out of people's love lives."

"But what would you do if a friend of yours was like Sofia and all you could think about was trying to cheer her up and get her out of her depression? I told you what happened to her some time ago when her ex broke up with her. That was before she met Jude, the guy who disappeared on their wedding day."

"Yes, you did. She tried to kill herself. But that was before she met the Lord. Has she ever tried to harm herself in any way since Jude left her? Even though you said she loved him very much?"

"I don't think so," Lily answered. "No... I am pretty sure she hasn't. But she has been very sad. I want her to move on and be happy again."

"And you think getting into a new relationship will help her be happy? What if the relationship also turns sour?"

"Everything good comes with risks, Taylor. You know that. I actually think she would be happy if she found true love again. I know because I feel like the happiest and luckiest woman in this world because I have you. Even with my fears and worries about my parents, I have been able to stay steady because of your love. I want the same for Sofia. I want her to have what we have, Taylor."

For a long moment, there was silence on the other end of the line, and Lily frowned. "Taylor, are you still there?"

"Yes, Lily. Wow! What you said was touching. I love you, honey, and you have made me the happiest man in this world, too."

Lily smiled, yearning to kiss Taylor. "So you see, I want this for my best friend."

"Okay. I guess I understand. I love that you want your friend to find love, but don't you think you should let her find someone by herself and in her own time? She might not be fully ready for another relationship yet."

"She told me she's had a series of bad dates recently. Her friend, Edith, set her up on those dates. Sofia said she knows she should move on but doesn't have the energy or motivation to do something about it on her own. And Edith is not doing a very good job of finding someone for her. Please, Taylor. Just think about a friend of yours who is single and who you think Sofia would get along with."

"Okay... I don't like the idea of interfering with other people's love lives, but for you, I will."

"Thank you, Taylor." She smiled and then asked him how the kids were doing and how his business trip in Florida had gone.

She leaned back and rested her head on the sofa as they talked.

I should leave for Dennis Hamilton's house, she kept telling herself, but she didn't. She wanted to talk with her husband just a little longer. His voice and words always soothed her.

He asked her what her plans were now. She had already told him everything that had happened when she'd gone to see Stella in Tucson, but she began to tell him about going to Dennis Hamilton's yesterday and the fight that had broken out with Daniel and one of the ex-leader's men.

"I was really scared that those men were going to hurt us," she said. "So was Sofia." She chuckled. "Daniel, as stubborn as ever, was prepared to stay there and fight them all. I decided not to go with him today."

"Are you sure that's a good idea?" Taylor asked. "I wish you were going with Daniel. At least you'd have someone to protect you if anything happens."

Lily frowned. Taylor sounded really worried. She had to put his mind at ease. "Taylor, stop that. Stop worrying about me. Nothing is going to happen. Besides, I think I'll be safer without Daniel. I certainly don't want another fight to break out because of his hot-headedness."

"You have a point. But maybe he could go with you and stop some distance away from Dennis Hamilton's. Anyway, are you going with Sofia?"

"No, I am not. She's still asleep, and I want her to rest. There's no need for her to go with me today."

Taylor told her to call him as soon as she left Dennis Hamilton's, and then the conversation shifted back to the kids. They talked for another ten minutes, and then Lily ended the call. She stood up to leave the house and turned around when she heard footsteps behind her.

"Lily, where are you going?" Sofia asked. "Don't tell me you are leaving for Dennis Hamilton's house without telling me? I thought we were supposed to go together."

"I came to your room and saw you were still asleep. I thought you needed to sleep in today. I mean, that was why you came to Fallow Creek with me. To rest."

"And I also came to spend time with my best friend and to help you look for your parents."

Lily raised her eyebrows as she looked Sofia over. "I can see you're already dressed up to go out." Sofia was wearing a fitted teal dress and strappy black heels. Lily smiled. "You look great as always, but this is hardly a suitable outfit for a casual outing in Fallow Creek." She didn't want to add that it was hardly a suitable outfit to visit the ex-leader in. Dennis Hamilton and his forebears had instituted the present drab dress code for women, and as much as Dennis had no more power in the town to enforce the dress code, he might not be very pleased. On the other hand, the man was a chronic womanizer, hence his many wives. Sofia was beautiful and single, and this dress showed off her figure. He might shamelessly make lewd advances toward Sofia. That would be really troubling.

Sofia looked down at her dress. "But I am dressed simply!" She looked at Lily and shook her head. "Actually, I should be the one complaining about your outfit. I thought I had elevated your dress sense some, but you have reverted back to these awful gowns now that you're in this place. Why, Lily?"

Lily smiled in amusement. "Because they are very comfortable. As much as I don't miss living in Fallow Creek, I kinda miss these simple dresses." She touched Sofia's arm hoping to indirectly convince her to change her dress. "I mean look at what you're wearing, Sofia. It's so tight and those shoes don't look comfortable at all."

Sofia giggled. "They are actually very comfortable. Most of all, I love what I am wearing, and you are not going to convince me to change." She took Lily's hand. "I have just the dress that would look great on you but will still be appropriate for our outing."

She began to pull Lily toward the guestroom, but Lily laughed and pulled her hand away. "No. I'm also not going to change my dress. Let's just go."

They walked out of the house chatting and laughing about random stuff, and Lily could not help smiling. Sofia looked like she was in a better mood this morning.

Sofia arched her eyebrows. "Why are you looking at me like that?"

"I'm just pleased that you look much happier today. You seemed a little depressed last night. I know you were thinking about Jude again."

"Yes. When I turned the TV on, it was on a news channel that was showing images of war from Jude's country. The war is getting worse there, and it scared me. I feel better today. I'm still worried about Jude, but I have to believe he's okay." Sofia sighed and bit her lip.

Lily put her arm around her friend. She didn't want Sofia to dwell on this sadness again, so she quickly said, "I just called Taylor now. I asked him to set you up with one of his friends when we get to California."

"Lily! Why did you do that?"

"You told me it was time you moved on, and

I agree with you. Taylor has good friends in California, and you said you wanted someone like Taylor or Jude, didn't you?"

Sofia groaned, and then she smiled at Lily. "Well, you're right. I guess Taylor's friends would be better than the guys that Edith has been setting me up with."

Lily laughed, and she was glad when Sofia laughed along with her. They continued to talk until they got to the building that Taylor had given Dennis Hamilton and his men. Lily walked straight to the gate and was about to knock when one of Dennis's men, a young ex-squad member, came out and asked what she wanted.

"We came here yesterday," she said. "We were told that Dennis wasn't around but would be back this morning. Is he home now?"

The man stared at Lily for a short moment and then turned to Sofia. He looked her over and the nonchalant look on his face turned to curiosity. He finally faced Lily again. "Wait here. I'll be back." He entered the gate, closing it behind him.

Lily tapped her foot impatiently.

Sofia said, "I hope Dennis Hamilton has some information that will help you find your parents."

The gate opened again, and the young man told Lily that Dennis would see her now. She and Sofia walked through the gates and followed the man into the large building. When they got inside, Lily looked around, surprised. Dennis had taken out the furniture that had been here when Taylor had given the building to him. Taylor had told her that the place was sparsely furnished, but this room was empty. Maybe this was the only place where Dennis had removed the furniture for some reason. There wasn't even a bench to sit down on. It was just a vast empty space now.

Dennis walked out and came toward Lily. His beard was even longer and bushier than it had been before, but his eyes were still cold and calculating. When he reached her, he gave her a small smile. "I heard you came here looking for me yesterday. Something about wanting to know where your parents are?"

"Yes," Lily said.

Dennis said, "I would not have agreed to see you if not for Taylor." He frowned and looked her over.

She cringed. She could guess what was on his mind right now. He was probably recalling the day she'd rejected him and he'd had her thrown out of town. His ego was so huge that she knew he would never forget the rejection. From the look on his face, her exile from Fallow Creek had not been enough. Without a doubt, if it wasn't for all Taylor had done for him, not only would he not have agreed to see her, he might actually have plotted some sort of revenge once he'd found out she was in town. But then, Keith had said something about Dennis being a changed man. That was to be seen.

She said, "Please, if you know anything about their whereabouts, I would like to know. I have been looking for them for ages."

He stared at her for a brief moment and then turned to look at Sofia. He blinked and his eyes lit up. He studied Sofia, from the top of her head to the soles of her feet and a lustful smile appeared on his face.

Lily frowned in annoyance. She had been right to

be concerned about Sofia back at the house. He was still the same disgusting, lustful man he had been when he was the leader of Fallow Creek. Keith was wrong. He hadn't changed at all. His many wives, as far as she knew, were still here in Fallow Creek, living in his old house, and here he was staring at Sofia as if she were a piece of meat. Lily took a deep breath to try to let go of her annoyance and once more asked Dennis if he knew where her parents were.

He finally tore his gaze from Sofia and faced her. "I don't know where they are." He looked at her with disdain, and she could clearly see he was trying to let her know without saying it that he had not forgotten how she had disgraced him, and that he did indeed know where her parents were but would not tell her anything.

She bit her lip as desperation rose within her. She began to plead with him to tell her what he knew about where her parents had gone during the mass exodus.

He looked at her with a smile on his face and told her once more that he had no idea where they were.

She felt like screaming at him, knowing he was lying, but she knew that doing so would not help at all. She took a deep breath to let go of her anger and said, "Please, Dennis. I really need to find them. Please tell me where they are."

Sofia placed her hand on Lily's back and whispered in her ear, "He said he doesn't know where your parents are, Lily."

"He's lying!" Lily yelled, finally unable to control her anger and frustration. She glared at him. "You are lying, Dennis. You know where they are. Tell me where they are now!"

Sofia took her hand. "Lily, maybe we should go."

"You definitely should go," Dennis said coldly. He turned to one of his men who was standing at the entrance of the building and beckoned to him. "See them out of here," he said. He gave Sofia a brazen smile.

It took everything in Lily not to slap the lewd smile off his face.

Dennis's man moved close to Lily and Sofia and said, "You heard him. You leave now, or I bundle you both out of here."

Lily glowered at the guard and marched out of the building with Sofia beside her.

Outside the gate, she paused, closed her eyes, and took deep breaths to try to let go of her annoyance. But she couldn't stop fuming. She propped her hands on her hips and shook her head. "How can someone be so wicked?" she said to Sofia. "He knows where my parents are. I am pretty sure of that. I could see it in his eyes."

"What are you going to do then?" Sofia placed a hand on Lily's shoulder.

Lily thought about Sofia's question for a few seconds and then said, "I'm going to call Taylor." She took her phone out of her purse and called Taylor. When he answered her call, she told him what Dennis had said and what she believed — that Dennis Hamilton knew exactly where her parents were but did not want to tell her. She said to Taylor. "He would not be alive and living where he is now without your help. Can you speak to him for me?"

"Definitely," Taylor said. "Give him the phone now."

"Hold on, baby. Let me go inside again." She went to the gate once more and began to bang on it.

A guard came and opened the gate. He scowled at her. "What are you doing? I thought you were sent away from here. Why are you knocking so loudly?"

"I have to see Dennis again." She held out her phone. "Someone important wants to speak to him on the phone."

The guard barked. "He doesn't want to see you or speak to anyone."

She glared at the squad guard. "Tell him *that* Taylor Dalton — you know, Taylor Dalton, the man who helped him and you out when you were stranded in the river? The one who owns this building you're all staying in? My husband? Tell him that Taylor Dalton wants to speak to him."

The guard blinked rapidly and then quickly withdrew inside. He came back less than a minute later and opened the gate. "Dennis Hamilton will see you now."

Lily nodded. She and Sofia entered the gate and followed the guard into the building and strode to the middle of the empty room where Dennis was standing with his back to them. He turned around just as they reached him, and Lily handed the phone to him. "Taylor wants to speak to you."

Dennis glowered at her and huffed. He snatched the phone from her hand and put it to his ear. "Yes? What is it, Taylor Dalton?"

Lily waited as Dennis listened to Taylor on the other end of the line. Dennis shut his eyes briefly, a scowl on his face, and then he sighed loudly. "Fine! I know where they are." He listened again and stared angrily at Lily. Finally, he handed the phone back to her and groaned. "So Taylor Dalton will never let me forget how he saved my life and gave me this building."

Lily laughed harshly. "So you do remember all that my husband has done for you." She shook her head as she glared at him. "Will you tell me where my parents are now?" She turned and smiled briefly as Sofia put her arm around her and then faced Dennis again.

For a long moment, he pressed his lips tightly together as he eyed her. Finally, with obvious reluctance, he said, "Your parents came to me for help when everyone was leaving and said they had nowhere to go. Since your father and I used to be good friends before you spoiled our friendship with your rebellion, I decided to help them. I got them the address of one of the elders who had already found a house outside Fallow Creek, and they went there. I'm not sure if they're there now, but that was where I told your father to go."

"And where exactly is that?" Lily asked.

"Utah. In a small town called Noble." He waved one of his men who was standing just outside the door over. "Get me a notebook and a pen."

The man hastened away and came back seconds later. He handed Dennis a notebook and a pen and backed away.

Dennis tore out a sheet of paper from the notebook and scribbled something on it. He handed the paper to Lily. "Here is the address."

Lily eagerly took the piece of paper from him and studied the address Dennis had written for her. "Utah," she said. She felt like weeping with relief mixed in with a bit of sadness. "All this time my parents have been in a small town in Utah," she said as tears filled her eyes. She sighed, overwhelming relief settling over her. When Sofia drew her close, she held her friend tightly. She drew back from Sofia and looked at Dennis Hamilton. "Thank you," she said.

He nodded and then again turned his gaze to Sofia.

Lily felt her blood boil with anger again at the lustful look in Dennis's eyes as he studied Sofia. She took Sofia's hand, but before they could turn around to leave, he asked, "What is your friend's name?"

Sofia frowned, and Lily ignored him. They both walked out of the building and out the gate together. And then Lily took a deep breath. She looked at the address on the piece of paper and laughed. "Finally! An actual address where I can find my parents!"

"I'm ecstatic for you, Lily," Sofia said. She smiled widely as Lily hugged her again. "So, when are we going to Utah?"

"Tomorrow," Lily said. "First thing tomorrow."

EIGHT

Dennis Hamilton walked into the room he had converted into his study and locked the door. He took his cell phone out of his pants pocket, sat behind his desk, and dialed Cliff Hunter's number. On the first ring, Cliff answered.

"I have done what you requested," Dennis said. "Your daughter will be far away from Fallow Creek and safely in your custody before our plans to take our town back from that woman is put in motion. Now you have to keep your end of the bargain."

Cliff sighed loudly. "I hope she doesn't suspect a thing. Knowing how stubborn Lily is, if she even gets a whiff of our plans, everything will be ruined."

"I made sure she wouldn't suspect anything," Dennis said. "I made her believe I didn't want her to know where you and your wife were. I knew she would call Taylor Dalton and get him to persuade me to tell her where you are. That way, she will think going to Utah is totally her idea and has nothing to do with me."

"Thank you, Dennis," Cliff said sounding

relieved. "At least she will be safe until our plans are fully carried out. My brother will make sure she remains in the house in Utah."

"Listen, Cliff, don't thank me. Just make sure you keep your part of this plan. Gather as many Fallow Creek men with as you can and tell them about our plans, and then you all meet me in Prospect in a few days. I have instructed the other elders to do the same." Dennis looked out the window at Fallow Creek, his hometown; the town he loved but which had been ruined by that Rachel woman. His mind went to Lily and her beautiful friend again, and he added, "There is a girl she came here with..."

"Who?"

"Who else? Your daughter. She came to my house with a girl I haven't seen before. I want that girl."

"But how am I supposed to get you a girl I don't even know?"

"She is your daughter's friend, and I believe she will go to Utah with Lily. Since you already plan to hold them there, I am sure you can find a way to *convince* her to marry me."

Cliff said nothing, and Dennis narrowed his eyes in anger. "Did you hear what I said, Cliff Hunter?"

"I still don't know how you want me to convince the girl to marry you. Remember, I wasn't even able to convince my own daughter to do that."

"I am sure you will find a way. And don't remind me of your daughter's rejection. The only reason I am not taking revenge for how she disgraced me is because of you. But one word from me and she will be back here, caught up in the war we are about to unleash."

Cliff groaned.

"Don't sound so defeated, Cliff. Soon, Fallow Creek will be restored back to its former glory and everyone can return. All I am asking you to do is get me one girl... and, of course, gather as many men as you can find that are willing to help us. That can't be too hard."

"I will try."

"Don't try! Just do it." Dennis clicked his phone off and leaned back in his seat. Soon, with the help of his men here and the others scattered around the country, Fallow Creek would be returned to him, and then he would take revenge on all those who had mocked and disgraced him. Rachel and Keith, those women at the Restoration House who had willingly and joyfully thrown everything they'd been taught since childhood away to be under the leadership of Rachel's false teachings, and even Lily and her parents.

***

After Lily had called Taylor to update him on what Dennis Hamilton had told her and informed him that she would be going to Utah to find her parents, she went with Sofia to see Rachel and Keith.

"Do you want me to come with you, Lily," Rachel asked as Lily sat in Rachel and Keith's apartment.

Lily smiled at Rachel. She glanced briefly at Sofia and then faced Rachel again. "No, you don't have to. I'll be going with Sofia, so I'll have company."

They changed topics and talked about the trip to Europe Lily and Taylor were planning to take with their kids. After that, Keith joined them and talked about his life in his hometown of Destiny and his plans to go for a visit with Rachel soon. They went from one topic to the other. When Lily got up to leave with Sofia, Rachel insisted that they stay for lunch, which soon turned to dinner.

Lily and Sofia finally left Rachel and Keith's apartment at a few minutes past ten o'clock. As soon as they got back to the house, Lily said goodnight to Sofia, went to her bedroom, changed into her pajamas, and climbed into bed. She immediately fell asleep.

Very early the next morning, she got into the rental car with Sofia and began to drive out of Fallow Creek. She turned to Sofia and smiled. "Did you think you would be taking a road trip with me to Utah when you agreed to come to Fallow Creek with me?"

"No, I can say I certainly didn't, Lily." She smiled. "I wonder what I would be doing now if I had decided to stay in Tucson?"

"I am really glad you didn't decide to," Lily said. "I am so happy you are here with me."

Sofia grinned.

From the corner of her eye, Lily noticed Sofia was staring at her and turned to look at her briefly. "Why are you smiling like that? What are you thinking about?"

"You, Lily. You're going to drive all the way to Utah. You could not hold a steering wheel properly when I met you a year ago." She chuckled. "What am I even saying? You had never gotten behind a steering wheel. You did not even know that women could drive." She chuckled again. "You've come a long way, my sister."

Lily roared with laughter. "Well, I had some

practice with your car and living with kids. You have to learn how to drive if you are a mother because you have to transport your kids from one place to the other."

Sofia laughed. "I thought your rich husband had a chauffeur that drives everyone around."

"Well, sometimes I want to spend time with the kids alone when their father is away on business trips, or at work."

"Lily, you're so lucky that you have a guy who loves you and a family of your own now."

Lily took her eyes off the road for a few seconds to look at Sofia. She faced the road again as she made her way out of Fallow Creek and said, "It will happen for you soon, Sofia. You'll see. Very soon, you will meet someone who loves you as much as Taylor loves me."

"Sometimes I don't even know if I want to meet anyone," Sofia said. "I don't think anyone will ever love me as much as Jude did, or that I will ever love anyone as much as I love him."

"That's not true," Lily said. "There's someone out there for you. I know that. His name might even be Ryan." She glanced at Sofia and smiled.

Sofia giggled. "Who on earth is Ryan, Lily?" She shook her head. "No, don't tell me. Ryan is one of Taylor's friends. Am I right?"

"Yes, you are. Ryan is the single friend of Taylor's that I have had in mind for you for a while now. He's good looking and a Christian and he's a really good guy."

Sofia groaned. "I don't know, Lily. I guess we'll have to see when we get to California."

Lily reached out her hand, took Sofia's, squeezed

it, and then gripped the steering wheel with both hands again. "It will all work out, I am sure," she said. She looked at the map on Sofia's lap. "Now, you have to concentrate on giving me directions to where we're going so we don't get lost. We have a long drive ahead of us."

They chatted as Lily drove and then stopped briefly in the town after Prospect to get some food. After that, Lily took to the steering wheel again. She smiled with pleasure as the wind blew through her hair and beamed at the sound of Sofia's laughter as they talked.

Lord, please help my friend heal completely from her heartbreak, she prayed silently as they continued to talk. *And thank you for allowing her to come along with me as my companion as I go to find my parents.*

Lily soon grew tired of driving and Sofia took over from her. Sitting in the passenger seat, she slept for about half an hour and then woke up and smiled at Sofia.

"Would you like us to stop again to get some food?" Sofia asked. "It's almost noon."

"I would prefer for us to drive on so we can get to Utah quickly and I can see my parents at last."

"I know you're eager to see them, but we need to eat," Sofia said. "I'm starving."

"Okay, then." Lily smiled and looked out the window. "We can stop to get some food."

They drove for about ten minutes more and found a small restaurant in Mount Carmel. They sat at the restaurant talking while they ate their food. Sofia had ordered mushroom rice, while Lily had ordered pasta. They talked about everything from Lily's time at the House of Refuge to Sofia's recent artworks.

The conversation turned to Dennis Hamilton, and Lily sighed. "Did you see the way he was looking at you when we went to see him? I felt like slapping him. You know he already has almost half a dozen wives and he's still not satisfied."

Sofia shrugged and said with a straight face, "You know… not too long ago, he was exactly my type, and I would have considered dating him." She burst out laughing at the look on Lily's face and added, "Okay, that wasn't funny. But you know what I mean, Lily."

"You are talking about your ex, George. Where is he now anyway?"

"Who knows," Sofia said. "I've chosen to forget about that period of my life. It was also awful. But if I could guess where George is now, I would probably say that he's divorced and dating another younger woman. His wife probably stripped him of most of his money, so I don't know if that would be possible though. Now that I think about it, his real selling point was his money — all he bought and did for me. I just lied to myself at the time that I loved him for him."

Lily could not help laughing out loud.

Sofia shook her head. "Lily! Why are you laughing? It is so not funny." But she soon joined in. She shook her head again. "This is so wrong of us. We shouldn't be laughing like this." Sobering, she said, "After I spilled my guts to his wife, telling her everything about our affair, I felt remorseful when I got home. It wasn't like he was the only one involved in the affair. I was partly to blame for it. I didn't care that he was married or that our relationship might eventually lead to the breakdown of his family. In fact, I wanted his marriage to end."

"Well, thank God you have walked away from all that."

Sofia's expression turned sad, and she put down her fork. "Only to fall into Jude's arms right after." She bit her lip and looked down at her plate without eating.

Lily hurt for Sofia. She looked so miserable. Taking Sofia's hand on the table, Lily said, "It wasn't the same, though. You truly loved Jude, Sofia. And from all you told me about him, I am pretty sure he loved you. Most of all, he was single."

"I know." Sofia sighed again.

"Do you wish you had never met Jude?" Lily asked softly.

Sofia shook her head. "In spite of the pain his disappearance caused me and still causes me, I will never give up the memory of the time we spent together. That's why I am hesitant about moving on and dating other people. I don't know if I can ever stop loving him."

Lily smiled sadly. "Give it time. You will meet someone who will sweep you off your feet, and then you will forget about the pain you feel over Jude now."

They finally finished their food and set out again. Sofia insisted on driving, and Lily sat beside her, studying the map, and giving directions to their destination.

The closer they got to the small town her parents were in, the more Lily's excitement grew. Soon, she would be reunited with her parents. She smiled as she looked out the window. She couldn't wait to see them again.

As they got closer to Noble, the small town Dennis Hamilton had directed her to, she turned and beamed at Sofia. "I'm glad you're here with me."

Sofia smiled. "I'm glad, too. You will finally get to see your parents again after looking for them for so long, and I will get to see that. I can't wait to see them, too."

Lily smiled and looked out the window again. She had so much to tell her parents. She saw the signpost a short distance away and her heart began to pound. Looking at the map once again, she saw there was no way to find the address through the map. They would have to ask someone for the specific house her parents were staying at.

Sofia slowed to a crawl in the tiny town. There didn't seem to be anyone here. All they saw were stretches of land and then a lake. They kept on and saw a man dressed in black jeans and a white T-shirt. He was the first person they'd seen so far. Lily showed him the address on the piece of paper, and he immediately told them how to get to the house.

She thanked him, and they went on again and found the house not too far away. Lily blinked as they stopped in front of a two-story house, painted off-white. This town seemed to be a ghost town with only this house. She told Sofia what she was thinking.

"Maybe there are other houses farther down the road," Sofia said.

"Maybe." Lily looked up at the house. Dennis had told her it belonged to someone from Fallow

Creek. She wondered if her parents were staying with that person or if they'd been given the house to use as theirs until they could get a place of their own. Dennis had not filled her in on that, and she had not thought to ask. But it didn't matter. All she wanted was to see her parents now.

She got out of the car with Sofia and walked to the front door. Knocking, she smiled at Sofia and then shifted her feet nervously as she waited for the door to open. Less than a minute later, a middle-aged woman with long braided hair opened the door and stared at them.

"Hi," Lily said. "I came to see my parents —Cliff and Anna Hunter. My name is Lily."

"Oh... okay. They are expecting you," the woman said, looking intently at Lily and then at Sofia. She opened the door wide and said, "Come in. Let me go get them for you."

Lily stepped into the house, with Sofia behind her. She stood studying the living room they had entered. It was a surprisingly colorful space with light brown sofas and green and orange throw pillows. Again, she wondered about the house and if her parents had had a hand in the choice of décor. Probably not. Her mom or dad would not add so much color to their living room. They preferred monotones.

As she walked toward the center of the living room to study a painting on the wall, someone grabbed her roughly from behind. She opened her mouth to scream, and a handkerchief covered her mouth and her nose. She struggled to break free, but the person who had grabbed her held on tightly and pressed the handkerchief firmly over her face.

Gradually, she began to feel faint and started to struggle again with the little strength she had. *Lord, please help me,* she prayed. She felt herself growing weaker and weaker. Just before she passed out, she saw Sofia on the floor, looking lifeless. A feeling of sheer terror settled over her, and then she blanked out.

NINE

Jude frowned as he watched his father praying yet again. As much as he did not want to hear what his father was saying, a part of him was curious to hear the exact words. He drew closer, while silently scolding himself for his curiosity, and listened. His father was asking God for a miracle as he usually did. Asking that they would be released somehow from their captivity.

Rage boiled in him, and he could not stop himself from crying in outrage, "I wish you would stop praying for a miracle! You've been asking the same thing since I was brought here almost a year ago. I don't know why you keep praying to a God who doesn't listen. By now it should have dawned on you that we are not going to get a miracle. Did you not hear what Keziah said when she came here? We are going to die in this prison!"

His father opened his eyes and stared intently at him.

He sighed and looked away, feeling ashamed of his tirade. But everything he said, he still believed.

He just wished he had not spoken so angrily to his dad and tried to extract the thread of hope his father had that they would be freed from this prison. Even though he had no hope of that happening, especially after what Keziah had said, he had no right to snatch his dad's.

"So what if I stop praying for a miracle?" Dad said. "What if I stop believing that God will hear me and bring us out of this cell? Will that change our situation? Will that change the fact that we have been here for a very long time?"

Jude shut his eyes and then opened them again. "I know it won't change anything, but at least we will not keep believing in the lie that God is listening to your prayers. Because He's not. You've been asking me to pray and trust God, and some days ago, I did. Do you remember? I said that if God did a miracle and freed us that day, I would believe in him again. But he didn't. Which of course I knew He wouldn't."

"And why would he hear you when your prayers are said mockingly?" his father asked.

"And what about your prayers that have been so sincere? Has God answered them? Aren't we still here in this stinking cell? I don't know when you will finally realize that God isn't listening! And He isn't listening because He's not there!"

There. I said it.

His dad glared at him. "What happened to you, Jude? How did you become this person? I know it's been a long time, but you used to love God. You believed that there was nothing God couldn't do. What changed that?"

"You want to know what happened? Let me tell you what happened. You were suddenly taken away from me. It was not enough that I lost Mom at a young age, but you were also taken, and I thought you were dead. I was all alone and God did nothing about it. That was what happened. I realized that God did not hear my prayers, or anyone else's for that matter. You loved and were dedicated to God and yet you spent years being tortured in prison."

Dad stood up and walked to him. "But we found each other again, didn't we? God did that. Can't you see?"

"No, I can't." Jude turned away from his father again. "If it really was God who worked a miracle and brought us back together, then He would not have allowed us to be taken to prison in order to wait to be killed."

"You don't know that we will be killed," his father said.

"Dad! Again, you remember what Keziah said, don't you?"

Dad waved his hand dismissively. "I have been in a dire situation before and you know it. When I was at death's door, I trusted in God and he delivered me. If he did it then, I know he will do it again."

Jude groaned and shook his head. He walked away from his dad, sat down on the floor, and leaned his back against the wall. There was no reasoning with his father. Why did he even bother?

Dad came to sit beside him and put his hand on his shoulder. "Jude, I know you're scared, and I understand your anger. But I think..."

"No, you don't understand." A wave of anguish washed over him, and Sofia's face appeared in his mind. "We will be killed in this cell, Dad, and the worst thing is that I will never get to see the woman

I love again. I will never get to explain to her why I left her on our wedding day with no explanation whatsoever. The thought of that is unbearable to me."

For a long moment, his father said nothing and then he began to pray again. Jude stared at him, but his father's eyes were closed. His dad prayed once more that God would deliver them, that Jude would get to see Sofia again so he could explain to her what happened, and that they would get back together again somehow.

Jude gritted his teeth in anger but said nothing. His father was incorrigible. Nothing he said would change the man's mind. For a long moment, his father kept praying, while he held his anger in check and forced himself not to say anything he would regret. He shifted away from his dad, pressed his back against the other side of the wall, and thought about Sofia. What was she doing now? Was she dating again? Had she found someone new?

The thought of her with someone else pierced his heart, but at the same time, he wished that for her.

"I'm so sorry, Sofia," he whispered, and then jumped as a loud explosion pierced the air. Another one sounded and another, shaking the foundations of the cell. A series of loud gunshots followed, and Jude swallowed his dread and rushed to look out the window. His father immediately went to him and pulled him away as though he were a little boy.

"Dad! I just wanted to see what's happening."

The gunshots began to get closer and closer. Usually, the explosions and gunshots, though loud, were so far away from their isolated cell. But this seemed close. Much too close.

The gunshots got even louder, and soon loud voices sounded outside as well. But not just voices. Screams of outrage and pain.

Jude gasped as their cell door flung open. Three men dressed in the National Army uniform strode into the cell with their guns pointed. Jude blinked and stepped back. He put his arm around his father and looked at the men, his heart pounding. Maybe this was the end then. He shut his eyes.

One of the military men looked at his father. "Gideon Daniels?"

Jude's father pushed away from him and walked forward before Jude could stop him. He said boldly, "Yes, that's me."

"My name is Sergeant Obed Peters. We were sent by a friend of yours high up in the government to get you out of this prison." They looked at Jude. "Is this your son?"

"Yes."

"Both of you are to come with us." The man who appeared to be the leader turned to the men behind him and said, "Help them get out of this place. I'll cover you as we go." He turned and faced Jude's father again. "Are both of you strong enough to run?" He looked at Jude and his dad with piercing eyes. His gaze was not sympathetic, just practical. Jude was sure that they looked pathetic and, as Keziah said, smelled bad. "We can move as fast as we need to," he answered.

Obed nodded and beckoned to his men. One took hold of Jude's arms, the other his dad's. Jude's heart began to race as they led them out of the cell, down a long dark hallway, and down a flight of stairs. He was astounded by how much noise came from the other prisoners in the cellblock. Inside their own cell, maybe because of the metal door, they hadn't heard any of the other prisoners and would not have known there were any others if it weren't for the fact that they had seen them the first time they were brought here. He wondered how many of them were innocent except for the fact that they refused to help madmen in their violent quest for power by any means. He wasn't exactly a fan of the present administration, but he did not support the systematic killing of the leaders by Felix and people like him in order to take over.

They finally walked out of the main prison into the open and Jude immediately closed his eyes as the sun almost blinded him. He slowly opened them again but had to shade his eyes with his hand.

They soon got to a dense forest some distance away from the cell block, and the men began to lead him and his father through it. Gunshots continued to ring behind them — clearly Seargent Obed trying to fight off the guards who were coming after them to prevent them from escaping.

For the first time in a long time, Jude began to pray that God would enable them to successfully escape. Hope ran through him as they made their way through the forest. Gunshots still sounded in the distance, but it seemed they were going to make their escape.

He wanted to turn around and see if they were still being followed, but he knew the best thing to do was to keep moving quickly with the men.

He turned to look at his dad, who was ahead of him with the other soldier. His father turned around briefly, and Jude saw that hope shone in his eyes. It was clear that his dad believed they would make it, but Jude wasn't totally sure. Obed and another soldier had been fighting off a group of guys behind them. If the other men overpowered Obed and these army men, or even killed them, that would be the end of their escape... and probably of their lives. Because it was unlikely Felix would let them live after this.

His father's words kept repeating in his mind. *Why won't you trust that God can work a miracle for us?*

Was it God who had sent these men to free them from prison? Maybe it was or maybe it wasn't. It was left to be seen if they would successfully escape or be killed today. And as much as he didn't want to, he could not stop himself from uttering another prayer for help.

The gunshots drew closer and closer to them. And then the guards began to gain ground. The soldiers who had broken Jude and his dad out told them to run while they stayed back to fight off the guards.

Jude started to run and then slowed and turned back when he saw his father was lagging behind. He became worried. His father was finding it difficult to keep up. Jude slowed in order to take his father by the hand, but the soldiers who had been covering them asked them to keep running.

"They are closing in and there are many of them!" one of the soldiers shouted. "We have lost three men, including Sergeant Obed."

Jude heard loud voices of the guards in hot pursuit and the soldier began to shoot again.

Lord, please help us! Jude prayed as he continued to run with his dad. He could hear the guards getting closer, but the remaining soldier was managing to engage them and keep them from gaining on Jude and his father.

They soon burst out of the forest, and Jude's heart drummed as he saw a black Jeep parked a foot away. An army man ran toward them and hurriedly led Jude and his father to the waiting Jeep, while the soldier behind them kept shooting, trying to keep the guards away until they could make their escape.

"Get in quickly," the man said as he opened the door for Jude and his father.

They got into the back seat with blood rushing through Jude's ears and hope soaring in him for the first time in a year. The army man opened the door to get into the driver's seat and then paused and collapsed to the ground.

Jude's mouth fell open, and he popped his head out of the window and stared at the man in horror. Blood gushed from a large hole in his chest. He was dead.

"No, no!" his father said, looking out the window at the guard.

Terror seized Jude as a dozen prison guards barged toward them, pointing their guns at them.

"Get out of the car now!" one of the guards shouted.

They opened the Jeep, roughly pulled Jude and his father out of the car, and flung them to the ground. One of the men held Jude down and pointed his rifle at his head.

Jude bit his lip, trying to press down his fear,

and then turned to look at his father, who was also being held at gunpoint beside him.

They were both going to die now.

Jude shut his eyes, waiting to hear the gunshot and feel the excruciating pain. Once again, Sofia's face appeared in his mind, followed by immeasurable anguish. And then he thought about his father and what he had told him about God and where he would spend eternity.

Fear gripped him again, but even more intense than the fear of dying. Where indeed would he spend eternity when he died?

Knowing he did not have much time left, he uttered a quick prayer of forgiveness. He wasn't sure it would be enough for God to accept him into heaven after being so rebellious, but there was no time for a longer prayer. Any moment now, he would be shot and that would be it for him.

He looked at his father beside him. If only they would spare his dad, but he was sure they would not. The cold steel edge of a rifle pressed into his temple, and once again he pushed down the overwhelming anguish that rose up in him at the thought of never seeing Sofia again.

Forgive me, Sofia, he thought. *And Lord, please forgive me.*

The guard holding the gun to his head cocked it.

"Wait!"

Jude blinked. Was that...?

"Don't kill them yet."

Jude pressed his lips together. It was definitely Felix. He groaned. He opened his eyes and looked up at his former friend. Felix was staring down at him with a frown.

"So they tried to break you out of prison?" Felix said, sounding amused. "I guess we will have to move you." He turned to look at Jude's dad and then turned to Jude. "Pick him up," he ordered one of the guards.

The guard lifted Jude off the ground, and Felix walked over to him. He stood right in front of Jude. "You thought you could escape," he snapped his fingers, "just like that?"

Jude frowned at him. "What are you going to do with us?" He looked at the gun Felix was holding.

Felix gave him a wicked smile. "Don't worry, I won't kill you or your father. But don't look so relieved. Even though we will keep you both alive, at least for now, you will wish I had killed you today." Felix pointed at one of the guards. "We will have to move them to the other location."

Jude's heart began to race wildly. What plans did Felix have for him and his father?

The guards pulled him toward a Jeep parked some distance from where they stood. His father was right in front of him, two guards leading him. Jude could not see his face, but from his demeanor, Jude could tell he was praying again. But this time, he did not feel angry or offended by it. Not even a little. But he still felt dread at whatever Felix had in store for them. His father's prayers had not stopped them from being recaptured, and neither had his. But strangely, he did not feel anger toward God anymore. Maybe he had resigned himself to his fate, or maybe it just took too much energy to keep being angry with God.

But as they kept walking to the Jeep, their pace slow because of his dad, Jude knew it was neither.

Even though he still feared whatever was coming, there was a thread of supernatural peace running through him, reminding him of a Bible verse he'd memorized as a child. *And the peace of God that passes all understanding will keep and guard your hearts in Christ Jesus.*

The feeling of peace that was even now spreading through him was one he didn't understand because he was sure Felix was not bluffing. They were going to be severely punished for this botched escape attempt. And yet, he could not help but think God was still in control, no matter what happened to them. It was totally contrary to what he'd have believed an hour ago. Maybe something had happened to him between the time he thought they were definitely going to be killed and now.

And then Sofia's face flashed through his mind again. When they were escaping, he had begun to have some hope that he would see her again, but now, his hope had been taken away. Maybe Felix was right. Maybe it was better to die right now than live knowing he would never see her again.

The guard walking beside him opened the door of the white Jeep and pushed him into the backseat. His father was pushed in beside him. Two guards got in beside them, squashing them together.

Jude turned to look at his father and sighed sadly, feeling sorry for him. He was too old for this sort of thing. He reached out and put his arm around his father. "I'm sorry, Dad," he whispered.

"It's not your fault," his father said. "Why are you apologizing?"

But a huge part of him blamed himself. His father was here because of him, at least partly.

"Oh Lord, please help us," he whispered again, and then sighed. The car began to move, and he put his head down and bleakly surrendered to whatever fate awaited him.

TEN

Lily slowly opened her eyes and winced in pain. She inhaled and placed her hands on her temples. Her head was pounding. She looked around her surroundings and noticed she was lying on a queen-size bed with red-and-gold bedding and matching curtains. There was a large, ornate armoire a few feet away in the large room and, on the floor, a gold-and-red Persian rug. Whoever owned this house loved bright colors.

She blinked and sat up on the bed as she remembered someone pressing a handkerchief over her nose and mouth when they'd arrived here. And then she remembered seeing Sofia lying on the ground, lifeless. Terror seized her. "No! Sofia!"

Her heart drummed with fear as she looked fully around the room and noticed another bed at the far end. Her fear dissipated slightly when she saw Sofia lying on the bed. Slowly, she swung her legs down, stood on unsteady feet, and went to Sofia. Sighing with relief when she saw Sofia was breathing, she gently shook her shoulder. "Wake up, Sofia!"

Sofia moaned and her eyes flew open. She looked at Lily and then glanced around the room. She sat up on the bed, rubbing her eyes, and shook her head. Looking at Lily again, she asked groggily, "Where are we? What happened?" And then her eyes grew round. "I remember someone pressing a handkerchief to my nose and mouth. We must have been drugged."

Lily nodded. "Yes. But the question is why? Why were we drugged and brought in here to this room?" Her heart began to race wildly again. "Where are my parents?" She hurried to the door and tried to open it. It was locked. She banged on the door and screamed, "Who is there? Let us out! Please let us go!"

She kept banging on the door until she finally grew tired. She wrung her hands and paced the gold-tiled floor. How were they supposed to get out of here? Clearly, this was Dennis Hamilton's doing. He had lied to her about her parents being in Utah; in this house. But why would he do that? Why would he send her all the way from Fallow Creek to this place to have her and Sofia locked up in this room?

"How are we going to get out of here?" Sofia asked.

"I don't know," Lily said, and then walked to the window. She threw back the curtains and groaned. The windows had iron bars. There was no escaping this room. She looked down and saw two men dressed in fatigues that looked like the ones the security squad members used to wear. Frustration and hopelessness washed over her, and she sighed and backed away from the window.

Sofia rose from the bed and went to her. "We have to get out of here," she said, sounding almost desperate. "We can't stay locked in here, Lily."

"I know." Lily gasped. "Where is my purse?" If she could get to her phone, she might be able to get someone to help them. She went to the bed she had been lying on and searched the covers and sheets to see if her phone was anywhere on it. When she didn't see it, she turned to Sofia and bit her lip. "Whoever brought us here has taken it. What about yours, Sofia? Is it still with you?"

Sofia went to check her own bed and shook her head. "It's not here. They took it too."

Lily searched the room again for their purses, but she didn't find them. The person or people who'd brought them up to this room had made sure to take their purses and their phones so they would not be able to contact anyone.

"That Dennis Hamilton is an evil man!" Sofia said.

Lily narrowed her eyes. "But again... why would he do this? What does he want from us?" She sat on the bed and held her head in her hands. Overwhelming distress settled over her. Taylor would have already tried to call her. Without getting through to her, he would soon start to worry. So would Rachel and Keith. She had to get out of this place. She and Sofia. She turned and faced Sofia again. "I'm so sorry. Because of me, you're locked up here. Maybe I should not have brought you along. You should have stayed in Fallow Creek." She placed her hand on her forehead. "Why did we come here? I should have known Dennis Hamilton couldn't be trusted."

Sofia put her arm around Lily's shoulder. "Stop! It's not your fault. How could you have known that this would happen?"

Lily raised her head and looked at the door. Anger rose up in her, and she stood and marched to the door. She began to pound on it with her fists. "Open up! Open this door right now!" She stepped back from it and shut her eyes. What were the people who brought them here planning to do with them? She turned to Sofia. Were they planning to harm her and Sofia? Was this some sort of revenge by Dennis Hamilton for rejecting him two years ago? Clearly, the man had a long memory, but she wasn't surprised by that. What she was surprised by was that he'd made her and Sofia come all the way here just to mete out his punishment for her rejection.

Sofia went to the door and shook the doorknob. She sighed and turned to Lily with fear in her eyes. "We are never going to get out of here," she said.

Lily shook her head. "We will get out... somehow!"

"How, Lily? There is no way to escape this place."

"There has to be a way out," Lily said to Sofia, who was breathing in and out, clearly trying to control her nerves. "Calm down, Sofia. Let me think. There has to be a way to get out of here." She stood up and looked around the room again for a point of escape. But there was no way out.

Lord, why oh why did I trust a man like Dennis Hamilton? She should have known that such a man would do something like this. He had not led them to her parents at all. Instead, he had deceived her and led her and Sofia here for some reason best known to him. She didn't know exactly why they were here, but she knew the reason they had been brought here was not a good one. Without a doubt, they were in danger.

Sofia strode over to her and sat down next to her on the bed. She sighed loudly and said in a surprisingly calm voice, "At least Rachel, Keith, and Taylor know that Dennis Hamilton gave us an address to find your parents. If we don't come back soon or they don't hear from us, they will come looking for us here." Her eyes grew wide again and she searched Lily's. "Tell me you showed Keith and Rachel the address that evil man gave us."

Lily groaned and shook her head, regret filling her heart. "No, I did not remember to show them. What have I done? I probably didn't remember because I didn't think it was important to show them the address. I just didn't think that something like this would happen." She put her hand on her forehead. "I'm so stupid."

"Lily, you are not stupid. Neither of us imagined that this would happen. At least they know Dennis Hamilton was the one who gave us the address. They will go and ask him about it."

"Yes, but even if they do, I am sure that will not help. He might give them another address, or insist that he doesn't know where we are and that we never reached the address he gave us. He can tell them that we went missing on our way here or something. There will be no proof that we actually got here and are being held captive."

Sofia moaned and stood up. She walked to the window, threw the curtains back, and looked out.

Lily sat looking at the wall in front of her, despair

and desperation warring in her heart. She sighed as she thought about Taylor trying to get to her and being worried that he'd not been able to reach her. She soon got tired of worrying about Taylor, stood up, and went to the window to stand beside Sofia. She looked out of the window. Below were the squad members she'd seen earlier, still walking in front of the building, their guns beside them.

Lily groaned again. What was it with these men and their constant need to have armed guards everywhere?

Another man dressed in jeans and a navy blue shirt walked up to one of the guards, and Lily blinked. The man looked familiar. He looked up and she gasped. She stepped away from the window as her heart began to drum.

Sofia turned to look at her. "What is it, Lily? You look like you've seen a ghost."

"I know that man down there." She walked back to the window, slowly opened the curtain, and looked down once more. The man was still looking up, and their eyes met. She gasped again. "It can't be." The man narrowed his eyes and began to stride toward the house. Lily immediately shrank back from the window.

Sofia put her hand on Lily's shoulder. "What's the matter? Who is the man you said you know?"

"He is coming up here... I think," Lily said.

Sofia's hands dropped from her shoulders. She backed away until her back was against the wall.

She stood staring at the door, her pulse racing. She would confront him and ask why he had brought them here. Because she was even more confused about that now.

The doorknob turned slowly and the door flew open. The man walked in and fixed his eyes on Lily.

Lily narrowed her eyes in confusion. "Uncle Matthew!" She stared at her father's much younger brother and then looked at the gun in his hand. Blinking, she looked into his eyes. "Why? Why are you holding us here against our will? Where are my parents?"

"Lily, your parents are fine. Don't worry about them."

She glared at him as anger began to burn in her. "What have you done, Uncle Matthew? Where are my parents? What do you plan to do with us?"

"Lily, do you really think I would hurt your parents in any way, especially my older brother? And I will never hurt you. You know that." Lily looked at the gun in his hands again, and he stared at it before tucking it into his belt. He looked at her once more and said evenly, "Your parents were the ones who asked me to keep you here when you arrived."

"That's a lie!" Lily glowered at him. "Why would my parents ask you to hold me captive in this place?" She stepped closer to her uncle. "Where are they, Uncle Matthew? If you know where they are, please, I would like to see them now. Are you 'keeping' them here as well?"

"They are not here," he said coldly. "And I told you that your parents were the ones who asked me not to let you leave this house."

She refused to believe him. "If they are not here, then let my friend and I go. Why would you keep us here anyway? What do you hope to gain?"

Uncle Matthew sighed and said exasperatedly,

"What can I do to convince you that it was your parents, your father specifically, who asked me to make sure you remain in this house?"

Lily searched his eyes and frowned. He looked like he was telling the truth, and yet why would her own father lock her up in this house? That couldn't be. She said, "Why would you lie to me, Uncle Matthew? My father would never ask you to keep me here against my will."

"He did, Lily. It's for your own good."

Lily's confusion deepened. "What do you mean by that? I know without a doubt that Dennis Hamilton is involved in this. Why would my father connive with Dennis Hamilton to bring me here and hold me captive in this house? It doesn't make any sense. I don't believe you."

Uncle Matthew walked slightly away from her and looked at Sofia, whose back was still pressed against the wall. His eyes lit up for just a brief moment, and then he turned and faced Lily again. "It's true, Lily. Your father planned for you to be far away from Fallow Creek in order to keep you safe. And knowing how stubborn you are, he asked me to keep you here by any means, even if I have to hold you down physically."

"My father planned for me to be far away from Fallow Creek to keep me safe?" Lily stared at her uncle. "Safe from what?"

Uncle Matthew's forehead creased and his mouth tipped. He looked at her without saying anything for a long moment, and then he said, "A battle is coming to Fallow Creek. All the families that left, the men at least, are in support of it. We want to take back our town from that Rachel woman and put Dennis Hamilton back in as the leader, just as it should be. We all want to be able to live as we used to, before that woman changed everything and wrecked our precious town."

Lily's mouth dropped open and she stared incredulously at her uncle, unable to speak. Finally, after a minute, she found her voice and said, "You cannot be serious! Tell me that you are just kidding. Please."

"I am not joking, Lily. I am dead serious. Your father had an agreement with Dennis Hamilton to get you out of Fallow Creek before our plans for a takeover started. We plan to remove Rachel and that man she married and get rid of anyone who resists Dennis Hamilton as the true leader of our town."

Lily's mouth dropped open again, and she stared at her uncle in total disbelief. And then overwhelming fear and panic seized her at what she'd just heard. She shook her head. There was no way this could be true. She would not believe it. "Uncle Matthew, you would not think about doing such a thing. Neither would my father. Tell me it's not true."

"It is, Lily. We are tired of living in other parts of this country because we were forced out of our town. Fallow Creek is our home and always will be. We will not continue to allow some woman to keep us away from our hometown."

"But Rachel is not keeping anyone away from Fallow Creek."

Uncle Matthew laughed harshly. "Of course she is. But I know you will not understand. You are a woman, and a stubborn one at that. You support that Rachel woman, don't you? Of course you do. You married her brother. You've always had a rebellious spirit. It wasn't enough that you were exiled from town, but you had to go back and show your support for the equally rebellious Rachel and the man she's living with now. It was why your father had to take extreme measures to get you out of there."

Lily bit her lip and her legs began to shake as the full import of what her uncle had just told her settled on her. Her vision blurred and she felt like she would drop to the floor at any moment. She placed her hand on the wall to steady herself and shut her eyes for just a brief moment before opening them again. "You cannot all be planning to do what I think you are," she said, her panic rising.

"I told you the battle is coming to Fallow Creek. If a true battle is what you're thinking, then you're right."

"No." She shook her head. "No, no, no! You cannot do such a thing. Rachel! Keith! All those women in the House of Refuge." They had all suffered so much. She screamed, "What right has Dennis Hamilton to take Fallow Creek from Rachel and Keith when it doesn't belong to him?"

"We the people decide who it belongs to," her uncle said. "And as far as we are concerned, Dennis Hamilton is our leader and it belongs to him. No woman can take that away from him."

"And why do you have to harm Rachel and Keith or any of the women in the House of Refuge?"

"Rachel and Keith forcefully removed Dennis from his place as our leader and caused most of us to move out of town. We are scattered all over the country, and many lost their livelihoods when they moved. It was Rachel's fault. We want to go back, but never under that woman, or any woman for that matter."

"And so how does that translate into harming them?"

"Did you not hear what I just said? They took everything away from us. They deserve whatever is coming to them."

"No, they don't! You left because of your stupid pride. Rachel and Keith never asked anyone to leave." She felt repulsed as she stared at her uncle. "And what about the women who live at the House of Refuge? What did they do to any of you? Why are you planning to harm them?"

"Who said anything about harming them? We plan to assimilate them back into Fallow Creek. The Fallow Creek we all knew and loved. As long as they agree to our terms and don't resist, none of them will be harmed."

She looked into her uncle's eyes. "How did you become so evil? And how do you plan to assimilate the women?" Her uncle smiled, and she bit her lip, as she immediately knew how they planned to do it. She knew the men of Fallow Creek well enough to know how they thought and what they were capable of. She knew what plans they had for the women at the House of Refuge. Before her uncle could say anything, she shook her head and said, "Don't tell me. I already know. The men plan on taking the women as second, or third or fourth wives... adding to the ones they already have. Am I right? That's the suitable punishment you think they deserve for being rebellious and standing with

Rachel."

"Punishment?" Uncle Matthew laughed and shook his head. "When did marriage become a punishment? You see, this is why we have to remove Rachel. She has filled the heads of our women with nonsense. They've all turned into loose and ungodly women, but we will remedy that. Marrying them will rescue them from their erroneous, sinful beliefs and teachings that Rachel has filled their minds with." He looked at Sofia again. This time there was a lascivious look in his eyes. He gave her a small smile and nodded.

Sofia glared at him in clear anger, but that did not seem to faze him any.

Lily's blood boiled with anger. Knowing this man, she knew what was going on in his mind. Over her dead body would she let him or anyone else come near her friend. It was her fault that Sofia had come to Fallow Creek and then to this place. She would not let anything happen to her friend. Not on her watch. And she could not let anything happen to Rachel or Keith. She had to find a way to warn them about this coming battle her uncle had told her about before it was too late.

Her uncle turned around to leave and she shouted, "Uncle Matthew, please don't do this! Think about what you and all those men are about to do." She moaned. "I cannot believe my father would be involved in something like this."

"He's helping to gather all the men for a meeting with Dennis Hamilton as we speak." Uncle Matthew said. "You'd better believe it. Soon we will be able to return to Fallow Creek. Including you, Lily."

She screamed at him. "If you harm Rachel or

Keith...!"

"What do you plan to do about it?" Uncle Matthew glared at her. "I'm not going to let you," he looked at Sofia and then faced Lily again, "or your friend, out of this house or even out of this room." He waved his hand. "This room is comfortable enough to spend weeks in, don't you think?"

She stared at him in horror. "Weeks?"

"We plan to attack very soon, but it might take weeks to put everything back in place in Fallow Creek. Only then can I let you go."

"You cannot keep us locked in here for that long!" Sofia yelled.

He blinked and looked at Sofia. His eyes moved over her, and then he looked at Lily again. "Just like I told you, your dad got you out of Fallow Creek for your protection, and he made the right decision. It will be much easier for you two to stay here quietly like good girls. Food will be brought up for you soon." He began to turn around again, and Lily knew she had to act now, though she didn't know exactly what she was going to do.

Without considering that he had a gun, she sprang forward, still not sure of what she was doing but knowing she had to do something, anything, to save Rachel and Keith and the women of the House of Refuge. Without thinking, she reached out to snatch the gun that was tucked into her uncle's belt, but he grabbed up her hand and flung her on the bed like a piece of rag.

He stared at her and shook his head. "Don't ever do that again, Lily! I don't want to hurt you."

Lily narrowed her eyes as she stared up at him. She took a deep breath and said, "At least give us our phones back."

Uncle Matthew laughed. "You know I cannot do that. You will call Rachel or Keith and warn them about what we're planning to do." He walked over to the bed, patted her head as though she were a little girl, turned around, and walked out of the room.

She flew across the room to the door, but he had already shut and locked it. She banged on the door and screamed, "Uncle Matthew. Let us out! please!"

She kept banging on the door for a long time, and then she stopped. No one was going to open for her. A sob rose in her throat at the realization that they were stuck in here while a major disaster was about to happen. She sank to the floor, weary and heartbroken. Her head hurt as she pictured Rachel and Keith and many of her friends at the House of Refuge. Her uncle had called what they were about to unleash a battle, but it really wasn't. In a battle, the other side had the strength and weapons to fight. That wasn't so with Rachel and Keith and the women in the House. It was more like an invasion and conquest. Their lives were on the line, and Lily couldn't do anything about it.

"Lord, why? Why is this happening?"

Sofia walked over to her and knelt beside her. When she put her arm around Lily's waist, Lily buried her head on Sofia's shoulders and wept.

ELEVEN

Sofia felt like screaming. Of all the times to be locked in a small space, this wasn't it. She had been descending into a pit of depression before Lily had come and gotten her out by asking her to go to Fallow Creek with her. She had been mostly keeping the depression at bay by immersing herself in all that Fallow Creek offered and trying to help Lily find her parents. But now, being held captive in this room, she could feel herself once more going down that pit. She tried to hold down the anger and hopelessness she felt, but she couldn't. She began to hyperventilate and then calmed down a little when Lily came and put her arms around her. She smiled at Lily gratefully, took a deep breath and told herself to stop freaking out.

"I should never have asked you to come with me," Lily said yet again.

"It's not your fault, Lily. I wish you would stop blaming yourself." To try to lighten Lily's mood, she mustered up a smile for her friend, even though she was still immensely troubled on the inside.

"Besides what would you have done if I was not here with you?"

Lily raised her eyebrows but said nothing.

The door opened, and Lily's uncle Matthew walked into the room. She glanced briefly at him and saw his eyes were on her. She turned away, choosing to ignore him. Once again, she sighed and tried to resist the depression that was pressing in on her. She blinked when she felt Matthew's eyes on her. Yesterday she had also noticed him staring, but only briefly. Why was he still looking at her? She turned and looked at the man who was holding them captive in this house. He was gazing at her with curiosity in his eyes… and something else.

She frowned. She knew this look. She had seen it in the eyes of many men who looked at her, including that evil Dennis Hamilton. Lust. She narrowed her eyes as she stared back at him, and then blinked in surprise. Maybe it wasn't quite lust. The look in his eyes was more like real attraction… but that did not change the fact that he had no right to keep them locked up in this place. She glowered at him, hoping it would make him stop staring at her, but it didn't. She sighed and turned her face away and focused once more on Lily.

"What is your friend's name, Lily?" he asked.

Lily faced her uncle. "Sofia. As you can see, she's having a hard time being locked in here. Please, Uncle Matthew, you have to let us go."

"You know I cannot do that."

Lily sighed wearily. "Please. At least let Sofia go. She has nothing to do with any of this."

Matthew shook his head slowly and said, "If I let her go, she will warn Keith or Rachel about our plans for Fallow Creek. As much as I want to, I cannot let her go." He looked at Sofia again and spoke tenderly to her. "I'm sorry for the difficulty this is causing you. Unfortunately, I have to keep you both locked in here, but if you need anything, anything at all, please let me know. I will try as much as possible to get it for you."

Sofia didn't answer.

Lily arched her brows. "Let me tell you what she needs, Uncle Matthew. She needs to go back to Tucson where she lives so she can continue to live her life." Lily put her hand on her chest. "And I need to get back to my husband. Thanks for asking."

Matthew chuckled. "No can do, Lily."

Sofia faced Lily's uncle and said, "There's one thing I need. Can I have my phone?"

Matthew looked into her eyes for a few seconds without speaking and then shook his head. "I wish I could get that for you, but I don't have it. The boss took both your phones away."

"The boss!" Lily said incredulously. "Who is this boss?" She walked up to him with her hands propped on her hips and stared at him. "Please don't tell me it's my father." When her uncle did not answer, Lily sighed loudly, stepped back, and sat heavily on the bed. She looked up at him with a clear look of loathing on her face.

Sofia said, "Okay, if you can't give me my phone, can I have art supplies for painting? Paper, some paint — acrylic or watercolor, brushes, a palette, varnish. I would like to paint something." She held her breath, praying he would accept her request. Her paintings had helped her through hard times in the past, and as she did not know when they would be released from this place, she needed all the help she could get not to fall back into that depressed state she'd found herself in last year. The emotional rollercoaster she'd gone through with the breakup and abandonment at the altar had been very hard. She never wanted her emotional state to get that bad again.

He frowned slightly. "Can you repeat that list again?"

She repeated the list of art supplies she needed and heaved a sigh of relief when he smiled and nodded. "Okay, I will get someone to buy those things for you. It might take some time to get them as there is no art store anywhere near here, but I will get them. Do you want anything else?"

Sofia turned to face Lily and found that Lily was looking from her to Matthew, an incredulous expression on her face. Sofia turned to Matthew again. "No, there's nothing else I want that you can get for us." He continued to look at her, and she turned away and went to sit down beside Lily.

He finally left the room, and Sofia looked up at the ceiling and groaned. "Great! We have no idea when we are going to leave this place."

Lily fell back on the bed, and Sofia jumped when she suddenly let out a scream.

Sofia turned to look at her Lily and put her arms around her to try to comfort her. She screamed again, and Sofia frowned.

"I don't know what to do," Lily said. "My sister-in-law and her husband are in danger and here I am, just sitting here unable to do anything to help them."

"Lily, please calm down."

"How can I calm down? Taylor will be trying to call me right now, worried out of his mind that he can't get through to me. I cannot even warn my sister-in-law about what is coming to Fallow Creek so she can get help. And all those women, Sofia. What if some of them refuse the lustful advances of those men? They might be in danger, or find themselves in the same situation we're in right now, only it will be permanent."

Sofia pressed her lips tightly together as misery encircled her. She didn't know Rachel that well, but the little she knew of her, she liked. Rachel and Keith were great people. The thought of anything happening to them left a terrible heaviness in her heart.

She stood up, went to the door, and turned the knob simply out of desperation. She already knew it was locked. She went and sat down beside Lily again. Taking her friend's hand, she squeezed it encouragingly and said, "I don't know what else we can do except pray. Let's ask the Lord to help us get out of here, or at least find a way to warn Rachel and Keith about the danger that is coming their way."

"But how will we warn them if we can't find a way out of here?" Lily asked hopelessly.

"That's why we should pray. God can give us a miracle and get us out of here. Even if he doesn't, he can give us the wisdom we need to find a way to warn your sister-in-law and her husband."

"I don't just want wisdom, I want a miracle," Lily said. "I want to get out of this place."

"I definitely want to leave this place as well," Sofia said. She briefly glanced around the room and then forced herself to smile at Lily. Closing her eyes with her hand in Lily's, she began to pray for a miracle for her and Lily, and especially for Rachel and Keith and all the women in the House of Refuge. When she finished praying, she smiled at Lily again.

Lily did not smile back.

"Lily, you're the one who always tries to encourage me and tell me that God will work it all out. I know this is a dire situation, but..."

"Taylor... our kids..." She stared at the wall in front of her as though she had not heard what Sofia had just said. "What have I done?"

"Lily, what you did was something good. You wanted to be reunited with your parents, and you were led to believe they were here."

"If only I had known that my parents, especially my dad, was the sort of person who would join Dennis Hamilton and plan to hurt innocent people, I would never have tried to find them. I don't know why I was not satisfied with the family I have now — with my husband and Bree and Josh."

"Lily, don't do this to yourself. Of course, you're satisfied with the family you have now, but that doesn't mean that you can't miss your parents. Anyone who loves their parents would have done what you did."

Lily spoke again as though she had not heard a word Sofia had said. "Bree and Josh. Did you know that Josh is about to start his summer holidays and we're all supposed to travel to France? Taylor and I promise to take him to Disneyland there."

"Lily, stop beating yourself up about this!"

Lily placed her hand on her forehead and looked at Sofia with pain in her eyes. "What am I doing? I'm talking about my husband and kids and Disneyland when my sister-in-law and her husband are in danger. As well as the women at the House of Refuge."

Sofia stood up and went to her again. "You cannot keep talking like this. Blaming yourself is not going to help anyone."

Lily stood up and paced the room, and Sofia sighed and sat down to watch her. A minute later, she sat down beside Sofia again, shook her head, and began to cry. "How can I help them, Sofia? How?"

"We prayed about that," Sofia said. "We have to trust that the Lord will make a way somehow." She reached out and gathered Lily in her arms.

Lily pulled away. "I'll have to try to plead with Uncle Matthew again to let us go so we can try to warn Rachel and Keith about the men's plan. The thing is, even if the Lord touches my uncle's heart and he agrees to let us go, I don't know if we will be on time to help them. Who knows, maybe Dennis and his men have already invaded Fallow Creek." Tears poured down her cheeks. "Maybe as we speak, something awful has happened to my sister-in-law and her husband. Maybe they are even..."

"Stop, Lily! Don't think like that. Have some faith." She put her arms around Lily again and rubbed her back to comfort her.

The door opened again, and Lily's uncle walked into the room with some plastic bags. Lily pulled away from Sofia. She went to her uncle and began to plead with him to let them go, but once more, he refused.

"Why can't you see that this plan you have to

invade Fallow Creek and hurt Rachel and Keith is wrong?" Lily said angrily. "Don't you people have an ounce of sympathy?"

"Rachel and Keith didn't have an ounce of sympathy when they took Dennis's place and left him and his men to drown in the river. But their plans did not work and God saved them. Dennis is right to take back what belongs to him."

"You're deluded, Uncle Matthew. First of all, you know that Fallow Creek does not belong to Dennis Hamilton. Secondly, Rachel and Keith did not hurt Dennis or any of those men in any way. It was Dennis Hamilton who tried to kill them, not the other way around. It was my husband, Taylor, who saved Dennis and his men." She propped her hands on her hips. "Now I wish he hadn't saved them," she said angrily. "I wish he had left them all to die that day!"

Sofia winced, and Uncle Matthew glared at Lily. "Your Taylor was just an instrument in God's hand. Since Rachel and her husband took over, has there ever been a time of prolonged peace in Fallow Creek or the Restoration House? I think those women in the Restoration House are innately rebellious and God just wanted them to have a taste of what it would be like to have an equally rebellious woman in charge."

Lily glared at him. "You're talking about what happened with Mike Cadwell last year? So you know about that."

"Of course I do. Everyone knows what happened. Remember that Dennis Hamilton was there and even tried to help out. All Rachel has brought to Fallow Creek is war and death. It shows that she has no right to be the leader of the town. It doesn't matter what anyone says."

"And is it not war and death you and Dennis Hamilton and all those men are about to bring to Fallow Creek?" Lily stared at her uncle with loathing.

Matthew shrugged. "Everything will be okay in the end," he said.

"No, it won't! You are all evil!"

Matthew said nothing, and Lily pleaded again. "Please, Uncle Matthew. Please, reconsider."

He turned away from her and walked up to Sofia on the bed. He handed her a bag and said, "Here are your art supplies." He turned to face Lily. "I brought some food for both of you." He gave Sofia one of the bags and dropped the other one beside Lily. Looking at Sofia again, he said, "If you need anything else, please let me know." He gave her a rueful smile and then opened the door to leave the room.

Lily flew after him and tried to force her way out. He pushed her back, exited the room, and slammed the door. Lily rushed to the door again. She shook the doorknob, but the door was already locked. She banged on it and then turned around, marched to the bed, and fell into it with a moan.

Sofia looked down at her and then took her hand and pulled out of bed. "Let's eat, Lily."

"Are you kidding me? How can I eat at a time like this?"

"We haven't eaten anything since this morning. Starving yourself will accomplish nothing. Besides, we need food in order to think properly and try to come up with an idea."

"I don't want to eat anything."

"Lily, you have to eat." She opened the bag of food and brought out two plastic bowls. The delicious aroma of the food wafted into her nose, and her stomach rumbled. She had not realized how much she'd been starving until now.

Lily glanced at the food and sighed loudly. She picked up the bag that her uncle had given her and brought out a bowl of spaghetti. She looked at Sofia's food and then at her own and raised her brows. "You have twice as much food, Sofia."

Sofia shrugged. "I'll share mine with you if you want more. I think your uncle must have made a mistake and bought an extra portion for me."

"No, he didn't make a mistake," Lily said dryly. "He gave you an extra portion because he likes you."

Sofia pressed her lips together and then said, "How do you know he likes me?"

Lily said off-handedly, "Because I see it in his eyes whenever he looks at you."

Sofia waved her hand dismissively. "I'm sure he doesn't like me, but what does it matter anyway?"

Lily put her hand on her forehead and sighed. "I wish my parents were here. I need to speak to them, especially my father. Maybe I could get him to listen to me and stop this madness somehow. I don't understand how he could be involved in such a thing. In something so wrong."

"You told me how the men of Fallow Creek are. They clearly want to move back to their town and get back to the way things were, and they believe they can't do that unless they get rid of Rachel and her husband."

Disgust was written on Lily's face. "Yes, and I

wish that getting rid of them didn't mean killing them." She dropped the food on the floor again and covered her face with her hand.

Sofia felt like throwing up. She couldn't imagine harm coming to Rachel and Keith. "Lord, please protect them," she whispered.

"I think Dennis Hamilton convinced them, my father included, that in order for them to reclaim all the things they had lost, they had to be ready to kill, or, specifically in their case, have the squad guards do it. It's the mob mentality, I think."

"We have to do something, Lily," Sofia said. Her heart raced wildly, and her stomach roiled at the thought of what might happen soon to Rachel and her husband and the women in the House of Refuge.

"That's what I've been saying, but what can we do when we are locked up in this place?"

Sofia looked up at the ceiling as an idea began to form in her mind. "I'm not sure it will work, but I think I have an idea."

TWELVE

"Where are you taking him?" Jude yelled at the guards who veered to the right and pushed his father into a black Jeep. Four guards had arrived at the cell earlier and led him and his father out. He kept asking them where they were going as they walked down the empty road, but they said nothing to him. Now two of them had pushed his father into a Jeep and driven away. He tried to free himself from the guards, who were holding him firmly by the elbows, but he couldn't.

Another black Jeep stood some distance away, and they led him to it and pushed him in. They drove for a short while down a winding road and then onto a dirt path that led to a two-story building.

He gasped as the Jeep parked in front of the building. His father was being led out of the other vehicle. One of the guards beside him opened the car door and he got out. He immediately began to walk toward his father, but the guards pulled him back and led him in the opposite direction.

He struggled and turned around just as his father was led into the large unpainted building. Fear grabbed him by the throat. What were they going to do with his father? Were they going to kill him? He began to shout, "Let him go!" but the guards forced his face around and ordered him to be quiet.

They led him down a dirt road until they came to a white single-story building, which was clearly freshly painted. Except for the building, there was nothing else around. The place was completely deserted.

A car approached from behind, and Jude turned. A black Mercedes moved to the front of the building and stopped. Felix got out of the car and came toward Jude. Without looking at him, he instructed one of the guards holding Jude to lock him up in the building.

Jude shouted at Felix, "Where did you take my father?"

Felix did not look at him.

The guards dragged Jude into the building while he continued to struggle to get away. He stopped struggling and looked around him, surprised to see a fully furnished living room. Who lived in a deserted place like this? There was no one else around except for the guards, and he guessed it was one of the houses in the country where Felix stayed.

Felix had told him he would wish he was dead once he faced the punishment waiting for him, but if he was to be held here, then this was definitely better than the place they had been kept for months.

The guard led him past the living room through the kitchen and then out the back door of the house. So, he was not going to be held in the house. They kept walking until they got to a forest again and then made their way through it, slapping back shrubs and plants as they did.

They continued on, and Jude began to get more and more tired. Leaves slapped his face and left marks on his cheeks and arms. Just as he thought they would walk forever in the jungle, they came to a tiny building that looked more like an outhouse. Apart from the building, there was nothing else anywhere around. Only the jungle surrounded it.

Jude's heart began to pound. This building was in the middle of nowhere. They were going to lock him up in complete isolation, in the middle of this jungle.

He started to struggle again, and the guards quickly unlocked the door of the building and pushed him into it. He fell to the ground and heard the door being locked. He pounded on it and groaned. Finally, he turned to look around the small building. He could barely see the place. Even though it was the middle of the afternoon, it was dark in here. He searched with his hands for a light switch but found none. Looking up, he found there was also no lightbulb. He laughed harshly. Felix had been true to his word. He would probably lose his sanity in a week locked up here alone.

He sat on the floor and pressed his back against the wall. Shutting his eyes, he groaned again. Sorrow threatened to suffocate him. What were they doing to his father now? Was he was even still alive?

Waves of fear crashed in on him. There was nothing he could do except pray.

"Lord, please help me and help my father." He said the prayer over and over again, not knowing what else to say. It was strange that just yesterday he had scoffed at the idea of praying to a God he thought did not hear him. Even though his prayers had not been answered and he and his dad had not been delivered, something had changed in him when he opened up his heart and cried out to God to save him. Somehow, he could feel God's presence next to him.

Just as his father had always prayed when they were locked up together, he asked for a miracle even though there was little chance of one now. "I know my situation seems impossible, but I believe there is nothing you can't do, God. You can deliver my father and me."

For some reason, he stopped praying and waited to see if something would happen. Nothing did and he sighed. What had he expected to happen anyway?

He jerked his head up as the door swung open. Someone shone a flashlight on his face and then around the room. He stood up as the room brightened and squinted at the door. Felix and Keziah stood before him, with two armed guards beside them.

"Where did you take my father, you wicked souls!" Jude yelled.

Felix shook his head and laughed. "Still as stubborn as ever, Jude."

"Where is my father? What have you done to him?"

"Your father is safe, Jude," Keziah said.

"For now," Felix added. "But that can change any

moment."

Jude shut his eyes briefly and moaned. He opened them and said, "Please, let him go. Your quarrel is with me alone."

"No, that's where you're wrong. You know what your father did. He was working for…"

"You've told me all that. I don't want to hear it anymore. You have punished him enough. Please let him go."

"As we've always told you, Jude — you have the power to free your father. Just say you will join us, and we will let both of you go. You will have great power once we fully take over the reign of this country."

Jude glared at Felix. "You want me to join you in committing your many atrocities. Never! I will never do that!"

"I knew you were stubborn, Jude, but I didn't know you were this stubborn." He glanced around the tiny building and then turned to look at Jude again. "I'll give you a few days. When you have stayed in here in isolation with no food, you will sing a different story."

Jude stared at him and felt intense hatred toward him. "You are a disgusting person, and you will get all that's coming to you," Jude said.

One of the guards behind Felix stepped up to Jude and punched him hard on the jaw. Jude staggered and fell over. The guard raised his boot to stomp on Jude, but Felix raised his hand and commanded him to stop.

"There's no need for this violence," Felix said. "It's not going to help change his mind." He looked at Jude. "We will be back in a few days, and by then you'll be begging to be released from here." He bent down and looked into Jude's eyes. "Your father is still alive, but barely. You have the power to save him, Jude. All you have to do is join us."

Jude coughed and moaned in pain. He narrowed his eyes and said, "Why are you so intent on me joining you, Felix?"

"Because we were once good friends, and I know what you'll bring to the table if you become one of the leaders of our great country. Like I said, my friend, I don't want to harm you because everyone who doesn't join us will be eliminated by the time the war is over. That means you will be killed. If not by me, then by someone else in our group. I don't want the same fate to befall you, but I will have no choice but to kill you and your father if you refuse our request." He straightened and sighed loudly. "I'll be back soon, Jude. I hope your answer to our request then will be the right one." He smiled at Keziah. "Let's go." Turning around, he began to walk to the door.

Jude looked up and saw Keziah staring down at him with sympathy in her eyes. He turned away from her and slowly rose to his feet. So this was Felix's plan and why he'd been brought here — to drive him to the point of insanity through isolation and starvation until he was forced to declare his allegiance to Felix and the opposition. If he hadn't been blessed with a conscience, he could save himself and his father. But he knew exactly what Felix and his group had done to people who opposed them. Even his own father had been held and tortured by them. Many had been killed. He could not join them. He would not.

He heard the door slam shut and he turned around. They had left and the place was dark. Once again he sat on the floor and sighed as overwhelming sadness washed over him. He felt like weeping for himself, for his father, for this country, and for Sofia.

Oh, Sofia. He would never see her again. That was for sure. He rested his head against the wall and shut his eyes as sorrow sat on his chest like a block of bricks. Soon, he began to feel drowsy, and he gave himself over to sleep in order to escape the unbearable emotional pain he felt.

A short while later, his eyes flew open when someone touched his shoulder. Blinking, he looked up. Keziah was looking down at him. A flashlight was in her left hand, while her right remained on his shoulder. For a brief moment, he stared into her eyes, and then he winced and shifted away from her. Her hand fell off his shoulder and he said, "Why are you here?"

She straightened and looked around the space. She turned and gazed at him again, the same look of sympathy in her eyes as earlier.

He shook his head. "I've already told you that I am not going to join you and Felix and your mad group. I don't know why you came back here, but there's nothing you can say that will convince me otherwise."

Tears swam in her eyes and fell down her cheeks.

He blinked in surprise. Was she really crying? Why?

She wiped the tears away. "I didn't come here to try to convince you to join us," she said. She looked back, and he followed her line of sight. She was looking at the door. No, at the guard who was standing near the door.

Jude looked quizzically at her and frowned.

"No, don't worry about him," she said. "He's loyal to me."

Jude's frown deepened. "Why are you really here, Keziah?"

"Jude, Felix is going to kill you when he comes back. That is if you don't die of starvation first. I came here to help you escape."

Jude's mouth fell open and he stared at her in disbelief. "Help me escape?"

"Yes, Jude. I cannot let harm come to you." Her eyes softened. "I still love you, Jude, just as I told you the other day. Even if you have refused to join us, I don't want to see you hurt."

He didn't know what to say or think. Was she really genuine or trying to set him up somehow? He looked into her eyes to try to read the truth and blinked in surprise again. He knew her well enough to know that she was being truthful and genuine. She still loved him and she did not want him to be hurt. But she was also part of that murderous group and a pretender. Could he really trust her?

She held her hand out to him. When he refused to take it, she looked back and called to the guard behind her. "Please help him up," she said.

The guard came to lift Jude up, but he waved the man away. Slowly, he struggled to stand up. When he finally did, he said to Keziah, "What about Felix? What about the other guards?"

"Don't worry about that, Jude. Felix has gone back to the capital with his other men. They won't be back for a few days. I told him I forgot something and would meet up with him later, but he doesn't know that I took the key to this place from his jacket pocket."

"Open the door," Keziah ordered the guard. He did, and she reached out to take Jude's hand, but he moved away from her. She might be helping him to escape because she said she still loved him, but that did not mean he trusted her in any way. He knew she would want something in return later, and he could guess what it was. For now, he would not think about it.

He walked out of the building slowly, still feeling some pain from Felix's guard's assault earlier. Just before he reached the door, two other guards walked in, and he winced when Felix also walked into the building.

His heart began to pound as Felix stared suspiciously at him and then at Keziah. "What's going on here?"

Keziah looked back at Jude and then faced Felix again.

Fear gripped Jude. This was it, then. Felix would find out what Keziah had planned to do and he would die. Had this been Keziah's plan all along? The reason she'd come here? To take revenge on him because he had refused her? To lead him right into Felix's trap so as to hasten his execution?

"You know Jude and I have history together," Keziah said to Felix, her voice soft and deliberate. "After I found what I was looking for, I had to come here to try to talk some sense into him so he could see the value of joining us. I told him that we could get married and make a life together peacefully in this country if he only joined us. I think he likes the idea."

Felix frowned. "But I thought Jude wasn't interested in you anymore?"

Keziah waved her hand in a nonchalant manner. "We've known each other since we were young, and he has loved me since secondary school. That thing with the American girl was temporary. Now that we are back in Bakali, he wants to make things work with me and start a family here." She turned and smiled at Jude. "Isn't that so, baby?"

For a brief moment, he was too surprised by all Keziah had said to speak, and then he nodded and croaked, "Yes. She's right, Felix."

Jude looked at Keziah as she smiled confidently at Felix. Hopefully his trust in her was not misplaced. He prayed he was not putting his trust in her only to find out she was playing him. Right now, he had no choice but to trust her and play along. He added for good measure. "I want to have a family with Keziah, right here in Bakali."

A smile broke out on Felix's face. "So you're going to join us?"

"Yes," Jude said, almost choking on the words. "Because of Keziah."

Felix grinned. He slapped Jude's back and exclaimed, "Finally! Keziah, you have done well. You have finally gotten him to join us." He looked at Jude. "It doesn't matter why you decided to join as long as you do. You will not regret it, I promise."

Jude said, "What about my father?" He looked from Keziah to Felix, still praying that he was not being played.

"We will release your father as soon as you make a public speech declaring that you are for us."

Jude blinked. "A public speech?" Not that it mattered anyway. He wasn't going to join their party.

"Yes. A speech at our next party meeting. Everyone who joins us has to give one. Don't worry about it. I'll let you know exactly what to say before then." He threw his arm around Jude's shoulder. "Come. We have a lot to talk about."

Jude looked back at Keziah, panicking. If he left with Felix, that might be it for him. He would never escape Bakali.

"Wait, Felix!" Keziah put her hand on Felix's shoulder. "I think Jude would like to rest, change, and freshen up before he's ready for any talk."

Felix blinked rapidly, and then he nodded. "You're right," he said. He looked at one of the guards behind him. "Take him to the house. Give him whatever he needs and let no one disturb him so he can rest properly. Tomorrow, drive him to the capital and meet us at my house there. Keziah, we have to head to the meeting at the capital together."

"Umm... I would like to stay with Jude for a while. Don't worry about me. I will come to the capital tomorrow. I don't think I'm needed at that meeting today."

Felix looked at her and nodded again. A knowing look appeared on his face, and he smiled. "I understand. You both would like some alone time together. Well, I'll leave you lovebirds today, but I'll be expecting you tomorrow." He smiled again and walked out of the building. The two guards followed him out as well.

After they left, Jude heaved a sigh of relief and looked at Keziah. "I don't know how to thank you," he said.

She gave him a wide smile.

He added, "But you know that I cannot..."

"Please, Jude, we don't have to talk about that right now. Let's just get you out of here safely."

"But where are we going to go? And what about you, Keziah? What will happen to you when Felix finds out you helped me escape. Because he will find soon enough that I had your help in leaving this place."

"It's what I have to talk to you about," she said. "To answer all your questions, I have a plan. A good plan." She searched his eyes. "But you're not going to like it very much."

Jude frowned. "What plan is that?"

She sighed and looked at her trusted guard who was standing at the door. "Go prepare the car," she said to him. He left and she faced Jude again. "We will talk about my plan when we get to the car. For now, we have to get out of here. Before Felix comes back."

THIRTEEN

Jude got out of the car after Keziah. He looked up at the two-story building that Keziah had told him was the safe house where he would stay for now. She had yet to tell him what her plan was that he would not like very much. He looked at her again and said, "Keziah, you still haven't told me what your plan is. I need to know."

She nodded. "Fine. Let's go in, and I will tell you."

The driver and her trusted guard stood near the car, while Jude went into the building with Keziah. Outside, the building looked nondescript, but he looked around as they walked in and it looked like a storage facility. There were rows of boxes stacked one on top of the other in the first large room they walked through. The second space was filled with all sorts of things, from furniture to farming tools and equipment. They walked through another space, larger than the first two. There were huge containers of who-knew-what. Jude's curiosity finally got the best of him, and he pointed and asked Keziah what they were.

She waved her hand dismissively. "Just stuff the party plans to use when we take over."

He didn't even want to ask what the 'stuff' was, especially what was in the huge containers.

They left the large room, walked down a corridor, and entered another room — an office this time, with a wooden desk and table, and a wall-to-wall bookcase filled with books. Keziah shut the door after Jude and pointed to the chair in front of the desk. When he sat, she took her seat in the chair behind the desk. She threaded her fingers together, her elbows resting on the desk, and leaned forward to look him in the eye.

He stared back at her and waited with bated breath for her to begin.

"Just as I said earlier, Jude, you might not like what I have to tell you, but it's the only way." She paused and searched his eyes. When he didn't say anything, she went on. "Just as you said before, we cannot remain in this country. You have to be sent away, and I have to come with you." Jude frowned, and she quickly added, "because when Felix finds out that I helped you escape, and he will find out very soon, my life will be in danger."

Jude sighed, and she continued, "I don't like the way Felix and the others in the party have gone about taking over this country. I agree with the ideology and all, but I don't like the violence that has been going on, and I certainly don't want to stay here and witness what is to come. Like you, I don't want to be a part of it any longer."

He stared at her in surprise. "I didn't know you felt this way," he said.

She shrugged. "How could you know? I just want

to get you out of here." She gave him a small smile and then took his hand on the table. "And I want to be with you."

He groaned and looked at their joined hands. He looked into her eyes again. She seemed so genuine and so sad that he could not bring himself to pull his hand away. But he had told her he was not interested and he hadn't changed his mind.

"Anyway, I have been making plans for quite some time to leave this country," she said. "Permanently this time. Since I lived in the U.S. for a long time and have a green card, it will be easy to relocate there. I packed up all my things and brought it here when I moved back to Bakali. I thought I was going to stay here forever, and the mistake I made was giving most of what I own to the cause. Thankfully, I have contacts in America who can provide the resources I needed to start a new life there." She looked deeply into his eyes. "Some time ago, I began to include you in my plans."

Jude narrowed his eyes at what she had said. "You did?"

"Yes, Jude. I want you to come with me." She bit her lip and looked into his eyes again. "I want you to come with me as my husband... or more specifically, my fiancé. That is the only way I know for you to escape this country safely and relocate to America."

His mouth dropped open, and he gaped at her.

She smiled sadly. "I know you don't like the idea, but right now you have very little choice. You come with me to America as my fiancé and we get married when we get there. My contacts there who have the resources to provide us with everything we need to start anew belong to some religious organization where you cannot live together without being married. They promised to provide every single thing we need — a town where we can stay below the radar until you can get your resident permit, a furnished house, food. Even jobs."

Jude could not speak. He kept staring at her, his emotions roiling. All he could think about as she talked about America was Sofia and the fact that he could be with her again. But not if he married Keziah. If he agreed to marry her, he would be giving up on the hope of ever being with Sofia. Besides, he had a lot of questions that Keziah had not answered yet. He finally found his voice and said, "I was an illegal immigrant before I left the U.S. I doubt I will be allowed back, even as a visitor."

"My contacts and I have our ways. Don't worry about that. I just want to know that you're okay with this plan." She took his hand again. "That you will agree to marry me so we can live in the U.S. as husband and wife."

He frowned. "But why do we have to get married? We can pretend that we are married for the sake of your contacts who belong to that religious organization. After all, you said your contacts have a way to help me to get into and stay in the country with no issues. You also said that we would be living under the radar. So I don't see why we should really get married."

She gave him a sad smile, and he sighed heavily. "You know what? You don't have to answer my question." He already knew the answer to it. He didn't want to listen to her tell him again how she felt about him. He sighed again and said, "Keziah, you know I told you I'm not in love with you anymore. I really appreciate what you want to do for me, but I don't want you to expect..."

She shook her head. "Don't say it, Jude. I don't expect you to do anything other than agree to marry me. That's all I want... for now."

He tilted his head and studied her. Finally, he said, "Why would you want to marry someone who doesn't love you the way you love him?"

"Because from experience I know that love can grow in time. Plus you once loved me. I believe there's still a part of you that cares deeply about me and that care can grow into love in no time."

He pressed his lips tightly together, still studying her. Should he tell her that he was still in love with Sofia and there was a chance that he would go looking for her once they got to America? No, not a chance, a certainty. He stared into her eyes and decided not to. It was not like either of them had a choice in this matter. They both had to leave the country for their safety. As for the marriage part, he wasn't yet sure how to answer her request, but if there was one criteria he had, it would be to take his father as well. Then he would have no choice but to oblige her... at least for now.

She was still waiting for him to answer her request.

He said, "And my father? You will get him to America as well?"

"Of course," she answered. "As soon as you agree to my proposal, I will send someone to get him over here. He can live with us in America."

For a long moment he thought about what she had asked. Not because he was thinking about refusing her request — there was no way he could as not only could she give him a way to leave Bakali and also save his father's life, there was a chance he would get to see Sofia again and explain to her why he had left on their wedding day — but he wondered if it was fair to her. He might agree to marry her now to get out of the country, but there was no way he would be in America and not long with every fiber in him to get back together with Sofia. That would not be fair to Keziah in spite of everything.

"Jude," she said. "Your answer."

He opened his mouth to tell her that he agreed to her proposal, but she added "I have one more condition to get you out of this country with your father."

Jude blinked. "What is it?"

"I know you're still in love with your ex." He winced as though she had slapped him, but she continued, "As much as I sympathize with you on that, my one condition is that you do not contact your ex at all. You cannot call her or try to see her."

Jude felt his head begin to pound. To go to America, to be in the same country that Sofia was, and not be able to speak to her? How could that be possible? How would he be able to do that?

"I'm sorry, Jude, but that is the only condition I have. I need you to agree to it in order to also get your father out of this country. I can't afford to take you and your father to America and then have you leave me for your ex."

He could not speak, and Keziah added, "Remember, you get your freedom and save your father's life. You both get to have a peaceful life out of this country. All I'm asking is that you don't contact your ex in any way. Who knows? Maybe she has moved on."

He shut his eyes against the pain that wracked his mind. A picture of Sofia appeared in his mind. He kept asking himself over and over how he could be in America and not contact her. And yet he didn't have a choice. He had to leave this country and take his father with him. He looked at Keziah. There was no point trying to plead with her concerning Sofia. Overwhelming sorrow gripped him. He knew he should not feel this way when he was being offered an opportunity to save his life and his Father's, but the thought of not seeing Sofia when he was in the same country as her was too much for him. He sighed. Once again, he had to choose to save his father's life and his as well. Maybe even Keziah's. Sofia may be better off without him.

Oh, Sofia. I'm so sorry.

"Jude! What are you going to do?"

"What if I promise not to see Sofia and then go see her in America without your knowledge?" Even as he spoke, he knew he would never do that.

"I know you, Jude. You would not do that. I trust your word."

He put his hand on his forehead, shut his eyes briefly, and then nodded. "Okay, Keziah. I will marry you once we get to America, and I won't contact or try to see Sofia."

She beamed at him. "Good!" She stood up. "I'll send someone to get your father and then start preparations for us to leave the country immediately."

***

Sofia sighed as she finished telling Lily about the plan she had for them to escape. "Now that I have spoken it out loud, I am not sure it will work out," she said.

"It might," Lily said, shrugging. "There's no harm in trying. It's not like we have any other option."

"But are we sure your uncle is going to come today?"

"We are not sure," Lily answered. "He might come, but there's a good chance that he won't. If he doesn't, we will have to postpone our plan and wait until he comes. But I hope we don't have to wait too long. We have to find a way out of here as soon as possible."

"That is the problem, isn't it?" Sofia said. "If your uncle doesn't come soon, who knows what will happen to Rachel and Keith."

Lily shook her head and pressed her lips tightly together. "Please, let's not even go there, Sofia. Just as you told me earlier, we have to keep hope alive." She prayed quietly, "Lord, please let Uncle Matthew come today. Please."

They continued to talk about their plan until the doorknob turned and the door opened. Uncle Matthew walked into the room, and Sofia sighed with relief. Maybe their plan would work out after all.

Without looking at Lily, he walked over to Sofia, his eyes fixed on her face. "How are you doing today?" he asked.

Before she could answer, Lily said, "Really, Uncle Matthew? You are really asking how Sofia is doing? How do you think she is doing when she has been locked in a room for two whole days? And as for me, I'm not doing well at all. Thank you for asking."

Matthew stared at Lily. "What's wrong?"

"How can you even ask me that question?" Lily glared at him. "We have been locked in here for two days. We need some fresh air."

He looked at her for a short moment and then went and threw the windows wide open. "There. Fresh air is coming into the room."

Sofia blanched. "We need to get out of here," she said.

He turned to look at her. "I'm sorry, but it's not something I can allow you to do."

She took a deep breath and began to pretend to hyperventilate. She put her hand on her chest, sank to the floor, and breathed loudly and quickly.

"What's wrong with her?" Uncle Matthew asked, sounding panicked. He rushed over to her and took her hand. "What is it?"

"She tends to get claustrophobic, Uncle Matthew," Lily said. "Whenever she's locked in a small space for a long time, she starts to lose it." Lily walked over to Sofia and knelt beside her uncle. "We don't want her to pass out like she has done before. When that happened some time last year, we had to get her to the hospital before we could we revive her. Please, she needs fresh air."

Sofia continued to breathe very fast while keeping one eye on Uncle Matthew and another on Lily.

"Please, Uncle," Lily pleaded again.

For a brief moment, Sofia thought he might just leave her lying on the floor. But he stood up and rushed to the door and unlocked it. He came back to her and lifted her up. He carried her out the door while Lily followed.

He climbed down the stairs, still carrying her, and they descended into the large living room and then out the front door. Sofia squinted as they got outside and the sun shone in her eyes.

He set her down on a seat on the patio and sat beside her.

She took another deep breath and then smiled and thanked him.

His hand was still on her back, his eyes fixed on her face. "Do you feel better now?" he asked with obvious concern.

"Yes, I'm feeling a little better." She looked at him. "Please can I have some water?" Hopefully, he would go get it himself rather than send one of the two guards who patrolled the compound. When he stood up and told her he would be right back with a glass of water, she nodded and sighed with relief after he left. She turned to Lily and said, "So, are you taking mental notes on how far the gate is from the house and how exactly the guards are patrolling the compound?"

"Yes," Lily said. "Hopefully, Uncle Matthew will let us stay for some time outside so we can memorize the frequency with which the guards patrol the area and if there is a pattern to the patrols. Maybe there's a specific time when neither of them is patrolling this area near the gate. That will be our chance to escape."

"Yes, but I still have to steal the key from your uncle," Sofia said. "Since neither of us has ever stolen anything, at least not in recent times, I don't know if I am going to be able to pull it off."

"Stop it," Lily said. "My uncle is enamored with

you. He will not even notice. Just do what we planned."

"Are you sure about that?" Sofia asked, worried.

The front door opened, and Matthew walked out with a tray, a glass of water set on it. He handed the glass to Sofia and sat beside her again.

She thanked him and took a sip of the water. Looking up at him, she found he was studying her and forced a smile as she groaned inwardly. He shifted even closer to her, and she sighed, regretting her decision to smile at him. Why couldn't he just shift away?

When she finished drinking her water, she put the glass back on the tray. When he smiled at her again and took her hand, she cringed. She forced herself not to snatch her hand away and gave him another smile. Their plan depended on him thinking that she returned his affection.

She turned to watch the guards as they patrolled the compound. She noticed that at no time did either of the guards leave the front of the house unpatrolled. She began to despair over their chances of escaping. It seemed impossible. She sighed. Was there any point trying to steal the keys from Lily's uncle if they could not get close enough to the gate to unlock it and make their escape?

Both the guards stopped in front of the gate, nodded at Matthew, and then walk away, probably to the back of the house.

Sofia blinked and then surreptitiously glanced at Lily. Lily nodded, and Sofia faced the gate again. There was no guard patrolling the front of the house.

She turned to Matthew. "Please, what time is it?"

He glanced at his wristwatch. "Six o'clock. Why?"

"Nothing," she said. "I was just wondering why it is already getting dark."

Two new guards walked to the front of the house and stood near the gate, and then they separated and patrolled the front of the house.

Sofia sighed again. It had taken less than three minutes for the new guards to replace the old. That meant if they could steal the key from Uncle Matthew, they would have to do it at just the right time, at about six o'clock, and they would have less than three minutes to unlock the gate and be as far away from the house as possible before a new set of guards appeared. That was a tall order, but they had no other choice. There was also the uncertainty of whether Lily's uncle would come by tomorrow. They had to pray that he did.

Matthew stood up and looked down at her and Lily. "I'm sorry, but both of you have to go inside. I think you've gotten enough fresh air."

Sofia stood up and smiled brightly at him. When she reached out to hug him, he blinked in surprise but put his arms around her.

She resisted the urge to pull away and, as fast as she could without drawing his attention, she put her hand in his pocket. The keys were in there. Tomorrow, she would have to do this again but take the keys. She pulled away and gave him another smile. Reaching out, she took Lily's hand and they entered the house together.

Matthew shut the door behind them and locked it. He led them upstairs to their room. Smiling, he said to Sofia, "I'll come by again tomorrow evening."

When he shut the door and locked it, Sofia sat

on the bed and gave a loud sigh. "It took everything in me not to slap your uncle when he put his arms around me."

"So you noticed what I did Sofia?" Lily asked.

"Yes," Sofia answered. "We have less than three minutes to make our escape." She exhaled. "And that is if I succeed in taking the keys from your uncle's pocket."

"Are you worried about that? He said he will come by tomorrow evening." Lily sat on the bed and covered her face with her hands. "I don't know if it will be too late by tomorrow." Her shoulders began to shake, and Sofia knew she was crying. She shifted closer to Lily and put her arm around her. "Let's believe it won't be too late, Lily. We have to keep praying and believe that God will keep those men away from Fallow Creek until we're able to warn Rachel and Keith."

Lily raised her head and smiled sadly at Sofia, tears swimming in her eyes. "I hope so," she said.

Sofia rubbed her back soothingly and once again prayed that Lily's uncle would come tomorrow and that their plans would succeed. She prayed that they could escape in time to warn Rachel and Keith. Because if not, she could not imagine the disaster that would follow.

FOURTEEN

Jude alighted from the plane, his heart racing with excitement. He took a long, deep breath and smiled. America. He could not believe it. He was in the United States again. He and his dad and Keziah had managed to escape from Bakali and were here now. Alive and free. Most of all, he was in the country where Sofia lived.

He pressed his lips together as he walked into the airport terminal between Keziah and his dad. An aching sadness settled in his heart. He was in America, but he could not see or talk to Sofia. They had taken the flight from Bakali to New York, as the only flight to America from Bakali was to New York. They would take a domestic flight to Arizona.

That was the worst thing. They were going to live in Arizona, the very state Sofia lived. He'd asked himself and the Lord over and over on the plane why the state they were going to live had to be Arizona, where he would be immensely tempted to try to see Sofia.

It shouldn't have surprised him, though. Keziah

had lived in Arizona when she was in America. He did not know yet where in Arizona they were going to stay. All he knew was that it wasn't Tucson anymore, but a small town he'd never heard of before.

His father took his hand and squeezed it as they walked through security. "I cannot believe we are out of Bakali and are free men," he said, smiling.

Jude smiled genuinely at his father. At least he had gotten his dad out of Bakali.

He felt nervous as they went through security, but Keziah handled everything. When they were finally through and had gone to claim their luggage, Jude heaved a sigh of relief. He had been holding his breath since they'd left the plane. They had encountered no issues going through security. He knew Keziah had forged some documents for him and his dad to enable them to get into the country, but he had asked for no details.

As they boarded a local flight that would take them to Arizona, his emotions roiled. He felt incredibly sad, but there was a thread of excitement running through his veins. He didn't know why, especially since there was no chance that he would see or speak to Sofia. He had given Keziah his word that he wouldn't contact her, and because of that, she had agreed to bring him and his dad here and help them settle and provide everything they needed. He could not go back on his word. Still, they were going to be in the same state. He began to feel sad about that, but he brushed aside the sadness and focused on what he was excited about — he and his dad were free men.

He strapped his father into his seat and then did

the same for himself.

Keziah sat in the aisle seat and said, "We will get married once we get to the small town where my contacts are."

He didn't look at her. She sounded excited, but he didn't know what she expected him to feel. He was going to marry her because he had no choice. He did not feel trapped or angry or used. All he felt about the inevitability of getting married to her was numbness.

He pictured Sofia in his mind. He'd thought about her every day since he'd left the U.S., but because at the time he'd suspected he would never see her again, he had tried not to, though he never succeeded. Now, since they'd stepped foot into this country, he had held her tightly in his mind.

Oh Sofia. How can I be here in America and not see you? He groaned on the inside. Why had he agreed to Keziah's proposal anyway? He turned to look at his father smiling and gazing out the window and sighed. This was why. And also because he probably would not have been alive by the end of this week if he had remained in Bakali. A thought came into his mind, but he immediately pushed it away. The Keziah he had known as a teenager and when they were together was gone. This one was dangerous. Aside from the fact that he had no money to live past a day here, Keziah would make sure he was caught and deported back to Bakali if he went back on his word and tried to see Sofia. Worst of all, he would put his father's life at risk. There was no escaping his fate now. He had no choice but to submit to it.

He looked at Keziah, and she turned and smiled

at him.

He forced a smile. Surely, there was a little of the Keziah he had loved somewhere in there. Just as she had told him, maybe gradually he would come to love her again. He didn't know right now if that would ever be possible, though. Not after all that she had done with Felix and their group. But he had to try. For his sake and his father's. And maybe one day, he would forget about Sofia completely.

Keziah took his hand in hers, and he did not resist. When she wove her fingers through his, he sighed softly and mustered a smile for her. She was going to be his wife in a matter of days. He had to learn not only to accept her touch, but welcome it. He forced himself to squeeze her hand and not withdraw his and tried to picture her the way she'd been when they were still together — sweet and loving, and not the woman who had participated in the deaths of many people. He would try to believe what she'd told him — that she had changed her mind about the violence going on in their country and wanted to be a better person. But he could not bring himself to reconcile the two — the Keziah he'd been engaged to and the one now were as different as his war-torn country was to this country. This was who he would be spending the rest of his life with and he would have to make it work, no matter what.

***

Lily stood beside Sofia and smiled. "Sofia, this is great! I don't know how you are able to memorize someone's face and draw them even when they're not here!"

Sofia looked back at Lily and groaned. "You're not supposed to look at it until I'm finish."

"Why not?" Lily asked. "It's not like it's my portrait. You are painting my uncle."

"Still, I didn't want you to see it until I had completely finished painting it."

"It looks finished to me. Uncle Matthew will love it. Most of all, it will help convince him that you actually return his feelings so he will allow us to go outside again today."

Sofia sighed. "That is if your uncle comes today."

"I know," Lily said. "I'm starting to worry again. If he doesn't come by today, our plans will not work. What will happen then to Rachel and Keith and the women at the House of Refuge? He just has to come today. He just has to."

Sofia pressed her lips together. She had been praying since morning that Lily's uncle would come today. He had briefly stopped by yesterday evening, and his eyes had been fixed on her throughout his brief visit. Today, they were going to try to convince him that she was just as into him as he was her. Hopefully, he would buy it.

"What if he comes today, Lily, but after six o'clock?" Sofia asked, looking up from her painting.

"Let's not think like that. I remember someone telling me just yesterday that we have to believe that God will work miracles on our behalf."

Sofia smiled. "I know I told you that, but I cannot help worrying that everything will go awry, Lily. So much is riding on our successfully escaping this house."

"I know," Lily said. "But we have to believe that

the Lord will help us leave and that we can find a way to call Keith and Rachel on time, before Dennis Hamilton and his men invade Fallow Creek."

Sofia went back to her painting, while Lily went to the window. A moment later, she stood up and joined Lily at the window. She looked out at the guards patrolling the front of the house and wondered where Lily's uncle was now. Was he in the house or was he out? They did not even know what time it was. The only way they could guess the time was by looking outside the window at how bright or dark it was. From what she could see now, it was probably three or four o'clock in the afternoon. But she could be wrong.

She kept on looking at the guards, praying that their shift schedules were exactly what she and Lily had surmised from observing them yesterday. Hopefully, even if they changed shifts before six o'clock, Matthew would have come by then and there would be some time in between the shifts for her and Lily to escape. After a while, she went back to her painting.

Some minutes later, clearly bored, Lily came to sit beside her.

"I'm finished," Sofia said, and handed the painting to her. "How does this look?"

"Exactly like my uncle. You're very talented, Sofia. I wish you had started to paint when we were living together in Tucson. Maybe you would have been able to open an art studio or show your pieces in an art gallery or something. Maybe then you would not have had to date George and depend on him for anything."

Sofia groaned. "Please, Lily, don't remind me of

George or the years I spent with him. I'm ashamed that I spent so long living off a married man. I wish I had met the Lord earlier. That is what I wish had happened. As for my painting, I would not have started if it weren't for Jude. He was the one who made me believe in myself again and in my talent."

"I know. You told me. You know I've never wanted to say anything to you because I know how much it hurts you, but from all you told me about Jude, even though I never met him, I don't believe he left you willingly at the altar."

Pain washed through Sofia.

Lily put her arm around Sofia and said ruefully, "I am sorry, Sofia. I should not have brought Jude up."

"You didn't bring him up. I did. And it's okay. I completely agree with you. I didn't want to tell myself the truth because the truth would mean that he had been deported, and since I haven't heard anything from him, that something bad has happened to him. But I finally had to be truthful with myself some weeks ago. I'm still worried about him, but I cannot dwell on that right now. We have to focus on the problem at hand. If I think about what could have happened to Jude, I don't think I would be able to go on."

Lily grinned at Sofia. "Well, this painting is really good," she said, looking at Sofia's portrait of her uncle. She turned and, pretending to glare angrily at Sofia, asked, "Why haven't you ever painted me before?"

Sofia laughed softly. "Why should I? I always have your face in my heart, and I get to see you from time to time, just like now. And you've never told me you wanted me to paint you. I will paint you now if you want me to."

"When we get out of this place, I think I'll commission you to paint Taylor and I and the kids together."

"Okay, I can do that. But I guess that will be in California."

Lily grimaced.

"What is it?" Sofia asked.

"Nothing… just worried. But I have to believe that our plan will work and I will be able to go back to Taylor and the kids soon."

"I hope so, too," Sofia said. Neither of them knew how long they would be kept here, and they didn't know what plans Lily's father and uncle had for her and Lily. The sooner they got out of here, the better.

"So should we run through the plan again before your uncle comes?" Sofia asked.

"Yes," Lily said.

Sofia pushed down the doubt that rose up in her as she and Lily ran through the plan they had laid out earlier in the day on how to escape. About fifteen minutes later, the doorknob turned and the door opened. Matthew walked in, and Sofia could not help smiling with relief. "Thank you, Lord," she whispered.

Lily walked up to her uncle. "You came here today?"

He gave her a small smile and turned his gaze to Sofia. His eyes widened as he walked over to her.

Sofia stood up and hid the painting of Uncle Matthew behind her.

He looked quizzically at her. "What do you have there, Sofia?"

Lily grinned as Sofia put on an embarrassed smile. "I have a gift for you," she said, in a tone she'd used plenty of times when she was still dating George.

Matthew blinked, looking surprised. "A gift for me?"

"Yes," Sofia answered. "But I don't know if you will like it."

Matthew gave her a curious smile. "I'm sure whatever you have for me I will like."

Sofia smiled and handed him the painting. His mouth dropped open and his eyes narrowed in concentration as he studied the painting. Finally, he looked up at her and shook his head slowly. "When did you do this? You actually painted me!" He looked amazed as he alternated between staring at her and studying the painting.

"I decided to paint you this morning because I could not get your face out of my mind."

He blinked rapidly and a huge smile appeared on his face. "Really?"

"Yes."

He looked at the painting again. "It's amazing, Sofia. Thank you so much." He looked up at her and then her hand, gazing into her eyes. "I will go and frame this and put it somewhere prominent."

Sofia nodded. She took a deep breath and looked around the room. She sighed sadly as she looked back at Matthew.

"What is it?" he asked.

"I am beginning to feel claustrophobic again," she answered.

He squeezed her hand and smiled. "Come with me." He took her hand and led her to the door while

Lily followed them. Opening the door, he led her out, and after Lily left the room, he closed the door again. He locked it with a bunch of keys he took out of his pocket and then dropped the keys back in.

They went downstairs together, and Matthew headed toward the front door, still holding Sofia's hand.

"No, I'll be okay just sitting in the living room," she said.

He stopped and looked at her. "Are you sure?"

"Yes, I am," she answered.

He led her to the couch and, just before she sat down, she reached out and hugged him tightly. "Thank you," she said. Slowly, with her heart racing, she reached into his pocket, pulled out the bunch of keys so they would not rattle, and closed her hand firmly around them. She considered taking his phone, but knew that would be too risky. Besides, where would she keep it without him sensing she'd taken it?

Lord please let him not hear or feel anything. When he did not react, she sighed with relief. She sat down and he sat beside her. Her heart continued to beat rapidly. They were not out of the woods yet. He might still notice that his keys were missing. Sofia smiled at him, but when he shifted closer to her, she felt very uncomfortable and had to force herself not to move away from him.

He turned on the TV, picked up the remote control, and began to flip through the channels. He finally stopped on a sports channel. He started to watch the football game and then looked at Sofia. "I'm sorry. Is there any particular program you want to watch? Do you enjoy football?"

Sofia shrugged. "I don't mind the game," she said, even though she'd never watched a full football game in her life. She lifted her feet onto the sofa and covered them with her dress. When Matthew put his arm around her, this time she could not pretend and shifted slightly away from him. She lay her head on the sofa and closed her eyes, pretending to go to sleep.

She could feel Matthew's eyes on her for a long moment, and then he said, "Lily, do you think Sofia is hungry? I could get you both some food."

"No, we are not hungry yet. We will eat later."

"Okay, then," Lily's uncle said. Sofia opened one eye to look at him and saw he'd turned to the TV set to watch his football game.

She began to breathe softly to give the full impression that she was asleep, but she made sure she did not fall asleep as she had to keep her wits about her.

It felt like an eternity before Lily finally asked, "What time is it, Uncle Matthew?"

"Umm... ten minutes to six," he said.

For another five minutes, Matthew continued to watch his football game. Sofia opened an eye again and looked over at Lily. She nodded discreetly and closed them again.

"Uncle Matthew, I think we will eat now," Lily said. "Sofia! Wake up. Do you want to eat now?"

Sofia slowly sat up and opened her eyes. She stretched and yawned. "I'm starving," she said, trying to sound groggy.

Matthew picked up his phone from the table. "Let me call one of the guards to get something for you. I don't think there's any food in this house."

"No, Uncle Matthew," Lily said. "I remember the chicken sandwiches you used to make for me and Stella when we were young. I want those."

Matthew narrowed his eyes and said to her, "Are you serious, Lily? You want me to go and make sandwiches for you."

"I told Sofia about your famous chicken sandwiches," she said. "She wants them too. Don't you, Sofia?"

"Yes, Lily told me about your famous sandwiches. I would love to try one." Sofia smiled. "Please?" She placed her palms together and looked into his eyes.

"Okay, then," he said smiling. "I will go and make you my chicken sandwiches."

"Thank you." Lily smiled.

Sofia gave him the sweetest smile she could muster.

"But you will have to help me out in the kitchen, Lily."

Sofia grimaced, while Lily's mouth fell open.

"What?" Matthew smiled and tilted his head toward Lily. "Did you think I would slave away in the kitchen while you sit here, relaxing?"

"But making sandwiches is hardly slaving away," Lily protested. "Besides, Sofia would not want me to leave her alone in the living room."

Sofia sighed. This was getting more complicated than they had imagined. Soon the guards would change shifts, if they hadn't already, and they would not be able to escape. She looked up at Matthew, who was looking expectantly at her. "I want... no, I need Lily here with me."

Lily shook her head. "And don't ask Sofia to go into the kitchen to make the sandwiches with you,

Uncle Matthew. You remember what I said about small spaces making her claustrophobic."

Matthew looked from Lily to Sofia, frowned in clear annoyance, and then marched out of the living room.

Sofia shot up from the couch. "Quick, Lily! Let's go."

Lily was already on her feet, heading toward the door. Sofia put Matthew's keys in the keyhole and unlocked the door. She slowly opened it, praying it would not make a creaking sound and alert Matthew. She looked back after opening the door. No one was coming behind. She walked out of the house and Lily followed.

Outside, there were no guards around.

"Thank God the guards are not anywhere around," Sofia said as they ran to the gate. She fumbled with the keys while Lily looked this way and that to make sure no one was coming.

"Hurry up, Sofia," Lily said. "The guards will soon come."

"I am trying, Lily," Sofia said, putting yet another key into the padlock to try to unlock it. "I can't find the right key."

Finally, Sofia unlocked the gate and opened it. They both looked back one last time and hurried out of the gate together. For a brief moment, Lily stood in front of the gate, her eyes wide.

"What is it?" Sofia asked.

"I should have known the rental car would not be here anymore," Lily said. She shook her head and began to run. Sofia ran after her.

They ran as fast as they could, looking back intermittently. Fear, relief, and worry warred in

Sofia's heart as they kept running. There were no houses or cars anywhere around.

"We have to find someone willing to take us as far away from this place as possible," Lily said.

"But there are no cars anywhere," Sofia told her.

They continued to run.

Lily said a minute later, "Hopefully, the guards at the gate will think it was Uncle Matthew who opened it to go out so they don't come after us. It will take Uncle Matthew about fifteen minutes to fix the sandwiches for us. When he comes out and doesn't see us, he will realize we took his keys and know we escaped. So we have just fifteen minutes to get as far as possible from that house. I don't know that we can do it on foot, especially as I am sure Uncle Matthew has a car parked somewhere at the back of that house."

"Then maybe we should have planned to steal the car instead," Sofia said.

Lily looked at Sofia. "Who are you?" she asked, but grinned. "You are right, though. But it's too late now."

"I know." Sofia sighed. "I wish a car would appear out of nowhere for us."

"It can, if we ask for a miracle," Lily said as they continued to run. Before Sofia could say anything, Lily said again, "Lord we need a miracle."

In spite of how dangerous their situation was, Sofia smiled. They could not stop to hold hands to pray, but the Lord would understand that this was the best they could do. Hope soared in her heart as a green truck began to speed in their direction.

Lily immediately stopped running just as Sofia did, and they both raised their hands and waved at the truck. Hopefully, the person behind the wheel was not a serial killer.

The truck slowed down, and Sofia said, "Thank you, Lord." And then her mouth dropped open and her heart sank as the truck sped up again past them.

Lily groaned. "Great! Just great!"

"What now?" Sofia sighed wearily.

Lily said, "We continue to run, that's what."

She began to run again. Sofia sighed once more and ran after her.

FIFTEEN

Dennis Hamilton leaned forward in his chair and glared at Cliff Hunter.

"Your anger is misplaced," he said. "Your brother was the one watching your daughter and her friend. There was no way they should have been able to escape. They were just two women in a house surrounded by guards. I don't know why you're angry with me when it was all your brother's fault. I did what I was supposed to do by sending your daughter to that house. I am not to blame. And no, I don't know where she is now."

Cliff narrowed his eyes as he stared at Dennis, and then he rose from his seat and paced the study. "Our plans will be ruined if Lily calls Rachel and tells her about what we want to do. And what if harm comes to my daughter?"

"Sit down, Cliff Hunter!" Dennis roared. "If you're not going to be reasonable so we can have a fruitful conversation, I don't know why you bothered coming all the way to Fallow Creek to see me. I don't know why you came at all. You took a great risk coming here, even if it was at night. Daniel Bacon patrols this town now, and even though he cannot patrol the whole of Fallow Creek, he could have easily spotted you. Next time, please call me before you decide to come all the way here."

Cliff stopped pacing the study and stared at Dennis. "Next time? Isn't that why we're making all these plans to invade Fallow Creek as soon as possible? Hopefully, I will soon be living here and will not have to call you from Prospect."

"Sit down, Cliff!" Dennis said again.

"How can I sit down when my daughter could be anywhere by now. Maybe she is hurt." He placed his hand on his forehead and frowned. "Those stupid guards at the house are a bit trigger happy from what I saw when I went there some days ago. What if they don't pay attention to orders and shoot my Lily?"

"They've been ordered not to shoot at all. You have nothing to worry about. Please sit down."

Cliff sat down on his seat at last. "Lily's mother heard that Lily escaped, and she isn't pleased at all."

Dennis frowned as he stared at Cliff. "Why are you telling me that? How is that any of my business?"

"She told me she wanted to come here to see you. I had to convince her that it wasn't safe to come to Fallow Creek yet."

Dennis groaned. "So not only is it you coming here without calling, your wife would have come with you as well. If Daniel Bacon was more studious about his patrols, or if there were more guards posted around town, you would definitely have been spotted and that would put our plan in jeopardy."

Dennis folded his arms on the table and shook his head. "It is yet another reason why that Rachel woman has to be removed. The town was now unguarded and could easily be invaded by anyone. It is why they need a man to take over once more as the leader of Fallow Creek. Why they need him to take over. Once he is in charge again, that would be the first thing he would do. Guards would be posted at every corner of town and Fallow Creek would be safe from any threat.

"So what if my daughter has already warned Rachel about our plans?" Cliff Hunter said. "Maybe our plans are already ruined."

"Really, Cliff!" Dennis laughed. "Even if she's already told Rachel, you know we have put everything in place to take back our town, and it's almost impossible for us to fail. There's someone watching the Restoration House now who will report back to me every move that Rachel and Keith make. They will not be allowed to get the police involved in any way before we have put our plans into action. However, we have to move forward now. Lily's escape has changed our timing."

"So what do I do?" Cliff asked.

"Gather the elders for another meeting in Prospect tomorrow morning. By midday, we should have all our troops in Fallow Creek for the takeover."

Cliff nodded and stood up. "I'll get on that right away."

"Do that."

After Cliff left, Dennis took a deep breath and focused his mind on what was to come the next day.

Finally, he would lead the people of Fallow Creek once again, and where he had been strict before Rachel took over, he would be ruthless this time. That was what was needed to make sure nobody else ever thought of taking what was his.

***

Lily stood beside Sofia on the side of the road and lifted her hands as another car sped down the road in their direction. "Lord, please let this one stop for us," she prayed quietly. She groaned in frustration as the car sped past them.

"Why won't any of these people stop?" She sighed loudly and sat on the ground, exhausted and angry. They'd been walking and trying to get a car to stop for what seemed like an eternity. There still weren't any houses anywhere around. Nowhere to rest or try to make the much-needed call to Rachel and Keith. For all she knew, they were already too late."

Sofia took hold of Lily's hand and squeezed it encouragingly. "We have to keep moving, Lily. Your uncle and those guards at that house have probably discovered we are gone and are out looking for us."

Lily pursed her lips and stood up again. They continued to jog, trying to wave down the occasional car that drove past. Worry was now Lily's constant companion. Without a doubt, it was only a matter of minutes before they were found out.

Lord, we need your help, she prayed silently.

A black truck approached, and a sliver of hope went through Lily. *Please let this one stop for us, Lord.* She immediately lifted her hands and began to wave, and Sofia did the same beside her. When the truck began to slow down, her heart leaped with hope. The truck stopped beside them and a man with a weathered face and a long red beard stuck his head out the window.

"You guys lost? You need a ride?"

For just a second, Lily hesitated. This was the very image she would conjure up in her mind if she were thinking of some backwater murderer who killed hitchhikers that got into his truck.

She sighed and moved toward the truck. They really had no choice. Before she could answer the man's question, Sofia said, "Yes, we do need a ride."

"Where are you headed to?"

"As far away from this place as we can go," Lily said.

"Get in then," the man smiled at her and then at Sofia. He was missing some of his teeth, and Lily shuddered as they got into the back of the truck.

Sofia got in beside her and shut the door. When the man pulled away from the curb, Lily leaned forward. "Please, do you have a cell phone? We need to make a very urgent call."

"No," the man said, smiling again. "I don't have a cellphone. I know you'll think that's strange. My friends tell me that I'm weird because I don't have a cellphone, but I have never understood the purpose of owning a cell phone when I can just visit the people I care about. And there are not many people I care about."

Lily pushed down a groan. If only this man would stop talking and move the truck. Thankfully, he soon picked up speed. She closed her eyes as she thought about Keith and Rachel hurt because she could not warn them of the danger coming to Fallow Creek quickly enough. Hopelessness flooded her, and she groaned. "I don't know what I would do if anything happened to Rachel or Keith. I know I would blame myself forever."

"Stop, Lily!" Sofia put her hand on Lily's shoulder. "You cannot give up now. See, the Lord brought someone to get us out of there. We will be able to call them before anything happens."

Lily shook her head. The Lord had brought them someone. Unfortunately, it was someone who didn't have a cell phone. She grumbled in her heart. *Why didn't you bring us someone with a phone so we could at least call Rachel and Keith, Lord? This is kinda useless to us.* And then she immediately felt remorseful. *Sorry, Lord. I am grateful.* Hopefully, they would find a payphone or something soon.

But as the man drove down winding roads, Lily's mood sank again. There was no single house anywhere near, let alone a payphone. Soon, she began to wonder where the man was taking them. What if he really was a murderer taking them somewhere very remote just to...

"Lily, what are you thinking about?" Sofia asked, breaking into her thoughts. "You look terrified."

Lily looked out the window and then turned to Sofia, her heart racing. "It's beginning to get dark, Sofia. You know we can make a run for it," she whispered. "Once he slows down, we can open this door and jump out of the car."

"Lily! What on earth are you talking about? And I thought I was the hysterical one and you the level-headed one."

"I am scared out of my wits," Lily said. "My sister-in-law, her husband, and maybe their child's lives are in danger. The women who live at the House of Refuge also. I feel terrified and totally helpless."

"I don't think the Lord would have helped us escape from the house if we were not able to do something to help them all," Sofia said.

Lily sighed and sat back on the seat and tried to calm her fears. She took a deep breath and tried to let Sofia's words sink in. Surely, the Lord would help them and protect Rachel and Keith and the women at the House of Refuge.

The bearded man continued to drive as the sky grew increasingly dark. About an hour later, he stopped in front of a small log house in a small town. "This is as far as I'm going, girls," he said. "This is my house. You are both invited to stay the night and then continue on to wherever you're going tomorrow."

Lily turned and looked at Sofia. She whispered, "Are we really going to go into his house with him?"

Sofia looked out the window. "I don't know if we have a choice, Lily." She looked at the man again. "I think you're overreacting. He looks safe enough."

"Are you kidding me!" Lily said. "He could be a…"

"Shh… don't say it, Lily!" Sofia whispered harshly. "Let's just get out of the truck. I'm going into the house with him. We will stay awake as long as we can. Maybe you can sleep while I stay awake and keep watch for some time, and then I sleep and you keep watch.

Lily shook her head, but she knew Sofia was right. They had no choice. "Lord, please protect us," she prayed for the umpteenth time and then got out of the truck with Sofia. They entered the small house behind the man. When he shut the door behind them, Lily shuddered. The man turned the lights on, and Lily looked around the small living room. It was plainly furnished but neat and surprisingly homey.

"I have a spare room you can share," he said. "There isn't much furniture in it except for a bed, but that's all I have."

"No problem," Sofia said. "Thank you so much."

"Let me show you to the room," he said.

Sofia immediately followed and Lily followed behind, her heart pumping. The man opened the door to a tiny room with only a bed and a side table. The bed had white sheets and a grey blanket. Even though it was small, it looked comfortable enough. Lily yawned and realized she was feeling very sleepy.

"I'll leave you two to sleep," the man said. He smiled at them and left the room.

Sofia looked around and climbed into bed. "I wish I could change into my pajamas. It's a shame they took our car with all our things."

Right now, Lily didn't really care about that. "Is the bed comfortable, Sofia?"

Sofia chuckled. "I don't know. I am so tired and sleepy, I could actually sleep on the floor." She closed her eyes and then opened them again. "Turn the light off when you're ready to sleep, Lily." She shut her eyes again and soon began to breathe softly.

Lily looked at Sofia for a long moment. Her heart kept racing. If not for the fact that she did not know where on earth they were right now, she would be out searching for a phone, night or no night. She yawned again and then sighed. She sat on the bed beside Sofia to keep watch for at least an hour but soon felt herself drifting off to sleep.

SIXTEEN

Rachel frowned with worry and gripped her cell phone tighter. "I've been trying to reach her as well, but I haven't been able to," she said to Taylor over the phone. "I thought she would have called you by now."

"No, she hasn't called. I have been calling for the past two days. I'm really worried about her, Rachel. It's not like her not to answer her calls or call me back. I have a feeling something bad has happened to her."

She had been thinking the same thing since this morning, but she'd refused to acknowledge it. She still couldn't. At least not to Taylor. "Don't say that," she told him. "I'm sure Lily is fine, wherever she is. Maybe the area she went to doesn't have cell phone service."

"I hope so," he said. "You said she went with her friend, Sofia. Do you by any chance have Sofia's phone number? I wish I did, but I don't."

Rachel sighed. "I don't have Sofia's number."

"I think even if the area where her parents are

staying now doesn't have cell phone service, Lily would still call. You know how she is. She'd try to find a way to get through to me. It's why I am so worried. But I'm going to try to believe that she's okay." He paused for a brief moment and then said, "You told me yesterday that you went to Dennis Hamilton to ask him for Lily's parents' address?"

"Yes, I did. I went this morning, but he still wasn't around. I only saw one of his guards, who told me he didn't know when Dennis would be back. I wish I had written it down when Lily told me she had gotten it from Dennis Hamilton. At least we would know where to look for her now if I had."

"Rachel, I don't like this at all. I'm canceling every business engagement I have, and I'm coming to Fallow Creek immediately. Meanwhile, keep going to Dennis Hamilton's to see if he's back so you can get that address, or at least a phone number from him. We have to find Lily."

"Taylor, are you sure you need to come? What about your kids?"

"They will stay with their nanny. I need to find my wife and make sure she's okay. You said the only thing you know about where she went is that she told you her parents are in Utah?"

"Yes. That's all I know. If only I had known things would turn out this way."

"Don't you think it's a little strange that Dennis Hamilton hasn't been back to Fallow Creek for the past two days since he gave Lily the address to her parents' new home?"

Rachel shrugged. "I don't really think so. Once in a while, Keith goes to his house and is told that he's traveling and will not be back for a few days. I don't know when the man comes and goes, but I guess he is out of town a lot." She took a deep breath to try to calm her nerves. Keith walked into the living room, sat beside her, and put his hand on her back. He rubbed her back soothingly, and she gave him a grateful smile.

"I'll be in Fallow Creek by tomorrow morning, Rachel," Taylor said, and hung up.

"I feel so awful," Rachel said. "Why didn't I ask Lily to give me the address that Dennis Hamilton gave her? Or at least a phone number."

Keith kept rubbing her back. "Don't be so hard on yourself. How could you have known that we would lose communication with your sister-in-law?"

"I'm scared, Keith. I don't understand why she's not answering her calls. And Taylor says it's completely unlike her. I'm hoping, though, that it's because the area she is in doesn't have cell phone service."

Keith smiled. "That is probably it. She doesn't have service, so she can't call you or Taylor. I think she's fine. She will call once she is able to."

"Taylor will be arriving here tomorrow," she said. "He wants us to try to get hold of Dennis Hamilton so we can get Lily's parents' new address from him." She took Keith's hand. "Will you go with me to Dennis's again this evening to see if he's back from wherever he went?"

"You know I will," Keith said. "Hopefully Dennis will be back by the time we go there."

Rachel sighed loudly. "If Dennis or Lily isn't back by tomorrow morning, we will have to go to Prospect to file for a missing person."

Keith nodded.

Rachel leaned back on the sofa and prayed that Lily and Sofia were okay. "Hopefully, it will not come to us having to go to the police station to report Lily and Sofia missing," she said to Keith. "By God's grace, Dennis will be back by the time we go to his house, and he will give us a number or an address. For now, I'm going to continue to pray and believe that my sister-in-law and her friend are okay.

***

Lily screamed as someone jerked her off the bed and grabbed her by the waist. "Let me go!" she shouted. She tried to turn around to see who it was, but the person tightened their hold on her. The room was dark and she could not see anything. Fear wrapped itself around her throat, threatening to suffocate her. *Lord, please help me,* she prayed silently, and then began to struggle again to try to break free. But she couldn't.

The light came on, and Lily saw one of the guards from the house where her uncle had kept her and Sofia captive standing at the door, holding Sofia around the waist with one hand while his other covered her mouth. Sofia struggled to try to free herself, and her eyes bulged as she looked at Lily. Fear shone in them.

Lily screamed again, and then tears of outrage flooded her eyes as the man who had grabbed her from behind covered her mouth with his hand. She tried to scream again, but he pressed his hand firmly over her mouth and began to drag her toward the door.

The man holding Sofia opened the door and pulled her out of the room while Lily struggled to be free of the man holding her. He held her even tighter and then pushed her out of the room as well.

Their host, the bearded man who had kindly given them a ride and a place to sleep for the night, knelt in the center of the living room, while a guard stood over him pointing a gun at his head.

Lily tried to cry out, but she could not. She began to pray silently. *Lord, please let them not kill him.* She and Sofia would be to blame if this man were killed for helping them. Terror gripped her and she began to hyperventilate. They dragged her and Sofia out of the house and to a black SUV. She kept struggling, trying to break free, until they pushed her into the car.

She continued to pray, asking God for help because she could not afford to be taken back to that house and held captive again. How would she contact Rachel and Keith and warn them about Dennis Hamilton's wicked plan? Fear, anger, and an intense feeling of betrayal flooded her heart. This was her uncle's doing, but worse, he was working on behalf of her father. Uncle Matthew had said her dad had led her to that house and was holding her captive to try to protect her, but she did not want his protection. He and the other elders of the town were going to harm the people she loved, and she was totally helpless to do anything about it. She didn't even know when they would let her go or when she would be able to see Taylor and their kids again.

They bundled her and Sofia into the back of the

SUV, and the guards sat beside them, hedging them in.

Lily blinked when she noticed the man sitting beside the driver. It was Uncle Matthew. She screamed again as the car began to move. "You! How could you do this to us?"

"You should not have run away Lily," he said. He turned and looked at her and then at Sofia. He said, "I told you we were keeping you in the house for your protection."

"I don't want your protection! I have to go back to Fallow Creek!"

Uncle Matthew said gruffly, "No, you don't. This time I'm locking both of you in that room, and the only time it will ever be opened is when a guard brings you food. You will not step out of the room until we are good and ready to let you go."

"I hate you, Uncle Matthew. You and my father are heartless."

Uncle Matthew shrugged. "We just want a better town for ourselves and our family. That Rachel woman has ruined Fallow Creek, but we will get it back to the way it used to be, and even better."

Anger began to boil in her and spilled out without control. She screamed and yelled and cursed him and all the men who were planning to harm Rachel and Keith. After that, she began to plead for him to let them go, but he refused. She finally gave up, put her head between her knees and cried.

***

Jude looked out the window as they drove into the small town called Prospect. This was where they were going to stay, he and Keziah and her father. At least for now. Keziah had said that when they got married, they would move to another small town where they would live permanently.

He turned to look at his father. His dad still looked excited. He could not blame the man. After years of being held captive in Bakali, he was now free — truly free and in a place where none of the people who had imprisoned him could find him. No wonder he couldn't stop smiling.

But Jude felt gloomy here and gloomier as the hours wore on. He had spent almost every waking hour thinking about Sofia and the fact that he was in the same country and state as her but would not get to see her.

The driver that had brought them from the airport to Prospect stopped in front of a small house, and Keziah thanked and paid him. His dad stepped out of the car and Jude got out after him. Keziah exited through the other door and went to grab her suitcase from the trunk of the car. He had no luggage of his own nor did his father. Jude took the suitcase from her, and they walked to the front of the small house.

Before Keziah knocked on the door, she said to Jude, "So my contacts hold meetings and such here. Since we are not married yet, I am sure our guests will get us to stay in different rooms." She looked at him with her eyes shining. "But once we get married, we will be given a small house in the next town where we will be living."

Jude tried not to think about the fact that he would have to marry Keziah. But it was all he thought about. The idea of marrying her did not repulse him as much as the idea of never being able to be with Sofia. He sighed heavily and then told himself to remember that he'd loved her once.

"And, Jude, before we go in, please remember we're supposed to be an engaged couple who love each other and cannot wait to get married," Keziah said. "Please try to smile and wipe that frown off your face."

Jude grunted and nodded.

"Keziah, I haven't thanked you properly for what you did for my son and me," Jude's father said. "Thank you."

Keziah gave him a small smile. "I love Jude, and when I decided that I'd had enough of the goings-on in the opposition party and decided to leave the country, I knew I had to get Jude out." She turned and grinned at Jude. "I'm glad I was able to get you and your dad out of Bakali and bring you here."

Jude knew he should thank her for what she'd done, but right now he didn't feel so grateful. He was ashamed of that, since she had saved his life and his dad's, but all he could think about was Sofia. He took a deep breath and said, "Thank you, Keziah. Thank you for putting your life at risk for me and my dad." He wanted to add grumpily, "Even if it was on the condition that I marry you," but he decided not to. Her conditions did not change the fact that she had put her life at risk in order to save his life and his father's.

She gave him a bright smile and then knocked at the door of the bungalow.

The door opened, and Jude blinked in surprise. An armed man dressed in a black T-shirt and military trousers and boots stared at them. Jude turned and looked at Keziah with suspicion.

"What do you want?" the man asked, his eyes on Keziah.

"My name is Keziah, and this is my fiancé and his father. I am here to see Cliff Hunter. A friend of mine connected us to him. He is expecting me today."

The guard looked at Jude, and then at his father, and then faced Keziah again. "I'll be right back," he said, and entered the house once more, closing the door behind him.

Jude looked at Keziah. "So, I see you are still running with the wrong crowd. What's with the armed guard in fatigues?"

Keziah shrugged. "One of the opposition members who also left is a friend of Cliff Hunter's, this man we came to see. We were introduced over the phone. We've been talking for some time, and he promised to give us a safe place to stay where we will be far away from the hands of the law — Bakali's and the United States'."

"I thought your forged documents and all that was impeccably done and there would be no problems," Jude said.

"Yes, it was. My guy in Bakali is an expert at such things. But you never know. That's why I took the offer my friend gave me to stay in this remote part of the United States. From what I gather, the town we are going to finally live in is even smaller and more remote than this one."

Jude raised his brows, but said nothing. There was nothing to say anyway. They had escaped their war-torn country and that was all that mattered. They could be living in some swamp or ghetto in the United States. As long as he was safe — and most of all, his dad was safe — that was all that counted.

The door opened, and the guard looked at them again. "You can come in," he said, and opened the door wide.

Keziah stepped in first, and Jude let his dad go in before him. He lifted Keziah's suitcase and stepped into the house.

They walked through a foyer and into a living room of polished wood. A bearded man dressed in a black shirt and pants walked into the room and looked at Jude and then his father. He turned to Keziah and gave her a small smile.

"Cliff Hunter?" Keziah said.

"And you are Keziah Samuel?"

"Yes," she answered.

"That means this must be Jude, your fiancé, and his father." He reached out and shook Jude's hands and then his dad's.

Jude was surprised that he did not shake Keziah's hand as well considering she was the one he knew. "

I'm sorry to keep you waiting," he said, his eyes still on Jude and his father alone. "I was in a meeting upstairs with some other men. I'm glad you all came.

As the man started to talk, it was as though Keziah wasn't in the room anymore. He spoke about the town they were going to live in. "It's called Fallow Creek," the man said.

Jude frowned. The name sounded familiar, but he didn't know where he had heard it before.

"The town was once booming and alive, but something serious happened and most people moved away. Soon, though, we will be moving back. At least the people we can get to go back. The problem is that half of the residents are not convinced they want to go back or have made lives for themselves in other parts of the United States and have decided not to go back to Fallow Creek. The town is empty as we speak, and when we — that is me and some of the men and their families — go back there, we will need more people to populate the town. When my friend told me about you and how resourceful you are and what you were trying to do for your country, I knew I wanted someone like you in Fallow Creek."

Jude frowned again. His words should be directed at Keziah, not at him. She was the one who had done all those things he was saying, yet the man was looking directly at him. That was a little strange.

The man named Cliff kept looking at Jude and his dad without looking at Keziah. Jude briefly glanced at her. She was glaring at Cliff with anger clearly written on her face.

Cliff went on talking about how great Fallow Creek had been. "At least, it was great until the mass exodus." He talked about how it would soon be once it was returned to its former glory. "When we move back, things will go back to the way they were and be even better."

"I'm glad to be here," Jude said. He could feel Keziah's anger. She was fuming beside him, but he understood why she said nothing even though it was unlike her not to air her grievances. This man was doing them a huge favor. Whatever his reason was for refusing to address her directly and address him instead, Keziah knew not to protest or show her anger.

"For now, you and your fiancée and your father will stay in this house until we reclaim Fallow Creek."

Jude tilted his head and stared at the man in curiosity. "Reclaim Fallow Creek?"

"Yes," Cliff Hunter said. "I cannot say much about it, but you'll find out everything soon enough. It's getting dark. Let me get my wife to show you to the rooms where you will stay."

Keziah looked up at him. "Please, my fiancé and I would like to get married as soon as possible." Jude sighed softly. From the sound of her voice, she was barely trying to control her anger. "We want a small wedding. Is there a minister or someone like that who can wed us?"

Cliff Hunter looked at her, smiled, and nodded. "I understand why you would want to get married quickly, but I suggest you wait for a few days until we get to Fallow Creek. There's a minister that can wed you easily there, as well as our chapel." Once again, his gaze returned to Jude. "You don't have to worry about anything because I will make sure that I get someone who will arrange everything for you both. Let me get my wife now."

When he left, Keziah huffed. "That man has problems! He was acting as though I wasn't even here!"

Jude chuckled. "I don't understand myself," he said.

"You said the man belongs to a religious organization where people aren't allowed to live together unless they are married," Jude's father said, a thoughtful expression on his face.

"Umm... Yes. Unmarried singles are not allowed to live together alone," Keziah said. "I guess since other people will be living here as well, we can live here in separate rooms without being married. At least until we get to Fallow Creek.

Jude was relieved that they would be in separate rooms, but for how long? In a short time, they would be married.

"I think I understand why he did not look at you," Jude's father said. "It's probably part of their religion. Maybe they don't address women directly."

"But I spoke to him on the phone while I was in Bakali a couple of times. I don't think it is that. They're not allowed to speak to women because they have chauvinistic ideas about men being better than women. I think he could have talked to me, but chose not to. He chose to talk to Jude and to you."

Jude chuckled. "And you want to live in that town, Fallow Creek. Knowing you, it won't be long before you decide you have had enough and move out of there."

She huffed again. "It's not like I have a choice right now. I am not going to let any man treat me as though I don't exist when I am in the same room as him." She frowned as she looked at Jude. "And you better not become that sort of man when we get married. I will not stand for it."

In spite of himself, Jude laughed. "Yes, ma'am."

A petite woman walked into the living room and smiled brightly at Keziah and then at Jude and his father. "My husband has told me everything about you," she said as she reached out and hugged Keziah.

When she pulled back, she said, "Unfortunately, the rooms in this house are very small and not very comfortable. When we move to Fallow Creek again, you will get somewhere more comfortable." She looked back and called out, "Tim, can you help carry their suitcases to their rooms?"

The guard that had opened the door for them came into the living room. He looked at Jude's suitcase, and just as he bent to pick it up, his eyes fell on Keziah's face. For a brief moment, they looked at each other, and then the guard straightened again and lifted the suitcase with him.

Jude narrowed his eyes. Was that a gleam of attraction he had seen in both the guard's and Keziah's eyes when they looked at each other, or was he imagining things?

He sighed and pushed the thought out of his mind, deciding it was just his imagination.

The guard, Tim, walked down a hallway behind Cliff Hunter's wife, while Jude walked beside Keziah and his father.

The woman opened a door and turned to Keziah. "This is your room," she said. "I suppose this is your suitcase as well?" She looked down at Keziah's large suitcase.

"Yes," Keziah answered.

Tim entered the room and dropped the suitcase. As he came out again, he glanced at Keziah, and once more Jude noticed a look between them. A look of clear attraction. He blinked once more and shook his head. Surely, he was imagining it, but maybe not. Keziah was beautiful. It wasn't a surprise that the guard found her attractive. But she had also looked at the guard with attraction in her eyes.

Stop thinking about this, Jude, he scolded himself. Maybe he was imagining such things because he was nervous about marrying Keziah.

The woman led him and his father to another room with a king-sized bed, a coffee-colored center rug, and a small walk-in closet. The room was larger than the one Keziah had been given.

"I hope you don't mind sharing," the woman said to Jude and to his dad. "There isn't any other room in the house right now."

"No, we don't mind. Thank you so much," he said to the gracious woman.

The woman beamed at him. "You are welcome. And congratulations on your upcoming marriage."

Jude forced himself to smile as he thanked her again. When she left, Jude sat down on the bed and his father sat beside him. "So, what do you think?" Jude asked his father.

"What do I think? I am the happiest man in the world. I am finally free, and it feels as though I have a new lease on life." His dad put his hand on Jude's shoulder. "I know you are not keen on marrying Keziah, and I also know it's because of that girl, Sofia, that you've told me about so many times."

"It's not just because of her," Jude said. "You know all that Keziah has done, or at least assented to."

"I know," his father said. "But you can see that she's changed, or at least she is changing. Just give it a chance. Give her a chance."

"It's not like I have a choice anyway," Jude said, sighing.

"Well, make the best of what you've been given," his father said. "You loved her once, Jude. You can learn to love her again."

Jude nodded and smiled at his father. But on the inside, he knew that it would not be possible, because he still loved Sofia with all his heart. And he was sure he would never stop loving her until he drew his last breath.

SEVENTEEN

Dennis Hamilton placed his hands on his desk and looked at the group of elders sitting in front of him. He took a deep breath and continued what he was saying. "Just like I told you, Cliff Hunter's daughter escaped from where she was being held. She has been found and returned to the house, but we are not sure she hasn't already warned Rachel and her husband. We have to bring our plans forward. As I speak, our men have already been posted around the Restoration House."

One of the elders, James Sanders, spoke out. "How do we know that Rachel woman or her husband hasn't contacted the police? And maybe one of the women at the Restoration House has seen one of the squad members around the place. We might be walking into a police trap."

"If the police have been contacted and were in Fallow Creek, one of our men would have spotted them and called to let me know. Even if Rachel has contacted them, they are not there now. It's the reason why we have to move in right away with our plans."

Dennis looked over at the men and then looked at Cliff Hunter as he walked into the room. He had excused himself half an hour ago because he had some visitors from out of town. Dennis said to him, "Have you been able to gather the other squad members from different parts of the country? We might need more than we have now, at least for later."

"Yes, and most of them have agreed to join us. And we have all the weapons we need ready as well."

Dennis nodded. Two of the squad members who had been with him since he'd been ousted had refused to join in and absconded, clearly afraid that what had happened some years ago when Rachel and Keith had taken over would happen again. They had a misguided idea that the flood that had swept them away had been a supernatural event. But Dennis knew it could not be, because God was on their side. Once he took over from Rachel, he would find the squad members that had absconded and deal with them. For now, they had more than enough men to retake the leadership of Fallow Creek, even if problems arose. Soon, everyone who'd left and who wanted to return would be able to do so.

Another elder said, "I have a niece in that Restoration House. I don't know how to get her to leave without making Rachel or Keith or the other women aware of our plans."

Dennis shrugged. "There's nothing we can do now. It's too late. I got my wives and children out of Fallow Creek some days ago. They are far, far away from here. So did a few of the men here like Cliff Hunter. Unfortunately, his daughter is too stubborn to stay away, hence why she had to be held captive. My own family is in Utah now with my first wife's parents. They are safely away because I made sure of it. You would have made sure anyone you loved was away from Fallow Creek long before now. Since you did not, whatever happens to them, happens."

He turned to look at the other elders. "In a few minutes, we will all be leaving for Fallow Creek with the squad members that have been gathered already. You all remember why we are doing what we plan to do. We have to take back our town and restore it to how it used to be. Every one of us misses living there, and we want the town that we knew back. The town where we can once again live as we used to. The way life is supposed to be lived."

The elders raised their voices in agreement.

Dennis continued to speak about what exactly they would do when they drove into town, what would happen once they took over the leadership of the town, and their plans to gradually rebuild the town spiritually and emotionally.

One of the squad guards stationed outside Dennis's study came in and walked up to Dennis. "I just got a call that most of our squad team are now heading toward Fallow Creek. I think we're all ready to go now."

"Good," Dennis said. He told the elders what the guard had said, and then stood up. "We all leave now."

All the elders stood as well, and they all walked out the door to head to Fallow Creek.

**

Rachel lifted her head as she heard a loud knock on the door. She grabbed the towel that was hanging on the bath, quickly dried Emily, and then lifted her out of the bathtub. The knock sounded again, and she wrapped Emily up in a fresh towel and hurried out of the bathroom. She reached the front door, opened it, and smiled as Taylor walked into the apartment.

"Rachel, how are you?" he asked, and hugged her and Emily together. He stepped back. There were worry lines on his forehead, and he said, "Have you heard from Lily?"

"No, Taylor. I haven't."

"And what about Dennis Hamilton? Have you been able to get ahold of him to ask him about Lily?"

"I went to his house again yesterday evening, but he still wasn't back. We've been trying to call him, but he is not answering."

Taylor frowned and sat down on the sofa. Rachel sat beside him and sat Emily on her lap.

Emily put her head on Rachel's chest and looked up at Taylor. He patted her head affectionately and then said to Rachel, "We should call the police." He took a deep breath. "Where on earth are you, Lily?"

"I agree with you, Taylor. We should go to the police. But which police department are we going to report Lily's disappearance to? We don't even know what state she is in."

He groaned. "We can call the police in Utah and also go to the police station in Prospect. We will tell them Lily and her friend were on their way to Utah and we're not sure they got there."

Rachel bit her lip. "I cannot believe we are searching for Lily now."

Taylor ran his fingers through his hair and groaned. "I have been so scared. I have had to force myself not to freak out because of the kids." He looked around the living room. "Where is Keith?"

"He went to Dennis Hamilton's again to see if he is back. It's unlikely, though, that he is."

"You know, Rachel, I saw something a little unusual when I was coming here."

"What?" Rachel asked.

"I saw two squad guards some distance away from the House of Refuge."

Rachel shrugged. "Maybe they are Dennis Hamilton's men. They usually don't leave his house or the area around it, but once in a while they have been spotted in different parts of Fallow Creek."

"Yes, but they were looking intently at the House of Refuge, as though they were watching for something or someone. I don't know. It just seemed strange to me. But maybe it's nothing." He stood up. "Should we call the police in Prospect or just go there?"

Rachel stood up with Emily in her arms. "I think we should go there. Could you just wait a minute? Keith will be back any minute. I have to give Emily to him to take care of her. The girl who usually watches her for us went out of town yesterday."

"Okay," Taylor said. He stuck his hands in his pockets and paced the living room.

Rachel ran her fingers slowly through Emily's hair as her heart raced with fear. Something bad had definitely happened to Lily and Sofia. This was now the end of the third day, and they'd heard no word from them. "Lord, please, I pray for your protection over Lily and Sofia," she whispered.

Soon, Emily began to breathe softly, and Rachel looked at her. Emily was asleep. Rachel smiled sadly. If only she was like a child, fearful of nothing, totally trusting God. But her heart was full of fear. Not only was she afraid of what might have happened to Lily and Sofia, but what Taylor had told her about the squad members troubled her a little.

She went to the window, opened the curtain with one hand, and looked out. Everything seemed normal as usual. She could see no squad guards anywhere around. Some of the women were outside, but most were in the House of Refuge as they had just finished having a general lunch. She moved back from the window when the front door opened.

Keith walked in with a grim look on his face. He briefly greeted Taylor and then went to Rachel and kissed her cheek. "I didn't see him," he said. "But I also didn't see any of the squad members there. There was no one there at all."

Taylor frowned. "That's strange, isn't it? They've all left that house without telling anyone."

"Maybe they went to meet Dennis wherever he is," Keith said.

"But I saw two of them a few feet away from the House of Refuge when I got here," Taylor said to Keith. "We have to get to the police station now, Keith." He looked at Rachel. "Let's go. The earlier we can make a report about Lily and her friend, the better the chances of them being found. I just hope that Lily's okay and that she just hasn't called because there is no service wherever she is."

Rachel could see from her brother's expression that he knew the chances of that being the case were slim but was holding on to hope. So was she. She handed Emily, who was still asleep, to Keith and then left the apartment with Taylor.

They walked out of the House of Refuge, talking about Lily and Sofia and holding on to hope that they were safe. They walked through the gates, and then Rachel's heart jumped into her throat. A fleet of black SUVs were moving toward the house. The SUVs looked like the ones the squad members had driven when Dennis Hamilton was still in charge of Fallow Creek. The fact that there were more than a dozen of them meant something was wrong. Something was very wrong.

The cars stopped in front of the House of Refuge, and then the doors opened and Rachel's eyes widened in horror. Squad members poured out of the cars with rifles. Some of the women who were standing in front of the gate screamed and ran into the House, while Rachel and Taylor stood staring at the sight before them in shock.

The squad team — more than two dozen men — stood in front of the House with their weapons. Rachel stared at them, her pulse racing. She grabbed Taylor's hand and whispered, "What is happening here?"

The doors of the last two cars opened, and the former elders of Fallow Creek, men she had not seen in years, the same men who had expelled her from town, came out of the cars. In front of them was Dennis Hamilton. She tightened her hold on

Taylor's hand as she took deep breaths to try to let go of her fear.

"Stay calm, Rachel," Taylor whispered to her.

She stared into Dennis Hamilton's eyes and knew that he had not come in peace. Her stomach roiled as she remembered how he had tried to kill her and Keith years ago. She knew what he was capable of doing. He was a wicked man and had no scruples about killing and maiming. She began to take deep breaths, fearful for her life and Taylor's, and the lives of the women in the House of Refuge.

"Not again, Lord," she whispered. It was just a year ago that dreadful event had happened, when Mike Cadwell had attacked them at the House of Refuge. The women here had been through enough. Why was this happening again?

Taylor whispered, "I'm sorry, Rachel. This is all my fault. If I had not saved Dennis Hamilton and his men and given them a place to stay in Fallow Creek, this might not be happening."

"It's not your fault, Taylor," she whispered back. "If you hadn't done all that, maybe this would have happened much earlier."

"What do you all want?" Taylor yelled as he stared at the squad members and then at Dennis Hamilton and the elders.

"You know what we want," Dennis said, walking up to Rachel and Taylor.

Rachel winced as the squad guards raised their guns and pointed them at her. And then she saw they were looking at someone behind her. She turned slowly and gasped. Daniel was standing at the gate, and he had his gun pointed at the men.

Rachel blinked. What was Daniel doing? He

was completely outnumbered. His actions now would only make things worse and start a shootout that could be deadly. That was the last thing they needed right now. "Daniel! Please put that thing down!" she shouted.

Daniel snarled, his face a mask of rage.

The men cocked their guns, and Rachel screamed again and ordered him to put his gun down.

At last, he lowered his gun to his side, and two of the squad members rushed up to him, grabbed the gun from him, and pinned him down to the ground.

"After all I did for you, Dennis, you repay me with this?" Taylor asked. "I saved you and your men when you were about to drown and gave you a house and everything you needed to live. This is how you repay me? By invading Fallow Creek and threatening my sister and the women here?"

"You didn't really save me, Taylor. God did. And your sister brought this upon herself. She has turned Fallow Creek into something completely different from what it was. All we loved about our town is gone because of her. She has destroyed the minds of our girls and poisoned the minds of the few men here," Dennis said, and glared at Daniel, who was struggling on the ground. He looked at Taylor. "Because of her, everyone moved out of this town that we have lived in for all our lives."

"She never asked you all to move out, did she?" Taylor glared at Dennis Hamilton and the elders.

"She didn't have to. Everything she said and did showed us that we were not welcome here. Besides, there was no way any of us could stay and live under her leadership, knowing that she's a rebellious woman."

"But you stayed, Dennis," Taylor said.

"I did because I refused to acknowledge her leadership. But most men could not." Dennis turned away from Taylor and Rachel and beckoned to one of the squad members, who was holding a microphone.

Rachel turned around, wondering what he was about to do.

He put the microphone to his mouth and announced, "None of you in the house should call the police. We have this place surrounded. If you call the police and they come here, there will be a shootout and, as you can see, we have more men than the tiny police station in Prospect could send. They will lose, and people will die here. So don't do it."

Someone yelled and ran toward Rachel from behind, and she turned. Keith paused in front of the gate, his eyes wide with fear, his mouth wide open, as he stared at all the squad members standing before them and then at Dennis and the elders.

"Dennis?" Keith blinked rapidly. "What are you doing?"

"What does it look like I am doing?" Dennis glowered at Keith. "Taking back Fallow Creek."

"I should have listened to Daniel and to everyone else who told me that you were deceiving me. But I really believed you had changed. I believed you wanted to draw closer to God and live a better life than the one you had always lived. You fooled me into holding all those prayer meetings with you when in actual fact you were scheming behind our backs."

Daniel screamed from where he lay on the ground, "I told you that you should never have trusted Him, Keith. I know him well. He is a snake."

"Listen, Dennis!" Taylor glared at the former leader. "Where is my wife?" He looked at Lily's father, Cliff Hunter, who was standing behind Dennis, and then faced Dennis again. "Where did you send her? If something bad has happened to her, I am going to kill you, Dennis Hamilton. I don't care what it costs me."

Dennis laughed out loud. "You're going to kill me? Let me see you try."

Taylor began to move toward him, but Rachel held him back.

"She is safe, Taylor," Cliff Hunter said. "I got her out of Fallow Creek to keep her safe because we were going to invade this place."

Taylor's mouth dropped open again, and Rachel's heart drummed. So there it was. They hadn't come to take over peacefully. They planned to harm her and Keith and maybe the women here. Still, she wanted to hear it from Dennis's mouth.

"What do you plan to do, Dennis?" she asked. Was it going to be like the time Dennis had kidnapped her and Keith to execute them? She began to pray silently and earnestly for a miracle, for God's deliverance, but fear wrapped itself around her like a heavy blanket, stealing her breath. What would happen to Emily if Dennis killed her and Keith? What would happen to the women here?

Dennis Hamilton said, "You, Rachel, will decide what happens here today."

She frowned. "How?"

"If you meet our demands, every one of our

demands, you and all the women in the House will live. If not, you will all die."

"And what are your demands?" Rachel asked, her heart beating fast.

"First of all, you know what I want. You know what we all want. I want the deed to Fallow Creek, and I want to take over as the leader of this place once again."

Rachel looked back at the House of Refuge and then at Keith. She took a deep breath and faced Dennis Hamilton. God had led her and Keith here. Through a harrowing experience, He had given them Fallow Creek and put her in charge of the women in this place. If He didn't want her in charge of this place anymore, then she would not fight it. She didn't have a choice anyway. She took another deep breath and said, "Fine. You can have Fallow Creek and become the leader again. But please, you have to let the women in the House of Refuge go. Let as many of them that want to leave town do so."

"I cannot do that," Dennis said. He turned to the elders and then turned back to Rachel. "You're not in any position to make demands."

"But you just said that you would let us go if I gave you the deed."

"I didn't say that." Dennis stared intently at her. "I said I would let you all live if you give me the deed to the town. I didn't say I would let anyone leave Fallow Creek."

"What?" Rachel stared at him and the elders in disbelief.

"The elders and I have plans for all the women in the Restoration House, including you Rachel. We cannot let any of you leave town."

"What plans do you have for us?" Rachel narrowed her eyes in anger as she continued to stare at Dennis Hamilton.

"I am glad you asked. You and all the women here have lived carelessly and in complete rebellion of all authority for too long. You have been living in rebellion to God. Women should not be free to run around and do whatever they please. To show your complete and total submission, we all agreed that the elders and I and the other men who come back will choose wives from the women here. Any woman that is chosen will marry the man who chooses her. There will be no protest, only complete submission. This way, the rebellion that you started will be squashed, and there will be peace and order."

Rachel blinked as she stared at the elders and Dennis. She could not believe what he had just told her. So it was either their lives or their freedom.

Keith and Taylor cried out in outrage, and Keith said, "We do not agree to your demands."

"Then you will die here today," Dennis said. "You all know what I am capable of doing."

Taylor growled, "You aren't real men. You are a collective blight to our existence."

Daniel began to kick and scream, trying to break free. His gaze was fixed on Dennis Hamilton, and his eyes sparkled with fury. The men holding him down scrambled to make sure he did not rise again, and two of them sat on him.

Rachel gritted her teeth in anger and then jumped as Dennis raised his gun and fired a shot into the air. There were loud screams from behind Rachel, and she turned around. A group of women were scrambling back into the house.

"All of you, stay inside that house!" Dennis announced again. "Nobody is to come out."

Rachel bit her lip and looked at Dennis Hamilton again. Disgust and loathing filled her as she continued to glare at him and the so-called elders. What kind of people did these kinds of things?

"So, Rachel, what is it going to be?" Dennis asked.

Rachel groaned and shut her eyes briefly. "Lord, please help us." She opened her eyes again looked at Dennis, and then said, "Please give me a moment to speak to the women."

Her heart began to beat rapidly as she waited for Dennis to give a reply to her request. If he agreed, she could buy some time. Not that she knew what exactly she would do with more time, but maybe a miracle would happen. If, however, Dennis didn't agree, then she wouldn't have any choice but to give her assent to his ridiculous demand. She prayed again, "Lord, please help us." She sighed as she continued to wait.

Dennis narrowed his eyes, a thoughtful expression on his face, and then he finally said, "Okay. But you have only thirty minutes."

Rachel nodded and then went into the house with Keith and Taylor.

EIGHTEEN

Rachel stood in the middle of the common room and said to Keith, "Please tell me the Lord has spoken to you about this. If there has ever been a time when we need a word from Him, it's right now."

Keith shut his eyes briefly and then opened them again. "I'm sorry, Rachel," he said, shaking his head and looking grim. "The Lord has said nothing to me. What about you? Do you have a word from God concerning this?"

"No," she answered. She sighed and sat down on the sofa near the entrance to the common room. Keith and Taylor sat next to her. "What Dennis Hamilton is asking for is completely crazy," she said. "There's no way we can give in to his demands." And yet she knew they had no choice.

"Maybe I should try to speak to Dennis, one on one," Keith said. "He appeared to listen to me when I used to go to his house to pray and share God's word with him."

"You just said it, Keith," Rachel said. "He appeared

to listen to you. But he wasn't really listening."

"Rachel is right. It will do no good." Taylor folded his arms across his chest. "You know that. Dennis deceived you, and he deceived me, too. I feel so terrible. I wish I had never helped him out. I wish I had let him and his men drown."

"Taylor!" Rachel looked at him. "You know that is not who you are."

"Well, at least I wish I had not let him stay on my property and provided everything he and his men needed. I cannot help blaming myself for all this."

"Stop blaming yourself, Taylor. It's not your fault," Keith said.

"At least we know that Lily and Sofia are safe," Taylor said, and sighed again.

"Yes, that gives me a measure of relief," Rachel said. "But it does not take away the fact that everyone here is still in danger."

"I cannot stand by and let Dennis physically and emotionally enslave these women again," Keith said. "And especially not you, Rachel. We cannot allow it."

"I know what they are asking for is terrible," Rachel said, "but what choice do we have but to give in?" She stood up. "It's time to go and speak with the women. We have to prepare their hearts for what is to come." She groaned. "Lord, why is this happening?"

Taylor asked, "Can't we find a way to call the police?"

"You know that would not be a wise decision, Taylor," Rachel said. "Just like Dennis said, the police department in Prospect is tiny and they will be outnumbered and outgunned here. We don't want a shootout that would put people's lives at risk. Unfortunately, the lives of the women here when Dennis takes over will be somewhat like a living death, especially since they have lived in complete freedom for a while now."

Keith looked up at the ceiling and shook his head. "I wish we had never come here, Rachel. All we've had since coming here is trouble. One trouble after another." He moaned. "What am I talking about? Not just troubles. We've had one life-threatening situation after another. Maybe we should have left Fallow Creek the way it was."

"You know we had very little choice. It was either we obeyed God and came here, or stayed in Destiny and continued to live in disobedience."

"But now, see what it's all come to," Keith said. "Dennis Hamilton and his men are going to take over this town and revert it back to the way it used to be."

"I still believe God has done something huge for this town. See how many of the women gave their lives to Christ. And their thoughts and way of thinking has been changed. I think God accomplished what he set out to do through us, Keith. We should be grateful for that."

"And what is going to happen to us when Dennis takes over, especially since he is saying that we cannot leave town."

"I don't know," Rachel said. She walked out of the common room, went up the stairs, and rang the bell to summon the women for a general assembly at the back of the House of Refuge. She hadn't rung the bell for more than a year. Today, though, she had to speak to all the women. And what she was going to tell them was very unpleasant.

Women began to pour out of their rooms, and Rachel said loudly, "To the assembly ground everyone." She went into her apartment, lifted Emily, who was still asleep, from her bed, and carried her down the stairs.

She waited with Keith and Taylor in the common room until the women had gone to the back of the house. Ten minutes later, she gave Emily to Keith and went to the assembly ground with Taylor. She stood on the platform in front of the women and raised her voice as loud as she could. "So, many of you have seen the security squad team in front of the house as well as the elders gathered there. You're wondering what exactly is happening. Dennis Hamilton and the elders have a message they want me to give to you all."

She sighed and began to tell the women everything Dennis Hamilton had said. There was total silence as she spoke, and she could see from the faces of many of the women that they were stunned speechless. Clearly, none of them had expected what they were hearing. When she finished speaking, she said to the women, "So this is a decision we have to make. And I know we don't have a choice but to agree to all they have said. It's either that or we face the worst." She looked at the women, her heartbreaking for them. "I'm so sorry," she said.

The women began to murmur again, and one of them said, "Why are you apologizing, Rachel? We don't regret following your leadership and counsel. We appreciate all that you have done for us."

The other women began to speak out in

agreement, and for a short moment, Rachel let them all speak. And then she raised her hand. "So, I guess this is it. Dennis Hamilton and the elders will take over and revert Fallow Creek back to the way it was. Most of you are unmarried, and I guess you will soon have..." She could not bring herself to say "husbands." Being married to men who already had wives was not having husbands. This was not right. No one should be forced to marry a man they didn't want to be with, especially a man who might already be married. She went on, knowing she had no choice but to do so. "Soon, you will all be 'married,' but don't ever forget all I have taught you. One day, I know you'll be free again. All of you."

The women began to murmur and complain, and then they started to protest loudly. Rachel raised her hands again, but they did not stop. Some of the women yelled different things: "We will not go back to the way things used to be, and we definitely won't be forced to marry people we don't want. This is the United States. We have our rights. We will not be forced to do anything we don't want to do! The Lord will protect us."

Rachel frowned with worry. "You don't understand. Our lives are at risk if we refuse their demands. There are more than a dozen squad members out there with guns. You remember what happened with Mike and his men. We don't want the same thing to happen, do we? And this time, it would be so much worse."

A middle-aged woman stepped out from amongst the others, and Rachel blinked. Dennis Hamilton's first wife, Patricia. What was she doing here? She did not live in the House of Refuge.

She still lived in Dennis Hamilton's old house. She raised her hand, and all the women stopped murmuring and complaining. She said, "I was in the House of Refuge, me and my daughter Cordelia over there, when Mike Cadwell besieged this place. I remember how afraid we were, how we scampered for our lives. But I think I speak for at least most of the women here when I say that we are through running. We want our freedom."

Cordelia, a raven-haired beauty in her early twenties, came out and stood beside her mother. Patricia said, "What Dennis and those elders are saying is that someone like my daughter here will be given to someone that she doesn't have feelings for and who is probably married and way older than she is. I'm not going to let that happen, and I'm sure Cordelia wants nothing to do with that." She turned to look at Rachel. "Since you became the leader, Rachel, we have come to understand the freedom we have in Christ. We now know better. We know what the elders are asking for is completely wrong, and we are not going to give in, are we?" She looked over the other women standing before them.

"No, we're not," the women shouted as one.

Rachel sighed. This was not good. And yet there might be hope with Patricia being here and speaking for them. But then, Dennis was a hard and wicked man. The rest of his family were not here. He might think nothing of getting rid of his first wife.

But then again, his daughter was here. Rachel ran her hand through her hair. Who knew what Dennis's reaction would be?

Another woman came out, a younger woman

named Sarah, and then another named Helen. Dennis's other wives. Rachel stared at them in surprise. When had they all gathered here? They stood beside Patricia and held hands with her. "We don't want to be married to Dennis anymore," they said.

Patricia said, "Dennis sent me, Helen, Sarah, and all his children, away to my parents' house in Utah. When he did that, I knew something was up. Knowing him, I guessed what he was planning to do, though I wasn't sure. We decided to come back here, so we left the young kids back at my parents'. If he wants to eliminate the women here, then he will have to start with us. We are going out there."

Helen and Sarah nodded.

Rachel's mouth dropped open, and she stared at Patricia. "You cannot do that."

"We've already decided to do it, didn't we?" Patricia turned to the wives.

"Yes, we did," Sarah and Helen answered.

"And I am coming with the three of you," Cordelia said.

Patricia stared at her. "I would prefer that you didn't."

"I am coming with you, mother. Don't try to convince me otherwise."

Taylor walked up to Patricia and the other wives. "You women cannot go out there. Your lives will be in danger. You can't protect any of these women. Dennis does not have to harm any of you. All he has to do is get his men to move you out of the way and then attack the house."

"Yes, but another thing I did not say is that my older brother, who I have not seen for a while and who left Fallow Creek years ago, is a police detective in the Utah police department. We reconciled during our visit to see my parents, and when I told him about my suspicions before I came back here, he said he was going to gather as many police officers as possible and come here as soon as he could. I don't know when they will get here, but I am going to make sure I stand my ground with Dennis and prevent him from doing anything until they do." She, the other wives, and Cordelia walked past Rachel and Taylor and made their way back into the house. Rachel protested, but they did not turn back. Instead, the other women followed them.

"This is not good, Taylor," Rachel said. "We need to try to stop them somehow."

"And how are you going to stop them?" Taylor asked. "Maybe this will work. As Patricia said, the police are on their way."

"And like Dennis said, if there is a shoot-out, the women might be caught in the crossfire."

"Not if enough police officers arrive and surround Dennis and his men. I know, Rachel. I don't like this either. But I don't know what else we can do."

They followed the women into the House of Refuge and out of the front door. They walked out of the gate with Patricia, Sarah, Helen, and Cordelia. Rachel and Taylor went to stand beside Patricia, the other wives, and Cordelia.

Rachel sighed. Well, she was not going to let Patricia and the wives stand-alone. If they were bold enough to do this, then she would stand with them to the end.

Dennis glared at them with an astonished look and roared, "What is the meaning of this?" He blinked rapidly and his mouth flew open as his gaze settled on Patricia and his wives and then on his daughter Cordelia. "What... what is this, Patricia? Helen, Sarah. Cordelia, what are you all doing here? I sent you out of Fallow Creek in order to protect you. Why are you here?"

"We heard what your demands were from Rachel," Patricia said. "We refuse them all. We are not going back to the way things used to be." She turned and looked back at all the women behind her and then smiled at Rachel. She faced Dennis again. "You can do whatever you want to us, but you will have to get through us first before having any of these women behind us. If you plan to kill these women, then you will have to kill us first."

The security squad team raised their guns and pointed them at the women, and Rachel swallowed. She took a deep breath and squared her shoulders, pushing down her fear. Whatever these men wanted to do to them, she would stand her ground.

"Put down your guns, you fools!" Dennis Hamilton barked at the squad team.

They put down their guns, and Dennis faced Patricia. "How could you betray me this way?" He looked at his other wives. "Why would you come here, Patricia... and with Cordelia? Do you know what you have done?"

"I've lived as your wife for years, Dennis, and also lived under your leadership of Fallow Creek. But never in my life have I felt so free and so happy than when Rachel took over and began to lead this place. At first, I was afraid that she would banish me and my children out of Fallow Creek because of what you did to her and her family. But she did not. Instead, she allowed me to go back and live in the house with the children. She let Helen and Sarah live there as well. And we have lived in peace ever since. Even the children have never been happier."

She sighed loudly and continued. "I have seen how happy and joyful all these women behind me are compared to how they were before. The House of Refuge was a prison before. Now it is a refuge and a place of celebration. None of us want things to go back to the way they were. And none of these women want to be married to random men. In fact, we don't want it *so* much that we are ready for whatever consequences you and your men will mete out."

The elders began to murmur amongst themselves.

"Dennis!" Cliff Hunter said. "I think you should listen to your wife. Maybe she has a point. Even my daughter was willing to give her life to come here just so they didn't have to go back to living the way things were. That should tell you a lot."

Then other elders glared at Cliff and began to berate him, and he said nothing more.

"So, what you're telling me, Patricia, is that you want Rachel to continue to lead this town. That means you don't want me anymore?"

"I have always loved you, Dennis, but you have treated me like property for years, and added more and more wives to what you have. Even now, you are planning to add more. I took it all because I believed that was God's will; that it was the way things were meant to be. But Rachel showed me a different way. She showed me it was not God's will at all. I don't care what you do now, but I will give my life so these women behind me will be free to live the way they want." She stood in front of the other women and linked her hands with Helen, Sarah, and Cordelia. "We are ready to give our lives," she said again.

Rachel took Cordelia's hand, and Taylor came and took hers.

"Dennis, we cannot back down now," the other elders said. "What do you want to do? Do you want to give your rightful place over to these women because of their childish antics?"

Dennis turned to the elder that had just spoken. "These women are my wives. Shut up and let me think." He turned and faced Patricia again. "You're really serious about this."

She nodded.

He looked at Rachel, and she could see the hatred in his eyes. "You are the cause of all this. You should be the first to die."

As soon as he spoke, the security squad team raised their guns again and leveled them at Rachel.

Dennis turned and shouted, "Put your guns down. She belongs to me!" He looked at Rachel with fire in his eyes and then raised his hand and pointed his gun to her head.

She closed her eyes. "Lord, is this it?"

A gunshot exploded, and she gasped and opened her eyes again. "No! Keith!"

Keith was standing in front of her, clearly to shield her with his body. He had been shot. Rachel held him. "Lord, no!" And then she blinked in surprise. Instead of Keith falling to the ground, Dennis fell, clutching his arm and writhing in pain.

As though the scene were playing in slow motion, she turned around and saw Daniel looking down at Dennis Hamilton, his gun beside him.

Some of the guards pointed their guns in Daniel's direction, some in the women's. They cocked their guns, and Rachel's heart jumped into her mouth.

Dennis yelled even as he writhed in pain on the ground, "Please, don't shoot! You might hurt my wives and my daughter." And then his eyes widened as police sirens pierced the air.

Rachel immediately jumped into action. "Everyone, inside! Now!" she screamed. Now that the police had arrived, the squad team might engage them in a gun battle, and she didn't want any of the women out here when that happened.

The women hurried as one into the House, with Keith, Taylor, and Daniel behind them. Rachel waited for them all to go in, and before she shut the gate, the squad team was already shooting at the police to try to escape.

The police fired back, and Rachel hurried into the House. "Stay away from the windows!" she yelled at the women. "Stay back!"

"Take cover wherever you can," Daniel shouted, and the women scrambled around. Some hid under the chairs in the common room, some under the table, but most ran upstairs to take cover in their rooms. Gunfire exploded outside for a long time, and then it stopped.

Rachel crawled out from under the sofa where she had taken cover while the gun battle went on. She went to the window and slowly opened a curtain. Taylor and Keith and Daniel came to stand beside her.

She sighed with relief as police officers herded the squad members and elders into the police cars. One of the officers pulled Dennis Hamilton up off the ground and hurled him toward a police vehicle. Just before he got in, he turned to the house and his eyes met Rachel's. The expression on his face was still full of hatred, but there was a sliver of respect there as well. She heaved another sigh of relief as the police officer pushed Dennis into the car, closed the door, and drove away.

Two police officers walked into the House of Refuge to take everyone's statement. They asked Rachel some general questions related to the attack, and then moved on to Keith and the other women in the House.

When the officers left and all the police cars were finally gone, Rachel turned to Keith and Taylor and nearly fell to the floor in relief. "It's all over," she said. "No more Dennis Hamilton to trouble us again." Tears pooled in her eyes and fell down her cheeks.

Keith reached out and pulled her into his arms. "I should have listened to you and Daniel when you voiced your suspicions about Dennis." He rubbed her back. "I'm just glad everyone is okay," he said.

The women who had gone upstairs began to make their way down. Rachel went to thank Patricia and Helen and Sarah, and then she came back to stand beside Keith and Taylor.

"We still don't know where Lily is," Taylor said. "At least I know she's safe, since her father said so, but I have to find her."

"The police will probably get the address of where she was taken from her father and Dennis

Hamilton," Rachel said.

"Yes." Taylor gave her a tired smile. "I am going to the police station in Prospect now. Do you two want to come with me?"

Rachel smiled. "I would like to, but I have to stay with Emily. Keith can go with you, though."

Keith nodded. "I'll come along, Taylor."

Keith and Taylor left the House of Refuge, while Rachel went to get Emily from the woman Keith had left her with. Hopefully, Taylor would find Lily soon and this whole nightmare would be over.

She walked up the stairs while lifting up a prayer of thanksgiving to the Lord for once again delivering them from an impossible situation.

NINETEEN

Jude woke up from a long nap and, for a brief moment, looked round the room, feeling disoriented. At first, he thought he was in the prison block in Bakali, in his cell with his father. And then he thought he was in the isolation building where he had been kept.

He shook his head as his grogginess began to clear up. Of course, they were in Cliff Hunter's house.

He reached out and turned on the light. The simply furnished room with the comfortable bed lit up brightly. He looked at the clock on the bedside table and blinked in surprise. He had only planned to take a short nap, but he had been sleeping for the past two hours. It was already five o'clock in the evening.

He drew the curtains back and turned off the light to let in the last rays of sunshine, and then he looked outside. He took a deep breath and smiled. For the first time since they'd come to America, it dawned on him that he was now a free man after more than a year of incarceration. He felt great.

He looked out the window again at the small store opposite the house. Talking about incarceration, he looked around the room wondering where his father was. His father was not here. He was probably somewhere in the house, maybe in the living room, talking with Cliff or Anna Hunter or someone else. Since they'd arrived yesterday, he'd noticed people trooping into the house and going out. There had been what seemed like an important meeting in the house when they'd arrived, but he had not seen the men in the meeting until after it was over. Most of them were older men and dressed almost identically in black jackets and pants.

Jude pulled on a T-shirt and a pair of black jeans. Just before he walked out the door, he glanced at the mirror and patted his head down. Suddenly, Sofia's face flashed in his mind, and he groaned. He remembered her smiling and patting his head down during one of their dates, when he'd gone to Edith's house to visit her. She had said something about him being more groomed and better looking than she was, but he couldn't remember the exact words she had spoken. What he did remember was their kiss. He sighed with pain, thinking about her being locked up in some house somewhere. He wished now that he could hold her and tell her that he loved her and that he'd left on their wedding day, not because he didn't, but because he'd had no choice. Most of all, he prayed with all his heart that she was happy. Truly happy.

He sighed again and pushed her face out of his mind. He had to focus on Keziah now. She was his soon-to-be wife. No matter how much he yearned for Sofia, he could not have her.

He walked out of the room, determined to find his father and walked down the corridor. He thought about Keziah. They still had a lot to talk about — their wedding plans and their life that would start soon in that town called Fallow Creek. What would he do for a living? And was Keziah planning on having children?

He felt troubled thinking about that, but once again he pushed down his worry. Why borrow trouble from the future?

Walking down the corridor, he got to Keziah's bedroom door and paused. It was closed. For a brief moment, he thought about knocking and entering into her room, but he changed his mind. He would go and find his father first, and then he would come back to speak with her.

Just as he'd thought, he found his father in the living room, but he was not speaking with anyone. Instead, he was reading a book. Jude looked around. The living room was empty except for his father. In fact, the whole house seemed empty, completely quiet, unlike yesterday when people had been coming and going and everywhere was very noisy. He wondered about that.

His father looked up at him and smiled. "Jude!" His dad pointed at the space beside him on the couch. "Sit beside me, Jude. Let's talk."

Jude smiled back and sat beside his father. He looked at the book his father was reading. "What is the book you are reading?

His father shrugged. "It's about city planning. Just a book I found on the coffee table when I came to the living room. After lunch I came in to talk to you, but I found you were already asleep, so I left you to find someone else to talk to. But everyone is apparently out. I don't know where they went."

"How long have they been out?" Jude asked. He knew his father had planned to talk to one of the men who had been here yesterday and must have been disappointed to find no one.

"Since after lunch. No actually, earlier. Cliff left the house with some men after breakfast. I thought he might have returned when I came to the living room but he hadn't. Anna left the house after lunch. I saw her leaving in a hurry and tried to speak with her, but she was already out the door before I could stop her to ask where she was rushing off to. We've been left on our own, I suppose." He smiled.

Jude picked up the book his father was reading and looked at it. It had the words *Town Planning & Management* written on the cover. "I didn't know this sort of thing held any interest for you," Jude said.

His dad smiled again. "I might be a pastor, but I don't just read the Bible, Jude. I read a lot of books on topics I truly find interesting."

Jude smiled at his father. Before he'd gone to America from Bakali for his Master's degree, he and his dad had had a good relationship, but it had simply been one of father and son, and nothing more. But during their time incarcerated together, they had gradually built a relationship of equality and friendship. Apart from Sofia, who had become his best friend before he'd had to leave America, his dad was his best friend. They'd had so many deep conversations in prison, and it was so strange sitting with him, here in this tastefully furnished living room, free to come and go as they pleased.

Well, not exactly free to go, but at least come as they pleased. They didn't really know anyone they could go visit, and with no resources, nowhere else to go as well. He was dependent on Keziah for most things. That was embarrassing. He hoped he could find a job quickly, once they settled down fully. He asked his father, "Do you know where Keziah is, Dad?"

His father narrowed his eyes as a thoughtful look appeared on his face. "I don't know where she is now. I think I saw her sometime after lunch going outside. I haven't seen her for about two hours now."

"I need to speak to her," Jude said. "I'll be right back." He stood and left his father in the living room. Walking out of the house, he looked at the patio and all around the front of the house, which was just a small grassland, but he didn't see her. As he walked to the side and the back of the house, he smiled in surprise. The land stretched far. If kids lived in this house, they would have a vast piece of land to play on and have fun.

He looked around, but Keziah was not at the back of the house anywhere in sight. He walked back into the house and saw his father was still reading on the couch. Walking down the corridor again, he stopped once more in front of Keziah's room. The door was still closed.

He knocked on the door and frowned slightly when she didn't open it. Maybe she was not even home. He began to move away, and then he heard her voice. It was as though she was speaking to someone else in the room. He came back to the door and called out her name.

"Jude! I'm coming!"

He frowned again. She sounded harried. He knocked again, and once more she told him in a voice that he'd hardly heard her use, a worried voice, that she was coming. And then, for some reason, he instantly knew why she sounded that way and why she had not opened the door for him. He wondered whether to just go away or wait. He decided to wait. Whatever she was hiding, he was curious to know exactly what it was and if his guess was right.

"Jude," she called out. "Can you come back later?"

He frowned again. "Keziah, open the door." He was itching to see whoever was inside that bedroom with her.

She finally came and opened the door, and he studied her face. He looked her over and then looked past her into the room. She tried to block his view, but he gave her a small smile and gently pushed her away from the door and entered the room. Someone was clearly hiding behind the curtain, and for some reason, he found it hilarious. Smiling, even though he didn't want to and knew he shouldn't, he opened the curtain and found that Tim, the guard who had looked at Keziah with clear attraction in his eyes yesterday, was behind it. And he was shirtless.

Jude stepped back as Tim quickly exited the room, and then looked at Keziah. He wasn't sure how to feel or what to think, or even what to say to her. She looked guilty, but he was not angry with her. For someone who was planning to marry her, that was not good. It was not good that he was not angry, nor did he mind that his fiancé was in her room with another man and clearly doing what a soon-to-be-married woman should not be doing. He knew he had to react so he did not seem totally uncaring, and said, "Keziah, what happened here? Why is that guy in your room, shirtless, and hiding behind a curtain?" He groaned inwardly. *You already know why, and she knows that you know, so why ask?*

She took a deep breath and said, "I'm sorry, Jude. It just happened. It won't happen again."

He didn't know what else to say, and he backed away and walked out the door.

He hurried down the corridor to the living room to sit with his father and try to process what he'd just seen. What did Keziah cheating on him really mean for their future? Were they going to go ahead and get married and pretend that what he'd seen had not really happened? Should he speak to her about it later on? He needed to speak to his father and seek his wise advice, but he wasn't sure he should tell his dad what he had seen.

Maybe he could tell his father about it without mentioning Keziah's name. Maybe he could pretend he'd heard about it happening to someone rather than to him.

He got to the living room, but before he could sit beside his father on the couch, he heard a commotion outside. And then a siren began to wail.

He blinked and dove toward the door just as his father got up. He went outside, and his mouth dropped open. The police were stomping toward the house, toward him. For a full minute he was unable to move, frozen with fear. Without a doubt they had found him and Keziah and his father. He and his dad were illegal immigrants and they would be deported.

"Lord, no." He would rather die than go back to Bakali and face all the violence and war going on there; rather than face Felix again, because Felix would be waiting at the airport to seize him once he arrived. He thought about running away, but the police were already on him. They got to the door and glared at him. "Who are you?" they asked. "We have a warrant to search this house." They held up a document that he didn't bother looking at.

He blinked in surprise as they walked past him into the house. Wasn't he the one they wanted?

Two more police officers entered the gate and ordered him back into the house. There were about half a dozen police officers in total, most with guns. The police officers told him and his father to sit on the couch. Two of them began to search the living room for something, while the others stomped away, clearly to continue their search in other parts of the house. He wanted to ask what they were looking for, but that would probably not be a good idea considering his precarious situation.

His father looked up at them with wonder and uncertainty in his eyes. He whispered to Jude, "What's going on? Are they here for us?"

Jude did not say anything, but who else could they be here for? The police came for those who had broken the law, and they — he, his father, and Keziah — were it. They would be bundled back to Bakali, and Felix would find and kill them.

One police officer came into the living room with Keziah and Tim walking in front of him. Keziah looked nonchalant, and Jude wondered how she managed to look or seem so calm. Tim looked afraid.

Soon the other policemen joined those in the living room. "We didn't find anything," they said.

The policemen began to shout and question them. "Where are the other occupants of this house? Are there other people here? Who exactly are you? Why are you here?"

Jude opened his mouth to tell them exactly who he was and where he had come from, but Keziah gave him a look that told him not to say anything.

She said to the policemen, "We're just friends of the people who live here. We came here to spend time with them yesterday. They left this morning without telling us where they were going. We have no idea where they are now."

They were asked how they knew the occupants of the house, and Keziah answered again, while Jude looked between her and the officers.

One of them frowned and said, "Your accent. Where are you all from?"

Keziah said nothing.

The police officer turned away from her to Jude. "Where are you from, young man?"

Jude bit his lip and then said, "Bakali."

"Can't say I've heard of that country before," the officer said. "And why are you here in America?"

"A short visit," Keziah answered. "As tourists."

The policemen ordered them to get their passports and followed them into their rooms. They checked Keziah's passport and handed it back to her. After that, they looked at his fathers' and then his.

His heart thudded as they studied his passport. When they finally handed it back to him, he hid a huge sigh of relief.

"You will have to come to the police station with us," one of the officers said.

"But we don't know anything," Keziah protested.

"It doesn't matter," the police officer said. "This place was used as a meeting point for some very bad men. We have to ask you more questions at the station. It won't take long. You'll be cleared if you have nothing to hide."

Jude groaned inwardly as they took him, his father, Keziah, and Tim outside and into their police cars.

At the police station, Keziah asked to make a phone call. Jude sat with a police officer, answering questions he had no answers to. All he could say to all their questions about the town called Fallow Creek and the people there was that he did not know because he did not live in America.

An hour after they were brought in, they let them go, clearing them of any wrongdoing. Jude shook his head and looked at his father. "Are you okay, Dad?"

"Yes," his father answered.

They headed out of the police station as two men walked by them. One of them was saying something about finding out where Lily and Sofia were.

Jude gasped and his heart began to race. *Lily and Sofia.* It could be a coincidence, but Sofia had a best friend named Lily. He had never met her because she lived in California, but he had heard so much about her that he felt like he knew her.

He looked back as the men walked past them into the station. He paused in front of the entrance of the police station, wondering what to do. Should he just leave it since it was likely to be a coincidence, or should he go after them and ask about Sofia. And what would Keziah say if he did? She had made him promise he would never contact Sofia again. And yet, he couldn't walk away without knowing.

"Jude? Are you coming?" his father asked.

Jude looked over at Keziah and frowned. She and Tim were standing close together, speaking in hushed tones. She looked over at Jude, and he said, "Please give me a minute. I need to do something important at the station." She opened her mouth, clearly to protest, but he walked away quickly and entered the station again.

He looked around the small police station and found the two men talking to a police officer. He waited for them to finish, his heart beating wildly. He felt very uncertain about what he was going to ask them, but he had to know if they were talking about his Sofia. It was unlikely, but maybe there was a chance that she was the one they were speaking about.

And what if they were talking about her? What will you do about it?

He did not know. All he knew was that he had heard her name, and he would not rest until he found out what he wanted.

The men walked briskly out of the police station, and he immediately moved toward them. "Excuse me," he said politely. He looked at the one he heard talking about Sofia and Lily and asked, "I'm sorry to disturb you, but I heard you talking about a girl called Sofia and her friend, Lily."

The two men's eyes widened in surprise, and they both stared at him. The man he had spoken to said, "Yes, I was. What about them? Do you know them?" He looked at Jude with clear suspicion in his eyes.

His heart raced. "The Sofia you're talking about. Is her full name Sofia Ross?"

The man frowned and looked up with a thoughtful expression on his face. "It's strange that I cannot remember my wife's best friend's last name, but I really can't."

Jude tried another question. "Does she live in Tucson?"

"Yes, she does."

"And her friend, Lily, does she live in California?

The man's mouth dropped open and he nodded. "Yes, you know my wife, Lily?"

Jude could not believe it. Was this really Sofia's best friend's husband? He immediately remembered Lily's husband's name. Sofia had talked quite a lot about him in relation to Lily and how much her friend Lily loved the man. "Is your name Taylor?"

The man beamed and nodded. "Yes, that's my name."

"My name is Jude."

The man laughed. "I can't believe this. You are the Jude Sofia talks about all the time." He blinked and stared at Jude in astonishment. "I thought you were deported back to your country. Bakali, am I right?"

Jude gave him a sad smile. "I wasn't exactly deported, but I did go back. It's a long story. Please, do you know if Sofia still lives in that apartment she lived in about a year ago?"

Taylor's face clouded over, and Jude frowned. His heart began to race wildly. *Lord, please no.*

Don't tell me something bad has happened to her. I could not take it.

"That is why we came to the police station," Taylor continued. "Some days ago, my wife and Sofia went to our hometown to look for her parents. She was told they were staying in a small town in Utah. She had gone to Tucson to visit Sofia and they'd both come to our hometown and decided to go to Utah together. They left some days ago, and since then we have heard nothing from them."

Jude gasped. "Nothing? They just disappeared?" Fear gripped him.

"We have involved the police to find out exactly where my wife and Sofia are. I think the police are trying to get information from her father and his associates to determine where exactly they might be."

Jude could not believe it. Sofia was missing. This could not be happening. He felt like screaming, but he held himself together. "Can I get your phone number, Taylor? I would like to know when the police find out where Sofia is."

"Of course," Taylor said.

Jude got his cell phone from his pocket and typed in Taylor's number. Taylor also took his. "We should know exactly where they are being held by tomorrow morning," Taylor added.

"Please tell me that nothing bad has happened to Sofia," Jude said, more to himself than Taylor.

Taylor smiled and put his hand on his shoulder. "I understand how you feel. Let me assure you that they are fine. Her father, Cliff Hunter, told me that much."

Jude's eyes widened, and his stomach began to

roil. "Wait… did you say Cliff Hunter?"

"Yes, that's my wife's father's name."

"I'm staying at his house," Jude said. "It was raided earlier today, and we were all brought to the police station, but we have been cleared. You are telling me that your wife's father kidnapped your wife and Sofia and kept them locked up somewhere?"

"Yes," Taylor said, looking as surprised as Jude was sure he looked.

Someone called Jude's name from behind him, and he turned. He saw his father and Keziah standing right behind. He smiled at Taylor, feeling an affinity to him. "I will call you tomorrow morning to find out what you know. Would that be okay?"

"Definitely," Taylor said. He put his hand on Jude's arm and smiled again. "The police will find them. I promise." He beamed at Jude. "I can tell you one thing. Sofia has missed you so much. I cannot imagine anyone who is more loved by someone that isn't in their lives as much as you are by Sofia."

Jude felt warmth in his stomach as he thought about Sofia, and he knew that nothing would keep him from finding her and being with her. He wished he could hold her now and tell her everything would be okay. Even though she'd only been locked up for a few days compared to his year in prison, he understood how she would feel.

He glanced back at Keziah and groaned. Keziah was the one person that could keep him from Sofia.

Lord what am I going to do? He had made a promise to her not to contact Sofia, but there was no way he wasn't going to see her after all this time, especially with all that was happening right now.

But then again, what would he do about Keziah? She could easily report him, and he would be deported. He and his father would be deported back to Bakali. That would be the end of their lives because they would be apprehended as soon as they landed.

Taylor smiled at him again, and Jude said, "It's been great meeting you. I have to go now. I'll call you later Taylor. And thank you so much."

Taylor nodded, and Jude turned around and walked away.

"Who were those men?" his father asked him.

Keziah did not say a word. She walked ahead of him, while Tim walked some distance away.

Jude frowned. Why was she walking so far apart from Tim? It looked deliberate. Was she really pretending that she did not have a thing with Tim when he'd seen them with his own eyes earlier today? He brushed the thoughts aside and settled his gaze on his father. "That was Taylor, Lily's husband."

His dad frowned. "Who is Taylor? And who is Lily?"

Jude shook his head and smiled. "Taylor is Lily's husband, and Lily is Sofia's best friend."

Dad's mouth flew open and he said, "Sofia! Your Sofia?"

"Yes."

"So I take it you are going to see Sofia?" Dad whispered. "What about Keziah? Are you sure it's a good idea to go and see your ex?"

Jude said "Now that I have heard about her, I don't think anything in this world could keep me away. But then again, I would be taking a huge risk because Keziah could use it to get us kicked out of America and back to Bakali."

Dad groaned. "That would not be good, Jude."

"I know." Jude nodded. "That is why I will have to have a long talk with her. For now, though, I cannot think of anything other than Sofia and when they will find her. I told Taylor to call me once they do."

"Find her? What do you mean find her? Is she missing?"

"It's a long story, Dad, but basically, she is. I'll tell you about it later." He prayed all the way to the house as he'd never prayed before. He knew he still loved Sofia, but he just realized now that he would not be able to go on if anything happened to her. "Lord, keep her safe," he said as they got into the house. "Bring her safely back home."

TWENTY

Taylor took his phone out of his pocket and excused himself from the company of the police officers he had been speaking with outside the Prospect police station. They were about to head to Utah for a joint rescue operation with the Utah police department to get Lily and Sofia out of the house they had been held in for almost a week.

Lily's father had given them the exact location of the house. He had tried to call his brother after the police arrested him and the other elders to tell him to let Lily and Sofia go, but his brother had switched off his phone and cut off all communications. Cliff believed his brother, Matthew, did not want to give up the girls, especially Sofia.

Taylor had convinced the police officers in Prospect to let him come along, but he would have to remain in the car when they went into the house. He wished Keith or Rachel could have come along with them, as well as Jude because of Sofia, but the police had refused when he'd asked. They told him they would only allow him to come along, and no one else.

He dialed Jude's number and waited for him to answer. He had been suspicious at first when Jude had approached him at the station yesterday and asked about Lily and Sofia, but it hadn't taken long for him to be convinced it was Sofia's Jude. Before Jude could fully ascertain that Taylor was Lily's husband, Taylor had already known it was Jude because he fit the description of the guy Lily had told him Sofia had been engaged to.

"Taylor!" Jude exclaimed on the other end of the line.

Taylor told him everything the police had said.

"So, you're heading there now?" Jude asked.

"Yes, we are."

"And you are sure there's no way I can come with you?"

"Just like I said, they refused to allow anyone else to come along. Don't worry, Jude. I will call you as soon as we get back to let you know how it went."

"Thank you so much," Jude said. "I don't know how I will be able to stay still until I get your call, but I will try. Again, thank you."

"No problem, Jude. And don't worry. The police will bring Lily and Sofia safe to us."

"I hope so. And, Taylor, please, can you promise me something?"

"What?" Taylor asked.

"Please don't tell Sofia that you saw me. I want to surprise her myself."

"I promise I won't tell her."

As soon as the call ended, Taylor sighed. It would be hard for him not to tell Lily that he'd seen and spoken to Jude, but he would not tell her. She would find it impossible to keep such news from Sofia. Again, he started to worry that they would not find Lily and Sofia in the house. The police were not entirely sure Lily and Sofia were still there. They thought there was a slim possibility that Lily and Sofia had been moved away after all the elders and Cliff Hunter were arrested.

For a short moment, he was consumed with worry, and then he finally pressed his concerns away. He had been praying constantly about it, and God was in control. Wherever the girls were, the Lord would lead them there. He went back to the police officers and found them talking to Rachel and Keith.

One of the officers said, "We will get to the station in Utah first of all and then go with the police officers to the address we were given." He looked at Rachel. "Don't worry, ma'am. We will find your sister-in-law and her friend."

Taylor hugged Keith and then Rachel.

"Be careful, Taylor," Rachel said, placing a palm on his cheek. "Bring Lily and Sofia back."

Taylor smiled. "I'm so nervous… but I cannot wait to see Lily again. I can't imagine the huge relief I will feel when I finally see her."

"I hope they are found in that house," Rachel said.

"There is a small possibility they will not be there, but the police think they still are. They also think there are armed guards there as well, and there might be a shootout. It's why they didn't want any other person to come along with them but me. There would be one too many people."

Rachel said again, "Please be careful, Taylor."

"I will be. I'm not allowed to get out of the car anyway." He looked into Rachel's eyes. "I'm scared, Rachel. I'm scared that something might go wrong and..."

"Don't say it," Rachel told him. "Nothing will go wrong. The police will get your wife and Sofia out of that house, and you will be happily reunited with her. Keith and I will be praying non-stop for the rescue operation to be successful."

"Thank you, Rachel," Taylor said. "We'll need all the prayers we can get. My poor Lily locked up in a house and unable to leave for days." He smiled. "You know how Lily is. She likes to go out, take walks. She says it's because of how long she lived locked in the Restoration House, and she would never want that kind of experience again."

Rachel smiled. "I know. I was with her in the House. She's with her best friend, though. So I think she is doing well in every way. They will keep each other healthy, mentally and otherwise."

"We have to go now," one of the officers called to him.

Taylor smiled at Rachel. "I've got to go. I will call you as soon as they are found. I have to call two people after we find them."

"Two?" Rachel asked. "Oh, Jude. Sofia's ex."

"I cannot say he's just her ex, because Lily says that Sofia talks about him all the time." He reached out and touched Rachel's arm. "I'll call you later." She smiled, and he hugged her again.

He walked away and got into one of the police cars. He knew it was a privilege that the police had allowed him to come along with them. He also knew that it was because the Prospect Police Department was small and informal. The department in Utah would definitely not have allowed him to come along if they were the only ones handling this rescue operation.

As they drove to their destination, all he could think about was seeing Lily again. He continued to pray earnestly that Lily and Sofia would still be at that house and that they were safe. Most of all, he prayed that the police would successfully get them out of the house and that no one would be hurt.

The drive to Utah took forever. It almost felt like going from one country to another. They stopped midway to get some food and then continued on. Sometimes, Taylor chatted with the police officer beside him, and at other times he simply thought about Lily and prayed for her safety.

They got to Utah at about three o'clock. As expected, the police department there was much bigger than the one in Prospect, and they were a lot more professional but less friendly and patient.

Taylor stood to the side as they talked with the police officers from Prospect. Some of the officers from the Utah police department kept looking at him while they talked... or argued with the police officers from Prospect. At last, two police cars with four police officers got into the Utah police department vehicles.

The police officers from Prospect got into the car, and Taylor got in with them. When he asked them why the officers from Utah had been pointing at him, one of the Prospect officers said, "They wanted to know why on earth you were coming with us." He looked pointedly at Taylor. "Remember, you have to stay in the car always. Anyway, Colt will stay here with you when we enter the house." He pointed at the young policeman who was in the driver's seat.

Some minutes later, they continued on their way.

It took an additional three hours or so to get to the tiny town of Noble. They finally parked in front of a white two-story building, and then the police officers soundlessly got out of the car.

"Remember, stay in the car," said the officer who'd sat beside him throughout the journey. He got his gun, put on his vest, and got out of the car.

Taylor watched them move stealthily toward the house, his heart beating wildly and threatening to burst out of his chest. "Lord, please protect Lily and bring her and Sofia out of that house safely," he prayed once again.

He watched as the policemen got to the front of the gates and knocked. They stood aside, their guns raised. Taylor pressed his lips together and looked away, too nervous to watch. Soon multiple gunshots rang in the air, and Taylor groaned. He had hoped that there would be no shots fired today, no casualties, and that there would be no armed men in the house, or if there were, that they would surrender to the police. The last thing he'd wanted was this gun battle. Not only had he seen way too much of it in recent times, he was scared that it might put Lily's and Sofia's lives in danger.

He continued to pray while his heart pounded along with the blasts of the gunshots. He looked once more toward the gate and found the police officers had entered and the gunshots were growing fewer. He continued to pray.

The gunshots stopped, but the policemen still

did not come out of the house. He kept looking and began to worry that they had been outgunned and were now dead or captured.

Lord, where are they?

From the corner of his eye, he saw something green move out from the back of the house. He turned around and his heart skipped a beat when he saw a woman being dragged away from the back of the house by a man in a green shirt who he soon recognized as Matthew, Lily's uncle. It had to be Sofia. He had a gun pointed at her. He'd bound her hands and gagged her and was pulling her toward the opposite side of the road.

Taylor's heart jumped into his throat, and he said to the driver, "Look! My wife's friend, Sofia! Look at her! He is trying to escape with her. We have to help her."

He began to get out of the car, but Colt ordered him to stay still. "I will go. Just stay in the car." Colt got out of the car with his gun and headed in the direction Taylor had pointed in.

The police officers began to come out of the gate, and Taylor's heart leaped with joy. One of them was holding Lily. She was weeping, pointing and arguing with one of the officers.

Taylor immediately got out of the car and ran to her. "Lily!"

Her eyes grew round when she saw him, and then she pulled away from the officer and flew into his arms. "Taylor! Oh Taylor! You're here." She began to cry hysterically. "He took Sofia! Uncle Matthew took her."

A gunshot rang out, and the police officers looked in the direction it had come from.

Fear gripped Taylor. What if Lily's uncle had shot Colt and was even now escaping with Sofia. Taylor pointed. "They went that way. He took Sofia, and Colt went to find him."

The officers nodded, and three of them went in the direction Taylor had pointed out, while the rest got into their cars. Lily got in beside Taylor, and he held her tightly, trying to comfort her while she continued to weep.

"They have to find her," she said. "They have to find Sofia."

Taylor ran his hand through her hair and rubbed her back. "They will find her, Lily. Don't you worry." He kissed her hair and thanked God for bringing her back to him.

"I've missed you so much," she said to him. She kissed him and then looked out the window, tears running down her cheeks.

"I have missed you too, Lily." He wiped her tears away with his thumb, and even though he was also scared, he said again, "They will find Sofia. You'll see."

Lily said frantically, "It's all my fault, Taylor. I never should have brought her here. And this is my father and my uncle's doing. How will I ever look her in the face again? Please," she looked at one of the officers who was sitting in front of the car, "please bring her back safely."

"They will bring her back, ma'am," the officer said.

"How could Uncle Matthew do such a thing?"

"I can't believe your Uncle Matthew took Sofia," Taylor said. "What was he thinking?"

"He was the one who held us captive in the

house."

"Yes, I know. The police found out about that yesterday."

"I cannot believe he would do such a thing," Lily said. "But maybe I should have seen it coming. He could not keep his eyes off Sofia. He was enamored with her." she began to cry again. "I will never forgive myself if they don't get Sofia back."

"Don't say that. First, you are not responsible for your uncle's or father's actions. Second, they will get Sofia back safely." Taylor looked out the window and his heart soared. He pointed, "Look, Lily! There she is. They have found her." He smiled widely.

Lily screamed, opened the door, and hopped out of the car. She rushed up to Sofia and they hugged tightly.

Taylor got out of the car and went and hugged Sofia, his heart filled with gratitude to God. "Thank God you're safe," he said. "I saw that man dragging you out of the back of the house. I was so scared, especially when I saw he had a gun. Are you okay?" he asked, looking into her eyes.

She smiled, tears falling down her cheeks. "I am fine. I'm just happy to be safe and out of that house."

Lily took her hand and then took Taylor's. They made their way to the police car together and got into the backseat. Taylor smiled at Sofia and gathered Lily into his arms. He kissed her for a long moment, grateful she was alive and safely with him again. When he pulled back, he said to her, "I am never letting you out of my sight again."

She laughed and wiped away the tears streaming down her cheeks. "That will mean you will never go on any of your business trips again… or even to work."

"Maybe I'll start taking you along with me," he said. "I plan to do more of that anyway. I want to start taking you and the kids with me whenever I travel on business. That way, we can spend more time together as a family."

"I love the idea, but what about Josh?" Lily asked. "He goes to school. He cannot miss school to go with you on your business trips."

Taylor said, "I will have to figure out a way to work his schooling into my trips. But I know I want to start taking you all with me." He turned briefly to look at Sofia. She was looking out the window, and she looked so sad that he almost told her about Jude. That would definitely lift her mood. But Jude had made him promise not to tell. He gently touched her arm, and she turned to him. "Are you okay, Sofia?"

"Not really," she said. "But I'll be fine." She gave him a small smile and said, "Well, this was one heck of a vacation."

Taylor laughed, and Lily laughed along with him. "At least your sense of humor is intact and your mood is lifting. You'll soon be completely fine." He sighed heavily. "I'm so sorry this happened to you."

Sofia shook her head. "I just want to forget about everything. But not the part about sharing this experience, no matter how bad it was, with Lily." She reached out and took Lily's hand.

"After everything that happened with me looking for my parents, I still don't know where they are, but now, I don't think I want to."

Taylor gave her a sad smile. He thought about

telling her that her father was in jail, but he changed his mind. She'd suffered enough. She would find out later.

"The police told me that Rachel and Keith and all the women at the House of Refuge are fine," Lily said. "We tried so hard to reach Rachel and Keith so we could warn them about the coming invasion. I'm glad they're all okay."

"You knew about that?" Taylor asked.

"Yes. Days ago, Uncle Matthew told me. We tried to escape so we could get to Rachel and Keith or call them so they could contact the police, but Uncle Mathew's men found us and brought us back here. Tell me, Taylor, what happened in Fallow Creek? Since everyone is fine, I take it that Dennis Hamilton, my father, and all those men were not able to invade the town?"

Taylor shook his head. "Actually, they did."

Lily's eyes widened in surprise. "They did? But everyone is safe? What happened?"

Taylor took a deep breath and began to tell her everything from the very beginning. When he got to the part about Patricia and the bravery of Dennis Hamilton's other wives, and the women's decision that they would not give in to the elders demands no matter what it cost them, Lily was amazed.

"They took such a great risk, but I applaud them," she said.

"Many of them said they would rather die than go back to the way things used to be. Even when the squad team pointed their guns at them, they did not back down."

Lily shook her head. "Wow!"

At last, he told her how the police had arrived

and how Dennis Hamilton and all the security squad members had been taken away. He almost told her about meeting Jude at the police station because he was so used to telling her everything, but he stopped himself just in time. He glanced at Sofia again and winked at Lily.

She tilted her head, gave him a quizzical look, and whispered, "What... what is it?"

"I'll tell you about it later," he said and smiled. Again, he pulled her close and kissed her and then leaned over to give Sofia a hug. "Thank you, Lord for bringing Lily and Sofia back home," he said, smiling. "Thank you."

TWENTY-ONE

Jude waited with bated breath for Taylor to call him and tell him that Sofia was okay. He could not eat, and he did not sleep that night at all. When his father came to ask him why he had not yet had breakfast, he shook his head, and said, "I will not eat until I know that Sofia is okay."

Anna Hunter, who had finally returned to the house from wherever she'd fled after her husband had been arrested, said, "You need to eat, Jude, to keep your strength up."

He gave her a sad smile, wondering how she was holding up. Now that Cliff Hunter had been taken to prison, Jude wondered what their future plans held. They couldn't remain in this house because Anna had told them when she'd returned that they only had until the end of this week to move out since the man who'd given them the house to live in didn't want them in it anymore as he didn't want to be associated with "criminals." Jude hadn't spoken to Keziah about it yet, but he would have to soon. With Cliff in prison, he wasn't certain that they would still have a place in that town, Fallow Creek.

Keziah walked into the living room, greeted Anna Hunter, and then looked at Jude. "You just talked about your ex, Sofia now, didn't you? You said you will not eat until you know she's okay." She glared at him with accusation in her eyes. "I told you not to contact her, Jude."

Jude shut his eyes for a split second and sighed. He opened them again and looked at Keziah. So she had found out. Was she going to report him and his dad and have them sent back to Bakali? Right now, because he'd talked about contacting Sofia, he and his father's stay in America was precarious. Keziah already had a green card and could remain here, but she wouldn't hesitate to get him and his dad thrown out. At least that was what she had said would happen if he contacted Sofia. The old Keziah might hesitate to do that, but this new Keziah was unpredictable.

He thought for just a second about pleading with her but knew begging would not help. It did not matter that she had cheated on him. Not that he minded anyway, but it would be great if only she would consider that as well. He waited for her to say what she was going to do, but she said nothing. Instead, she went to the dining table, sat down, and began to eat the breakfast that Anna Hunter had set out for them.

Tim walked into the living room and then into the dining area. He passed by Keziah and brushed his hand against hers. He clearly didn't mean for anyone to see, but Jude did. He frowned slightly. With the way things were going, they soon would not even bother to hide their relationship, if he could call it that. What was he going to do? If Keziah didn't send him and his father back to Bakali, was he meant to marry her and live with a not-so-private affair his wife was having?

A part of him was amused more than anything else, and yet another cried out against it. Not only would he marry someone he did not love, she would be having an affair. Was this her way of punishing him for refusing her a year ago, or did she genuinely care for Tim? He looked at her as she ate. He could not read this new Keziah as well as he could read the old one. She could be thinking about anything.

His mind went to Sofia again, and for the umpteenth time, he got his phone out of his pocket and checked to see if he had a missed call from Taylor or would receive a call from him now. He frowned when he saw no missed call.

Why hadn't Taylor called him? He was supposed to have called yesterday. Jude had tried calling him a couple of times, but Taylor had not answered any of his calls.

He sat beside his father and glanced at the TV show his dad was watching. It was the kind of show his dad liked watching. People talking about politics. In Bakali, it was about their country's political climate; here, about America's. He looked at Keziah again. She was still eating. Apart from their upcoming marriage, they still had a lot to discuss.

One very important issue was where they were going to stay now that they couldn't settle in Fallow Creek anymore.

Jude looked down at his phone again just as Keziah passed by him. She opened the front door and went out. A moment later, Tim walked out the door and shut it firmly after him.

Curious, Jude stood up and went to the window. He didn't see either Keziah or Tim outside and went to sit on the sofa again. A minute later, he grew thirsty. He stood up to get a glass of water and then jumped when his phone rang. Looking at it, he gasped and immediately answered. "Yes, Taylor? Is she okay?" He quickly walked out the door and stood outside the house.

Taylor spoke with laughter in his voice. "Sofia is fine. She's somewhere in the house. I'm outside so she doesn't hear me making this call. I'm so sorry I didn't call you yesterday. We had to give a lot of statements at the police station and so much was going on that I didn't have time to call. Plus, we got back really late."

Jude began to walk toward the back of the house. "That's okay," he said. "Where are you now? I would like to come over to see Sofia."

"I am in a small town called Fallow Creek. It's the next town to Prospect, where you are. You will find a taxi to take you from Prospect to Fallow Creek, though it might be a bit hard to get one."

Jude blinked. "Wait, did you just say Fallow Creek? That's the town my fiancée and I were supposed to move to." He pressed his lips together after he had spoken. Why had he told Taylor he had a fiancée? What would Taylor think of him? He would not understand.

"Fiancée?" Taylor asked, sounding incredulous. "You're getting married to someone else?

"It's a long story, Taylor. Please don't tell Sofia anything. I would like to tell her about it myself when I get there," he said. "She's inside your house now?"

"Yes."

"Please don't let her go anywhere. I'll be there as soon as possible."

"I hope you won't break Sofia's heart with this thing about a fiancée," Taylor said.

"I will explain everything to her when I get there."

"She will be ecstatic when she sees you."

Joy flooded Jude. "So Sofia isn't seeing anyone else?"

"Not that I know of. In fact I am sure of that. My wife was talking about setting her up with a friend of mine." Taylor chuckled. "You are lucky you came now, because that friend is a great guy. She wouldn't be single if my wife had gotten to introduce them."

Jude didn't say anything for a short moment, and Taylor laughed. "I was just joking. Sofia seems to still be crazy about you."

Jude smiled. "I cannot wait to see my Sofia." He blinked in surprise as Keziah emerged from behind a tree nearby with Tim and walked toward him. Her eyes widened, and he sighed. There was a mixture of guilt and accusation in her eyes. That meant she had heard him talk about seeing Sofia, and he had clearly seen her hand in hand with Tim.

What now?

She frowned at him, the expression on her face one of disapproval.

Fear gripped him. What if she reported him and sent him back to Bakali now that he was going to see Sofia?

"I'll call you when I get there, Taylor," he said. If

Keziah was going to send him back to Bakali, he would do one thing in America before he left and nobody would stop him. He would see Sofia and explain why he had disappeared on their wedding day.

His call ended, and Keziah whispered something in Tim's ear. Tim glared at him as though he were the one who was caught with another woman rather than Keziah. Tim walked away, and Keziah looked at Jude.

"We need to talk," she said, sighing heavily.

His heart began to race, but he forced himself to be still. She opened her mouth to speak, and he said quickly, "Keziah before you send my father and me back to Bakali, please just listen to me. You can send me back, but please leave my father here. He won't be able to handle whatever will be awaiting us there. He will…"

"Jude, I am not sending you back to Bakali!"

He blinked. "You are not?"

She chuckled. "Let's not pretend anymore. You saw me just now with Tim, and you saw us together yesterday." She sighed heavily. "I think I might love Tim. I know I just met him, but I feel a deep, strong connection to him, as though I have known him all my life." She gave Jude a sad smile. "I am so sorry, Jude. I cannot marry you. But I guess you will be happy with this, especially as you have connected already with your ex even when you promised that you wouldn't."

"Keziah, let me explain. I didn't go looking for her. I just saw…"

"You don't have to explain anything." She smiled. "There are no hard feelings. You will stay in America and be with the girl you love, and I will do the same for myself. How does that sound?"

Joy swept over him and, he couldn't stop himself. He hugged Keziah tightly and then pulled back. "Thank you," he said. "I was going to ask where we will live since we can't stay here anymore, but I guess everyone will have to make their own way."

"Yes. But you are resourceful Jude. You will be alright."

He hugged her again. "And I know you will thrive." He smiled widely at her. "I wish you all the best with Tim."

"And I wish you all the best with Sofia."

He could not contain himself and hugged Keziah again. Brimming with happiness, he ran into the house, called to his father, and said "I'll be back. I am going to Fallow Creek."

"Fallow Creek? What are you going to do in Fallow Creek?"

"I'll tell you when I get back," he said to his father, and hurried out the door again.

TWENTY-TWO

Sofia stood in front of the sink in Lily and Taylor's kitchen, washing the dishes she had just used for lunch. She looked out the window as she thought about her week-long captivity in Utah. As awful as that week had been, she had not been as traumatized as she was when Lily's uncle had tied her up and tried to escape the police with her. The look in his eyes when he'd forced her to go along with him had been terrifying. All she could think about was that she was going to die, and she would never see Lily again. Most of all, she would never see Jude.

The thought had surprised her considering she had not seen Jude in over a year. She realized now that she still held out hope that he would return one day. But she knew she had to discard that hope or be crushed by it.

Yet, she wasn't ready to discard it. Even now, she pictured Jude's face clearly in her mind. She smiled as she remembered how much they had loved each other even though they'd not known each other for long.

Fear flooded her heart as it sometimes did when she thought about him. She didn't even know if he was still alive. She immediately pushed away the morbid thought.

He's alive. I choose to believe that. Fear tried to knock on the door of her heart to tell her there was no way he could survive such violence going on in his country, but once more, she pushed the fear away and held on to hope. Maybe not hope that she would see him again, but hope that he was alive and well. After all, there were still people who were still alive in his country. Everyone wasn't dead. He was one of them.

But even if he is alive, is he happy?

The obvious answer to that question sent a shaft of pain through her. She wished with everything in her that he was happy, but how could he be in a war-torn country? Unless he had found a way to leave his country for another.

Conflicting thoughts and troubling emotions warred in her as she thought about Jude. She sighed heavily, washed her hands, and dried them. She went to the living room and plopped down on the sofa, weary from trying to fight the troubling thoughts.

Lord, where is Jude? Please, wherever he is, keep him safe. She bit her lip. Why couldn't she just forget about Jude? Why couldn't she just move on?

She began to feel slightly depressed again and stood up to go upstairs to talk to Lily. Talking to her best friend always helped her out. Besides, Taylor had gone out about twenty minutes ago and Lily might need some company.

Stay here and talk to me.

She blinked and then smiled. She'd heard God's voice a few times since she'd given her heart to Him, and the voice that had just whispered in her heart was definitely God's. She went and sat down on the sofa. "Okay, Lord, you want me to talk to you rather than Lily? Here goes. I still miss Jude very much even though I don't want to. I don't even know if he's still alive, though I have been praying for you to protect him since he left America more than a year ago."

She sighed. "Lord, I know I have been asking you to bring him back since he left, but I think it's time to let him go so I can move on with my life. I haven't been able to because I've held on to the hope that he will return someday." She sighed sadly and went on. "I am letting Jude go now, and…" Her heart skipped a beat as Lily screamed her name. She looked up the stairs and immediately began to head toward them, not panicking, because Lily sounded more excited than scared or troubled, just curious.

"What is it, Lily?"

She heard footsteps coming down the stairs and waited. Lily met her in the middle and said with a huge smile, "Have… did you see him, Sofia?"

"See who? Taylor?" She heard the front door open and smiled at Lily. "That must be Taylor. You would think that seeing your husband everyday would temper some of this excitement at the fact that he is home." She chuckled. "It's not like he left a week ago. It is more like twenty minutes."

"Sofia, I am not talking about Taylor!"

Sofia blinked and then shrugged. "I'm going upstairs, Lily. Whatever surprise Taylor got you wherever he went, you can tell me about it after I take my nap." She began to move past Lily, but Lily took her arm.

"Come with me, silly girl."

"Where to?" she asked, looking at Lily.

Taylor met them at the bottom of the stairs. He had a cheesy smile on his face. "Sofia, I got you a huge surprise from Prospect."

She blinked. What was happening here? "You mean Lily, don't you? You got Lily a huge surprise from Prospect."

"No, I mean you."

"But it is not my birthday today." She looked at Lily and Taylor, wondering why they looked so excited. And apparently, the excitement was over something Taylor had gotten her from Prospect. She yawned. "Guys, can't whatever it is wait until after my nap? I need my beauty sleep, you know."

"No, it can't," Taylor said.

"You mean, no *he* can't!" Lily said excitedly, and took her firmly by the hand and began to lead her toward the living room.

"He? What are you guys going on about? Please don't tell me all this excitement is for that guy you said you wanted to set me up with. Taylor's friend." She pulled her hand out of Lily's grasp. "Lily, he's here, isn't he? He is the one you went to get, Taylor. Right?" She sighed, exasperated. "I wish you guys hadn't done that. I don't think I am ready to date at this time."

Lily took her hand again. "It's not him, Sofia. And this particular guy you will definitely be ready to date right now."

"I doubt it," she said, and pulled her hand away. She dashed in the opposite direction.

Lily groaned loudly. "Go get her, Taylor!"

Taylor dashed after Sofia and caught her before she could climb the stairs. "Come, Sofia. Just trust us. You will want to see this guy."

"No, I won't!

"Yes, you will," Taylor and Lily said in unison.

"At least let me go and change and freshen up first. I was washing dishes and I look a mess. The last thing I need is for some guy to see me and think I am a slob." Before they could protest again, she snatched her hand from Taylor's and ran up the stairs.

Once she got to her room, she went into the ensuite bathroom to shower. "Why did they have to bring me a guy all the way from California?" she murmured. "Am I that pathetic now?"

She didn't want to see anyone. She sighed, deciding not to go downstairs. She would stay in her room after her shower and take that nap. Hopefully, that guy would be gone when she came downstairs this evening or even tomorrow morning.

She finished showering and looked around for her big towel. She sighed wearily. She had left it on top of her bed after she'd finished using it as a hair wrap. She picked up the small towel and began to dry herself and then paused, and her ears perked up. The sound of a creaking door caught her attention. She gasped as she heard her bedroom door open.

Lily whispered, "It's okay. She won't mind you being here in her bedroom. You can talk with no distractions."

Sofia's mouth dropped open. *I cannot believe this.* They had actually brought the guy up to her room? How was she going to come out of the bathroom now, with some guy in her bedroom? She looked at the small towel she'd used to dry her body. It would hardly go around her.

Lily, what have you done? How am I going to come out of here now, Lord?

She began to pace the bathroom. This was not good. Maybe she would sit down in the bathtub and wait until the guy got tired and left. Or she could ask him to hand her the gown on the bed. She changed her mind on the second option. She didn't want to tell a stranger that. For some reason she didn't feel comfortable with that.

She shook her head. Some reason? She wasn't comfortable with that because the guy in her room was a stranger. So, Lily had brought a stranger to her room. *I will kill that girl when I get out of here. Her and her husband.*

The only option she had was to stay here until the guy left.

Annoyed beyond words, she sat in the bathtub and waited, hoping she would hear the sound of her door opening again. But she heard nothing. The guy still had not left. She waited a few more minutes and then she stood up again and hissed. *Why won't this guy go?*

At last, she knew she had to ask the guy to pass her the dress on the bed. Angry that she had to ask a strange man for this, she vowed to give Lily a piece of her mind when she saw her again. She went to the bathroom door and drew it slightly open. She huffed and then called out, "Can you pass me the blue dress on the bed?"

Ten seconds later, a knock sounded on her bathroom door. She reached her hand through the slightly ajar door, grabbed her dress, and closed the door again. Gritting her teeth in anger and embarrassment, she put the long, knee-length dress she'd worn this morning back on. She took a deep breath, pulled herself together, and stepped out of the bathroom.

The guy was looking out the door with his back to her. She narrowed her eyes as she looked at him. And then she gasped and her heart began to race. Even standing with his back to her, she knew exactly who he was. But she could not believe it. The moment felt surreal, like a dream. How was it even possible that Jude was standing here in her room? Maybe she was longing for him so much that she was seeing him now rather than a strange guy.

She slowly walked to him, her heart pounding. Taking another deep breath, she whispered, "Jude?"

He turned around with a smile on his face, the same smile that she had seen countless times in her dreams.

"How are you here?" she stammered. "Tell me this is not a dream!"

He walked toward her until he reached her, and then he took her hand. He said, "Can you feel my hand in yours?"

She nodded, unable to speak as a sob rose up in her throat.

He ran his hands slowly up her bare arms, sending goosebumps down her back. "Can you feel this?"

She said nothing as she gazed at him, all the love she had for him rushing up.

He drew her close and kissed her hair, her cheeks. He opened his mouth to speak again, but she could not wait any longer. She smiled. "Yes… Jude, I can feel it all." She placed her palms alongside his face and kissed him. She drew back and laughed as joy filled her. How long had she dreamt of kissing him again? Now he was here. He was really here. She kissed him again.

For a long moment, they clung to each other, kissing. Intermittently, she drew back and they laughed, waves of delight washing over her. She could feel his joy as they laughed together before drawing into each other's arms again and kissing deeply and passionately.

Finally satisfied, they both drew back slightly, and he brushed his nose against hers. The smile melted off his face, and he took her hand. "Sofia, we have a lot to talk about." He sat on the bed, and she sat beside him.

She reached out and touched his cheek slowly. "I still can't fully believe you are here, Jude. Right here with me."

He smiled and said, "That is what we have to talk about. I need to tell you why I left America on our wedding day." He sighed. "It has haunted me since I left. The fact that you would be deeply hurt and think that I left because I had cold feet. But that wasn't the case at all."

She smiled sadly as she remembered that day. "I know it wasn't, Jude. I know how much you love me and wanted to marry me. At first I tried to convince myself that you had left because you developed cold feet, but it was just because I didn't want to deal with the fact that the only reason why you did not come to the courthouse that day was because you had been deported. I knew that would mean you had left for your war-torn country and that you might not survive the war. It was better to believe you had left than that you were dead. But I eventually had to tell myself the truth. You don't have to explain anything. I am just happy that you are alive and here with me."

He took her hand and gave her a sad smile. "I was not deported, Sofia."

She blinked rapidly. "You were not?"

"No, I wasn't." He began to tell her everything, from when he was abducted by Felix and his men, to all the suffering he and his dad went through, to breaking up with Keziah again today.

When he finished, she shook her head slowly. Tears fell down her face, and she began to weep. "This was what I was so afraid of. That you were dead or suffering intensely in your country." She reached out and caressed his cheek, her heart breaking for him, but at the same time, starting to heal from the wound caused by his disappearance.

"It's all behind me now," he said.

"So your father is really alive!"

He nodded. "Yes, he is. You can meet him tomorrow."

She fell into his arms again, and he held her tightly. "I love you, Jude." She kissed him. "I am so happy you finally came back to me. I am never letting you go again. Never."

He kissed her nose and her lips. "You won't ever have to if you marry me."

She laughed. "We should continue from where we left off before you left America. Unfortunately, I don't think our marriage license is still valid. But we will get a new one as soon as possible."

He laughed. "Okay."

Her excitement grew at the thought of finally marrying Jude. "You know… I still have the same dress I wore that day."

"And what about Edith? Are you still friends?"

"Yes, but I doubt she'll want to come to Fallow Creek in two days."

He chuckled. "In two days?"

"Yes, that is when we will get married." She raised her eyebrows, a smile on her face. "Any objections to that?"

"No," he said. "No objections."

They kissed again for a long moment, and then Sofia stood up and drew him up with her. "Let's go and share our good news with Lily and Taylor."

They left the room together, their arms still wrapped tightly around each other. It made moving much slower, but Sofia didn't mind, and she knew he didn't either. Never again would they be separated from each other. No matter what came their way, they would face it together as one.

TWENTY-THREE

Jude stood in front of the altar in the small chapel in Fallow Creek, waiting for Sofia to come into the church. He turned to look at Keith, who was standing in front of him and would be the officiating minister who would wed him and Sofia.

Keith gave him an encouraging smile, and he smiled back. Once again, he looked around the chapel. Lily, Taylor, and Rachel were sitting in the front row, but there was also a crowd made up of the women from the House of Refuge. He didn't know any of them, but that did not matter. They had embraced him and Sofia as their own. Most of all, Taylor and Lily, Rachel and Keith had embraced him as part of their family because of Sofia. They had even given him and Sofia a house in Fallow Creek for whenever they decided to visit. He was extremely grateful.

He turned to his dad, who was behind him acting as his best man, and his father smiled at him. "I am so proud of you, Jude," he said, placing his hand on Jude's shoulder. "Most of all, I am thrilled for you.

You have been dreaming of marrying Sofia for so long, and now you get to make her your wife."

Jude beamed. He felt like he was floating on a cloud. He couldn't wait to see Sofia. She would be such a beautiful bride.

The bridal song started, and Jude's heart began to pound in excitement. He turned around as the door to the chapel opened and his heart skipped a beat. Sofia entered the chapel looking as radiant as ever in a gorgeous fitted wedding dress. Without a doubt, she was the most beautiful bride he had ever seen. No, actually the most beautiful woman he had ever seen. He smiled widely as he fixed his eyes on her.

She began to walk down the aisle and his eyes remained fixed on her, just as her eyes were fixed on his. She gave him a tender smile, and he mouthed, "I love you."

She continued to walk down the aisle, and he stood watching her, enthralled by her beauty. He couldn't believe that in an hour or so, she would be fully his. "Thank you, Lord," he whispered.

She finally got to his side, and he immediately took her hand. "You look beautiful, Sofia," he said.

"And you look handsome in your suit."

The ceremony began, and Jude listened as Keith gave a short sermon about marriage. Soon, he asked them to repeat the vows. Jude repeated his first, and then Sofia. It all seemed surreal to Jude. Just a week ago, he was languishing in prison. Now, he was marrying the most beautiful woman he'd ever seen, the woman he loved more than anything or anyone in this world. He remembered what his dad had always said in prison about asking God for a miracle. His father had kept believing that God would free them from prison even when it seemed impossible. But God had far exceeded what Jude could have ever hoped for.

He regretted the years he had spent shaking his fist at God, angry at Him, and proclaiming later on that there was no God. All he could do now was fully dedicate his life to the One who had done so much for him.

After exchanging rings, Keith pronounced them man and wife, and Jude leaned in and tenderly kissed Sofia. He whispered, "We are married now, Sofia. Can you believe it?"

"Finally," she said, with tears in her eyes.

He took her in his arms and kissed her again, and the crowd erupted with cheers and claps.

They went outside to take photographs, and Jude took Sofia's hand and led her aside from the crowd pressing in on them. They stood alone at the back of the chapel, and he wrapped his arms around her. "We have come such a long way," he said, smiling at her and marveling at how smooth her skin looked.

"Yes, we have," she said. "How is it possible that I love you even more now than when we were to get married a year ago?"

He smiled. "I have never loved anyone and will never love anyone the way I love you." Running his hands down her arms, he said, "We have been through so much, Sofia. But God has brought us through every time. Let's go and join everyone else before they begin to look for us."

She smiled and nodded, and they made their way to the front of the chapel together.

***

Rachel put her arm around Keith's shoulder as they stood looking at the new church building in Destiny. She smiled at Taylor and Lily, who were standing to their left, and Sofia and Jude, who stood to their right. "So, guys, this is Destiny. This is the town where Keith and I met and got married."

Keith nodded. "This is where I grew up, and it's still a town that has my heart because this is where it all started for me. God called me to be a minister here. I still love this town."

Lily said, "So this is the church you were in the middle of building when the Lord told you and Rachel to leave everything and go to Fallow Creek?"

"Yes," Keith said.

Lily smiled. "Fallow Creek is so much richer and better because you obeyed the Lord's voice and went there. Everything has changed so much. We need to thank this town and people here for giving you to Fallow Creek."

Keith smiled. "But Fallow Creek already had Rachel, and she started it all because she wanted a different life not just for herself but for others in Fallow Creek." He looked deeply into Rachel's eyes. "I would never have done half of all I accomplished, especially in Fallow Creek, without you, Rachel." Rachel smiled back at him, and then he turned to Lily again. "She's really the one I owe all my thanks to, after the Lord."

For a long moment, Rachel couldn't take her eyes off Keith. Finally, overcome with emotion, she whispered, "I love you, Keith. With all my heart."

He kissed her lightly on the lips and whispered, "I love you, too."

For more than a minute, no one said anything as

each couple stared into each other's eyes, their love for one another clear for all to see. Finally, Taylor broke the silence and said, "I'm glad we decided to come to Destiny with you, Keith and Rachel. It's a lovely little town."

Jude said, "I'm also glad I came here with Sofia. You have all been like a real family to me. I want to say thank you for embracing me and treating me like your brother."

"You are our brother in Christ," Rachel said.

"Yes." Lily smiled. "Especially now that you're married to my best friend, you best believe that you're my brother, Jude."

They walked around the church premises talking about their lives and the past year. The talked about the challenges they had gone through and the triumphs. After a while, Keith said, 'Would you guys like to see the rest of the town? We have only seen a part of it."

They all agreed that they wanted to see the rest of Destiny. They left the church premises and walked around town, each of them hand in hand with their spouses, love brimming in their hearts for one another.

Sofia shook her head. "I can't believe this whole town was once destroyed by a hurricane."

"Yes," Keith said. "It has been fully rebuilt now." He turned and looked at Taylor, who was walking with Lily behind him and Rachel. "Thanks to you and the kindness of so many people, this town was returned to how it used to be… and even better. The church we just saw was finished because of Taylor's generous donations."

Taylor waved his hand dismissively. "I only did

what God wanted me to do."

They continued to walk around town. From time to time, Rachel and Keith raised their hands in greeting to different people who waved at them. Every few steps they took, they stopped to briefly talk or hug someone.

Rachel smiled as they walked past Eric and Paula's. They'd already visited their good friends, and Rachel was pleasantly surprised to see that two more children had been added to their family.

She tenderly caressed her stomach and smiled at Keith. They were expecting their own baby in seven months. Keith had been ecstatic the day she'd told him she was pregnant. All she'd told Emily was that she would be a big sister, too. They did not know the baby's gender because they had chosen not to do a scan. They wanted to be surprised. Rachel whispered a short prayer for their baby as she usually did, asking for God's protection and that His will for their child's life would be fully accomplished.

They soon began to approach a huge house, and Rachel felt a sense of misgiving come over her. She took a deep breath and pushed the feeling away. She would not allow the past to haunt her anymore. The Lord had given her a brand-new life, and she would leave every other thing that was not part of that life behind her.

Sofia pointed at the house. "That's a beautiful home," she said. "Do you know who lives there?"

Rachel gave her a sad smile. "I used to live here. I and Mike Cadwell."

Sofia's eyes widened open in clear surprise. The others also looked astonished, except for Keith.

"So this was where Mike Cadwell took you to when he fled Fallow Creek years ago," Lily said.

"Yes." Rachel looked up at the house and sighed at the unwelcome memories it brought. There was, however, one welcome memory. The memory of the first day she'd met Keith. She continued, "I lived here with Olivia and her kids as well."

She shuddered as she remembered the awful events of last year when Mike had threatened to destroy everyone at the House of Refuge. Now, he was dead, and Olivia and her kids still lived in Fallow Creek. She turned to look at Keith and an overwhelming love for him filled her heart. What would she have done if she had not met him? She probably would still be married to Mike now. She leaned in and kissed him. "I love you so much, Keith."

He tilted his head to study her face. "Wow!" he grinned. "What was that for, Rachel?"

"It's for being the best husband any woman could ever hope or dream of, and for how much you love me."

He beamed at her. "And you are the best wife any man could ever have." He pulled her close to his side and they kept walking until they found themselves once more on the church premises.

Alec, the new church pastor, came and greeted them and briefly talked about the church. "Our church has grown immeasurably," Alec said. "Almost everyone in Destiny attends service here now."

Keith smiled widely and said to him, "That was my ultimate dream when I lived in Destiny. God has brought it to pass, but he did not use me to do it.

He used you, Alec. As well as the people of Destiny." He looked at the huge church building. "Instead, the Lord sent Rachel and me to work on hard ground to get a harvest."

Rachel said, "It was very hard, but we ultimately reaped a bountiful harvest."

"All those years ago when God called me and Rachel to go to Fallow Creek, I never would have imagined everything that would happen. How hard it would be, but how fulfilling."

Rachel took his hand. "It's been really hard, but I would not trade all our experiences and all the Lord did through us for anything. I can say I am truly glad we went back to Fallow Creek. But I still have an affinity to Destiny, Keith. Maybe it's because this was where I met you and this was where it all started for me."

Sofia threw an arm around Jude and smiled. "We would like to explore the town on our own."

Rachel waved them away. "Go. Newlyweds should spend as much alone time together as possible."

They left, and Rachel laughed. "Those two can't keep their hands off each other."

Lily giggled. "Neither can you and Keith, Rachel. And you have been married for years."

"Look who's talking," Keith said.

Taylor wrapped his arm around Lily's waist. "We would also like to go alone to explore the town." He eyed Keith playfully. "Unlike Sofia and Jude, we are not asking for your permission."

Keith and Rachel laughed. "Well, what are you still standing here for then?" Rachel said. When Lily and Taylor left, Rachel laughed and threw her arm around Keith's shoulder.

"Let's go into the church again," Keith said to her.

They walked into the church and looked at the brand-new pews and the beautiful marble tiles. They called it the new church, but it had been fully built about two years ago. However, they had just remodeled some parts of the church again.

"I remember when building this church was my whole life. All I aspired to," Keith said. "When the Lord told us to go to Fallow Creek, the church building was one of the reasons why I first doubted that it was the Lord who had spoken to me. I was sure at the time that He wanted me to build the church building, and yet he was saying we should move to another town right in the middle of the building project. It did not make any sense to me. Remember?"

She chuckled. "I do. I'm so glad we obeyed the Lord, even though going back to Fallow Creek was the last thing we wanted at the time."

Keith took her hand, and they continued to go around the church. They got to the back of the building and noticed a much smaller building annexed to the church. Keith blinked and pointed. "Rachel, is that my old office?"

She smiled. "Yes, it is. It's exactly how it was when we were here. I thought they would have torn it down, but for some reason, they didn't."

They walked to the small building and found the door open. They walked in and looked around. It was empty now. Keith had sold the desk and chair during their yard sale, but it seemed every other thing may have been given to charity.

"I can remember the day the Lord gave me

that dream about Fallow Creek right here in this office," Keith said. "I was so afraid to tell you about it because I didn't know what you would say. No, actually, I thought for sure you were going to say no."

She smiled. "But the Lord had spoken to me already about it. He's such a great God."

Her eyes moved around the small office. There was nothing else to see and yet she did not want to leave. Apparently, neither did Keith because he took her hand and they moved to the center of the office.

"I have a feeling that the Lord has much more for us to do in the near future," she said, with a deep certainty she knew could only come from God."

"I feel that, too," he said. "God has much more for us in the future." He kissed her and added, "I cannot wait for what he has for us. But most of all, I can't wait to share that future with you, my love. You have been my rock through everything we've gone through."

She beamed and kissed him again. Their journey of reforming Fallow Creek had not started in her hometown, but in here, in this small office. She sensed that the next adventure the Lord had for them would be right here, in Destiny. She told Keith what she felt and he nodded. "The Lord is bringing us full circle, and it seems our destiny points to this town once again. To Destiny.

Rachel took his hand. "Let's go and find the others. I'm starving."

They left the office hand in hand, still as in love as they had been when they first got married. As they would be, by the grace of God, many years from now.

A LOOK AT: THE SISTERS OF ROSEFIELD SERIES

GOD HAS A PLAN FOR THE GARDNER SISTERS, BUT WILL THEY HEED HIS CALL, BEFORE IT'S TOO LATE?

Sienna Gardner lives a life most could only dream of. The socialite is engaged to one of New York's most eligible bachelors, and is paid a small fortune to grace the covers of high-end magazines. But her champagne existence comes to a screeching halt when she suffers a wake-up call that throws into question her values and choices.

Back in their hometown, Audrey Gardner is too busy working as a police officer to worry about her high-flying sister in New York. She's on the precipice of becoming Police Chief, when a new officer appears from Miami. He's handsome, experienced, and ready to step right into the role she's worked so hard for. God works in mysterious ways, but Audrey's not about to give up her dream without a fight.

Trisha Gardner Coleman pities her busy sisters and their loud, career-focused lives. She thanks

God for her husband Stan, and the family they hope to make together. But Stan has been keeping secrets, and Trisha is about to learn that her sweet, domestic existence is masking an ugly lie.

The three sisters are all approaching crises that will leave them questioning everything they believe. God's light can pierce the deepest darkness, but it will take courage and faith for Sienna, Audrey and Trisha to find their way.

Love is enough to make all their dreams come true, but are the three sisters worthy?

AVAILABLE NOW

ABOUT THE AUTHOR

Like the characters in her stories, Emma Easter juggles a range of identities.

In the low-income community where she works, Easter is known as a family medicine physician who treats patients of all ages and backgrounds.

College friends see her as an accomplished musician, having studied and mastered five classical instruments—but behind closed doors, she's just as comfortable rocking an air guitar to Creed. And when she isn't giving her heart, soul, and sanity to her three young children she's indulging in her most secret identity of all: meeting new characters, crafting fresh plots, and exploring every corner of her imagination.

Across all these different roles, one cohesive thread has tied everything together: her faith and love of Jesus Christ.

Find more great titles by Emma Easter and Christian Kindle News at https://christiankindlenews.com/our-authors/emma-easter/.